Other books by Sandra Moran . . .

Letters Never Sent
2014 Edmund White Award for Debut Fiction Finalist

Nudge
The Addendum

All We Lack

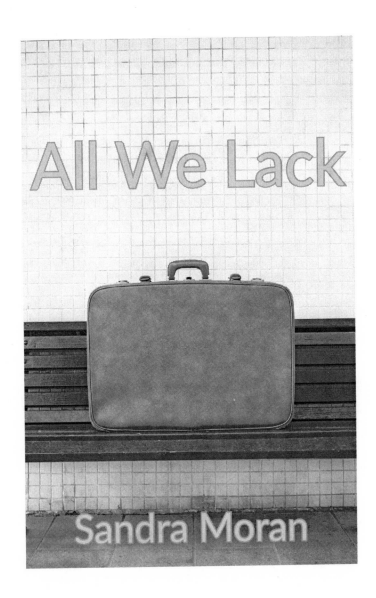

All We Lack

Sandra Moran

Bink Books

Bedazzled Ink Publishing Company • Fairfield, California

978-1-939562-92-0 paperback
978-1-939562-93-7 ebook

Cover Design
by

TreeHouseStudio

Bink Books
a division of
Bedazzled Ink Publishing Company
Fairfield, California
http://www.bedazzledink.com

To Cherie and Cheryl,
both of whom make me a better person.

Acknowledgments

I continue to be humbled by the people in my life who give so freely of their time to help me become a better writer by reading (and later re-reading my manuscripts). Thank you Kathy Belt, Jane Montgomery, Rebecca Maury, Annie Yamulla, Stephanie Smith, Catherine Smith Sherrill, Cheryl Pletcher, Deborah Bowers, John Moore, Betts Ballard, Patricia Decker, and Ines Molleda. Thank you to my paramedic "technical advisor," Courtney Wood; my social worker connection, Stephanie Smith; my "Catholic guilt advisor," Carleen Spry; and my Philadelphia chauffeur and partner in crime, Rebecca Maury. Many thanks to Jordan Chambers for designing and hosting my website. Thank you, too, to C.A. Casey and Claudia Wilde at Bedazzled Ink for giving me a chance to tell a story that is so different from *Letters Never Sent* and *Nudge*. I always appreciate your dedication to taking risks with the books you publish. Thank you to Ann McMan for being my mentor, friend, and for designing yet ANOTHER great cover. And thank you especially to everyone who has been so kind, encouraging, and supportive of my writing.

I would like to also take a moment to extend a special thank you to my mother, Cherie Moran, who reminds me frequently that she went through eighty-seven hours of excruciating labor and sacrificed not only her career at NASA, but also gave up her seat on the Apollo 8 mission to orbit the moon so she could give birth to me. Thank you, also, to Cheryl Pletcher, who puts up with my "creativity," and without whose love, patience, and support none of this would have been possible.

Prologue

Maggie

SO THIS IS how it ends.

That was the totality of Maggie Anthony's thoughts as the fifty-passenger express bus swerved, fishtailed, and then began what felt like a painfully slow series of barrel rolls down the steep embankment. She took a deep breath and gripped the armrests on either side of her seat. The woman in the seat next to her had done the same thing and their forearms touched.

"We're all going to die."

The murmured words were so low Maggie was surprised that she even heard them. She turned her head to stare at the woman next to her. Everything seemed to be happening in slow motion now and the elongation of time gave her an opportunity to take in the tiny details of the person with whom she had made pleasant conversation off and on for the past two hours.

The woman was small and efficient looking, with blondish hair that was glossy and probably very silky. She had green eyes . . . thick lashes . . . a blemish she had tried to cover with makeup. When the woman had slid apologetically into the seat next to her in New York City, Maggie had noticed that she had seemed anxious. *Helen*, Maggie thought suddenly. She had said her name was Helen.

The bus rotated and Maggie, who had the window seat, was thrown against Helen who let out a *whoosh* as Maggie's right elbow and shoulder slammed into her chest.

We're like those numbered balls in that round Bingo cage thing, Maggie thought as the force of the rotation flipped her upwards— or downwards given that the roof of the bus was suddenly below her. Helen was on top of her, but only for a second before they were separated and jerked sideways.

Everything happened faster now and suddenly, the noise was deafening—the groan of bending metal, the crunch of breaking glass, the screams and the rush of air as she was flung forward. Around her, the passengers bounced against each other and the seats of the bus. Purses and bags bounced, too, their contents spilling out and spraying like shrapnel.

"Grandma!"

It was, Maggie thought dimly, the little boy—the one she had seen with the sticker on his chest, his name written in Sharpie, sitting in the seat directly behind the driver. *Unaccompanied minor,* she had thought when she first saw him. Why that phrase occurred to her now, she didn't know.

"Fuck!"

This came from the heavyset man who had sat behind her. He had been on her connector bus to New York City. He'd boarded in Harrisburg, she remembered. She had gotten off the bus to stretch her legs and to use the bathroom at the station. When they got back on the bus, he had chosen to sit directly behind her. He had small brown eyes that were lost in the pale flesh of his face. Something about him made her uncomfortable and she had considered switching seats before deciding it would be too much work to move all of her things. When they changed buses in New York, he had again chosen the seat behind her.

Why these thoughts . . . not my life flashing before my eyes . . . tell Sarah.

The questions came to her in snatches—half-developed thoughts that she understood without completion.

The bus was flipping again, on the second, perhaps third rotation. Maggie wasn't sure. And there was Helen again, her eyes wide, her lipsticked mouth in a perfectly round O.

Maggie thrust her arms out to soften the impact of their bodies crashing together again. One or both of them groaned as they came together and Maggie thought, oddly, that at least Helen was softer than the hard angles of the seats. They held onto each other and once again, Maggie was on her back on the roof of the bus.

Around them, coins and pens and a hundred other bits and pieces from pockets and bags rained down. The bus had stopped rolling and was now just gently rocking from side to side. Then silence for what felt like ten seconds as everything and everyone came to rest. And then the moans and cries began. Helen was sprawled halfway on top of her, loose-limbed and unmoving.

I'm alive.

The thought occurred to Maggie just as a sharp pain shot through her head and down her spine. Her body tingled, every nerve suddenly aware and too sensitive. Adrenaline. Helen's weight was too much. She tried to move but didn't have the strength. *Move, dammit.* She tried again to force her body to do something . . . anything. She felt another stab of pain. This time it was excruciating and she moaned. She knew she had broken bones and likely internal injuries. She wondered what her face looked like.

I hope they do a good job on the restoration.

She imagined her naked body on the cold, shiny funeral home gurney—imagined the work that would go into making her broken body and damaged face look presentable. She should have gone with cremation. Besides, who would go to the funeral anyway? Ben? Sarah? Would Sarah even know that she had died? After the way Maggie had treated her, would she even care?

Now is not the time to feel sorry for yourself.

Maggie tried to raise her head again and gasped when the pain and nausea hit her simultaneously, followed by the white noise and tunnel vision. The chaos of the other passengers was obscured as she felt herself lose consciousness. The escape was welcome, she realized as she gave into it and felt herself let go.

Suddenly, she was looking down on the scene—at her bloody and broken body with Helen curled on top of her as if they were lovers. To her right was the man who had sat behind them. His face was bloody and his head was cocked at a strange angle. His eyes were open but he wasn't moving. Maggie knew that expression. Toward the front of the bus was the little boy, curled into a ball, crying. The old woman who had taken so long to board lay sprawled limply on her stomach, her limbs at unnatural angles. Maggie saw all of it and felt nothing. It was a nice change to see death and not to feel sadness.

Maybe dying is not so bad after all. Maybe . . . She had trouble forming the rest of the thought. The scene below her faded and then, before she could be troubled to summon up the words to describe what happened next, there was nothing.

Wednesday
November 12, 2014

Maggie

MAGGIE ANTHONY CLOSED her laptop and pushed her chair back from the ornate wooden desk. As she stood, her hands braced on the highly polished wood, she thought for the hundredth time that although it was pretty, the mahogany desk wasn't what she would have chosen for herself. It was too large . . . too substantial . . . too stuffy. When she had first taken over, she had considered replacing it, but ultimately hadn't. It had been her father's desk and his father's desk before him. It, like the business, was her heritage, even though she knew that deep down in his heart, her father had hoped one day Ben would change his mind and fulfill the promise of the Anthony & Son Funeral Home sign out front.

To his credit, Franklin Anthony had never made Maggie feel inferior to her brother. If anything, he had gone out of his way to show her how much he appreciated that at least one of his children wanted to follow in his footsteps. *Just not the right child*, she often thought.

Many people thought that funeral directors were historically men, but in fact, until the 1860s, women were the ones who'd had the responsibility of preparing the body for burial. Men, Maggie often said when people expressed surprise that she was in charge, historically dug the graves and built the coffins. It had been only in the last twenty to thirty years that women had begun to reassume their rightful place in the mortuary industry.

That said, in places like Seymour, Indiana, which were more southern in culture and mind-set and where Confederate flags still were flown with pride, Maggie was an anomaly.

"Betty Jo, I'm about to head out," Maggie called out, knowing her voice would easily carry to the outer office. "Is there anything I need to sign or—"

Maggie jumped as Betty Jo popped her head into the room. Her hair was a flaming shade of red that could only have come from Clairol and its almost violent intensity never ceased to startle Maggie.

"You don't need to shout, Margaret."

Betty Jo was one of the few people who still called Maggie by her birth name. She had been her father's office manager—and, she had learned when she was fifteen, mistress—since the late 1960s and took personal pleasure in reminding everyone that she knew the business as well as, if not better than, anyone else, including Maggie. Maggie didn't doubt it and was thankful that, despite being in her seventies, Betty Jo had agreed to stay on after Franklin's death.

"Sorry." Maggie bent to pick up the computer bag that leaned against the desk. She straightened and busied herself sliding the computer and various cords inside. "I'm getting ready to leave for the NFDA conference in Boston and I wanted to know if there was anything I need to sign or do before I leave."

Betty Jo shook her Aqua Netted head. "No. Though I do need the on-call schedule for while you're gone."

Maggie nodded and picked up a sheet of paper and extended toward Betty Jo. "Nick is on call today and Friday. Amber said she'd be fine with covering Thursday, Saturday, and Sunday."

Betty Jo frowned as she studied the schedule. "Are you sure you want to do that? She's just an intern."

"I know," Maggie said. "But I think she can handle it. And it's unfair to ask Nick to be on call for five days straight. Besides, I'm only a phone call away if there are problems."

Betty Jo nodded again, slowly, and then lowered her head to study the schedule, giving Maggie a clear view of her very gray roots. *Time for a touch-up*, she thought with a small smile.

Betty Jo looked up and caught Maggie's expression.

"What's so funny?" She self-consciously touched her brittle coif.

"Nothing," Maggie said quickly. "I was just thinking about how much I'm looking forward to getting away—even if it does involve public speaking."

Betty Jo's stern expression softened somewhat. "You'll do fine. And it's to the women's development group, so you'll be preaching to the choir."

"I know." Maggie laughed ruefully. "And let's face it, I'll have plenty of time to work on it."

Betty Jo's smile was sad. The funeral home staff knew that

Maggie was terrified of flying—a fear that had nothing to do with the fact her parents had been killed four years earlier in a plane crash. More than anything, it had to do with the claustrophobia of being trapped in a pressurized tube with no option for escape. There probably wasn't all that much difference traveling by bus or train, she knew, but being able to see trees, cars, and knowing she could open the window somehow made her feel less constricted. And hell, if bus or train travel was good enough for John Madden, who was notorious for his fear of flying, it was good enough for her.

"How long is the trip?" Betty Jo asked.

"Long," Maggie admitted. "I leave Indianapolis at four o'clock and get into Boston tomorrow at four-twenty in the afternoon." She sighed. "I wish Amtrak had a Wednesday train but with the meet and greet Thursday night . . ." She shrugged.

"Well, either way, try to get some rest." Betty Jo lifted her chin slightly. "You know how grumpy you get when you're tired."

Maggie nodded rather than replied. Unbeknownst to Betty Jo—or anyone for that matter—she had no intention of going to the mixer or, if her plan to see Sarah worked, getting any rest. Granted, Sarah didn't know she was coming into town and had been left with the impression that she would never hear from Maggie again. Still, Maggie would worry about that later.

"So, I'm going upstairs to pack and then I'm heading to Indy," Maggie said. "I'll have my phone if you need anything."

Betty Jo sniffed. "I've been running this place longer than you've been alive. I'm sure we can get along without you for a weekend."

Maggie stifled the urge to point out that wasn't what she meant and said simply, "Great."

She picked up the computer bag and the folder that contained the beginnings of her speech and walked around the side of the desk to where Betty Jo still stood. Impulsively, she leaned down and kissed the crusty woman on the cheek. "I know we're in good hands."

Maggie opened the door of the administrative offices and stepped into the hallway. She closed the door gently behind her. How, she wondered, had her father justified his relationship with Betty Jo when his wife and children lived just upstairs on the second floor of the funeral home? And how had her mother stood it, knowing that her romantic rival was in such close proximity? Her parents had always seemed happy enough. In fact, they had died while on vacation together. That had to say something . . . didn't it?

It says that being with one person for your entire life is unrealistic and love is . . . She shook her head at the unfinished thought and walked down the hallway to what had originally been an entryway. The room was quiet and cool. The afternoon light had moved to the back of the building and the front rooms, with only natural light, were shadowed.

Maggie stopped at the foot of the waterfall staircase and touched the polished newel. The dark wood was cool beneath her fingers and she smiled. She had always loved this room—this stairway. In fact, she loved almost everything about the rambling building with its warren of small rooms, carved mantles, and stained glass. Built in 1901, it had served not only as a residence, but also as a boarding school and, very briefly, a furniture store.

She had seen pictures of how it had looked in the past and the one commonality was that regardless of what it was being used for, the building always looked homey. And it was that sense of warmth and family that had made Anthony & Son so successful—that and the fact her father and grandfather had built a reputation for caring and integrity. It was a mind-set that Maggie was dedicated to keeping alive, despite the increasing pressure from one of the country's largest corporate funeral chains to buy the business.

Maggie closed her eyes, inhaled deeply through her nose, and, for a moment, was transported back to her childhood. Her mother, Jackie, was upstairs baking and her father was in the embalming room or doing paperwork in his office. Ben was at baseball practice. Everyone was safe. Everyone was present and accounted for. They all still loved each other. Or had they? Maggie opened her eyes. Had any of them ever really been fully present or had she been the only one living under the illusion that everything was fine? The familiar anger rose into her chest, her fingers tightened on the banister.

"Don't," she murmured.

She forced herself to relax her grip and climb the stairs to the second-floor living quarters. It was, she thought as she walked down the hallway to her bedroom, too large for one person. But, it would probably always be that way. She would never marry and have children. And there was no way she could ever live openly with a partner—not if she wanted to maintain the reputation of an upstanding, moral business owner. She was damned if she did and damned if she didn't. She pushed down the familiar anger. So what if it wasn't fair. She had made her decision long ago.

Inside her room, she surveyed the outfits she had chosen, but not yet packed for the trip. They lay neatly on the bed. The obligatory black suit. A gray suit. Blouses. Jeans. A couple of tops. Running clothes and shoes. She went to the dresser, pulled open her underwear drawer, and grabbed several bras and pairs of underwear.

Her hand hovered over the black, lacy nightgown. It was the one she had worn last year; the one she had worn the only time she had broken all of her rules. If she wore it this time, would Sarah remember it? She held the nightgown against her body and studied her reflection in the mirror. Black really was her best color. It accentuated the paleness of her skin and complimented the dark hair that hung to just below her shoulders. Her hair had been longer last year. Would Sarah notice the difference?

She leaned forward suddenly as she caught a glint in the brown. Was that a gray hair? She narrowed her eyes and peered at her reflection. She was only thirty-one, but she knew that they had a way of just appearing. She thought again of Betty Jo's dye job and promised herself that when she reached that age, she would never try to hide her gray. Or, she amended, if she did, she would at least do it gracefully with highlights.

As she straightened and leaned away from the mirror, Maggie caught the glowing red reflection of her alarm clock. The bus departed at four o'clock and she wanted to be early so she had her choice of seats. She did the math quickly in her head. She still had the hour-and-a-half drive from Seymour to the bus station in Indianapolis. She needed to leave.

Maggie glanced down at the scrap of lace in her hand and then turned and tossed it into her suitcase. Having choices was important.

Bug

BUG STOOD NEXT to the black, wrought iron fence that surrounded the playground and stared out at the cars parked up and down South 47th Street. Behind him, he could hear the other ten year olds as they ran and played, their games punctuated by occasional shrieks and disagreements.

"I don't think she's going to come."

Bug turned and looked at Tasha. She stood to his right, next to the red-and-white cinder block column that anchored the fence. She was his only friend at Lea Elementary School and the only one who knew he was living at the shelter.

Bug shrugged and returned his gaze to the sidewalks that ran in front of the red brick buildings across the street. The few times Rhonda had come to the school, her approach had been from the south. Of course, given that he didn't know the location of the rehab program she was in, there was no telling from which direction she would come. Like Rhonda herself, nothing was predictable.

"She will," he said finally. "If she finds out they're sending me to Aunt Sarah's, she might."

Bug didn't want to admit it, but he hoped more than anything his mother would suddenly appear, clean and sober, and rescue him from being sent to live with a woman he'd only met once. He hoped for it but as with most things concerning his mother, he didn't expect it.

Tasha touched the sleeve of his coat with her mittened hand. "I'm going to miss you, Sammy." Her voice was soft.

Bug nodded but didn't turn to meet her gaze.

Like him, Tasha suffered at the hands of bullies. Grandma Jean would have said it was because they were both "sensitive children" but Bug suspected there was more to it. The other kids sensed there was something wrong with them—that there was a weakness in them that made them targets. For Bug, that weakness was not only the fact that he was one of the few white kids in this part of West Philadelphia, but also the very visible vulnerability of neglect. For Tasha, it was her lazy eye and clubbed foot. They were both outcasts and too gentle for Walnut Hill's survival-of-the-fittest mentality.

"Thanks, Tasha," he mumbled. "I'm gonna miss you, too."

She leaned forward and grasped the bars of the fence. "I've never been to Boston. I wonder what it's like."

Bug blinked. He had never been to Boston either. Aside from Philadelphia, the only other place he knew was Harrisburg and he tried not to think of his life there because if he did, if he allowed himself to remember Grandma Jean and how happy he had been, it would make the present all that much more unbearable.

He shrugged again. "Probably like here. But colder maybe."

"You could go see where they did the tea party," Tasha said. "Maybe your Aunt—"

A group of boys had formed a half-circle around them. "Hey, *Bug*. You and your girlfriend havin' a good time over here all by yourselves?"

"Don't listen to them," Tasha said softly.

Bug didn't turn.

"Hey, Talbott, I'm talkin' to you!" The voice was Albert's. "Or, sorry . . . am I bugging you?"

Bug blinked but still didn't turn. He remembered with shame the day Albert and his friends had learned the nickname his mother had given him. She had shown up just as school was letting out. Rhonda—she didn't let him call her "mother" or "mom"—had been drunk and he'd tried to pretend he hadn't seen her, slinking down in his jacket and walking quickly past, but she had seen him and called out to him.

"Bug!" she yelled and waved. "Bug! Get your ass over here. I came to walk you home."

All the children standing around heard—including Albert and his pack of friends. Up until then, they had only known him by his real name, Sam.

"Bug," Albert had said in a singsong voice, "your mama's calling you."

His friends jumped in.

"Yeah, Bug." "Buuuuug." "Oh, Bug, give your mommy a kiss."

Bug stopped and turned. Even from where he stood he could

see that his mother's eyes were nothing but empty, black pupils. She was high, as well.

Somewhere in her brain though, she must have heard and registered some of what the boys were saying because she suddenly thrust out her skinny arms and said, "Give me a hug, Bug."

The rhyme seemed to amuse Albert and his friends who took the chant up immediately. "Hug Bug. Hug Bug."

Bug felt his face redden in embarrassment. His mother stamped her foot and wiggled her out thrust arms. He closed his eyes and walked toward her.

She seemed encouraged by the chant and said again, loudly, demandingly, "Give me a hug, Bug."

He could smell the alcohol as he got closer. It clung to her skin, oozing from her pores.

"Rhonda, please . . ." he began.

"Give me a fucking hug, Bug," she said, her voice hard and sharply edged. "Don't piss me off."

Cringing inwardly at the contact, Bug stepped forward. His mother stank of cigarettes, cheap whiskey, and unwashed skin. She wrapped her thin arms tightly around him and squeezed.

Bug could hear Albert and his friends hooting and making kissing noises in the background. He felt sick. Rhonda held him like that for several seconds before finally thrusting him away from her. Bug took a clumsy step backward, his balance thrown off by her sudden release of him. He refused to look at Albert and his friends, though he could see Tasha's scuffed orthopedic shoes and unnaturally twisted right foot in his peripheral vision. His ears burned with shame.

"Come on," Rhonda said as abruptly as she had released him. She started to walk away, not looking to see if Bug was following. He had turned and trailed after her.

"Maybe I could come see you."

Bug jerked his attention back to the present. He had forgotten that Tasha was there. "Maybe."

Bug glanced over his shoulder at Albert and his friends who appeared to have lost interest in taunting them and instead, had turned their attention to taking a basketball from two smaller boys who had been playing HORSE.

He looked back at Tasha. "I don't know if my aunt would let you. I've only seen her once—when Grandma died. She was . . ."

He shrugged, unsure how to describe the woman who looked so much like his mother, but had acted so differently. Rhonda had been angry, cursing at everyone and everything. Sarah had been the opposite. She had even seemed kind in a standoffish sort of way. Bug could tell she was uncomfortable around kids.

"I'll send you e-mails. And we can talk on the phone if you want." Tasha held up her battered pink Nokia. The adhesive gemstones she had used to decorate it caught the light in flashes of green, red, and white.

"I don't have a phone." It was one of many things other kids had that he didn't. It hadn't seemed like a big deal until now. "And I don't know if she has a computer."

"I'll bet she does." Tasha shoved the phone into her jacket pocket. "She's a teacher, right? Maybe she'd even get you your own."

Bug nodded without enthusiasm.

"It'll be okay." She touched his arm again and seemed about to say more when the school bell pealed loudly.

Bug looked once more at the street outside the school grounds and then turned to face the school. Most of the other students were heading toward the rundown red brick building. *Maybe Rhonda was going to come to the shelter to say goodbye.*

Tasha turned and moved unevenly toward the school. She stopped when she realized Bug wasn't behind her. "Sammy, we gotta go in."

She reached back for him and waited until he moved. They walked together, he in his habitual slow, hunched-over shuffle and she in an uneven, lopsided gait. By the time they reached the door, they were the only two still outside. The playground monitor waited impatiently at the door.

"Come on, you two," she said as she pulled up the sleeve of her coat and glanced down at her watch. "You're going to be late for class."

Bug didn't raise his head to meet her gaze but instead focused on the tiled floor of the hallway. It looked unnatural in the glare of the fluorescent lights.

"I'll see ya after school," Tasha said as they each turned to head down different hallways to their separate classrooms.

Bug's homeroom was two doors down and Mrs. Simmons

stood waiting. Other teachers were closing the doors to their rooms and Bug knew she wanted to do the same.

"Sam."

He recognized the tone. It was a command—a "hurry up."

"Sorry, Mrs. Simmons," he mumbled as he slipped into the room and headed for his desk.

His job was to do what he was told and not to complain. He had figured that much out. It was why he was going to Boston in less than twenty-four hours to live with a woman who he knew without a doubt didn't want him. It was his life and whether he liked it or not, he had learned to accept it.

Jimmy

JIMMY REILLY STUDIED his reflection in the full-length mirror and scowled.

"I don't even know why I bother," he muttered.

This was the third combination of clothes he had tried on and each had looked worse than the one before. Part of the problem, he knew, was he no longer wore anything but athletic warm-up pants and sweatshirts. With no real reason to go out or do anything but stay home, surf the net, and play online video games, he had no need for "real clothes." The other part of the problem was all the clothes he owned that were something other than sweats and t-shirts, were from before he had his accident and they no longer fit.

He stared at the jeans he had struggled to fit into. The waistband squeezed his hips below his belly, which hung uncomfortably over the cold buckle of his belt. The t-shirt he had once thought was trendy now looked dated and unflattering as it stretched over his bulk.

Jimmy sighed. He had never been thin. Even when he was in grade school, he'd had to wear husky-sized jeans. His mother said it was because he was just big boned and reassured him that it ran in the family. But Jimmy had always known the truth; he was the fat kid.

It made little difference that he made a formidable offensive lineman in high school or that he could bench press two-hundred-and-fifty pounds. What mattered was that off the football field and outside of the weight room, he was still the unpopular kid who couldn't get a date to any of the dances. He was still the socially awkward boy (and eventual man) who made people uncomfortable; the guy who laughed at the wrong time and never really fit in.

Jimmy frowned again at his reflection. The two weeks of dieting had done little to slim his physique. He quickly tallied his credit card balances. The bus ticket to Boston and the room at the Comfort Inn had already pushed him over the limit. There was no room for new clothes. There wasn't even really enough money to take Helen out to dinner if, once she learned the truth, she forgave him for the lies he'd told her.

He turned and walked back to his closet. He could wear his sweatshirt and warm-ups on the bus. And, he could stand his too-tight jeans for one day, even if it meant being uncomfortable. He scanned the clothing that hung limply from wire hangers and noticed the oxford shirt in the back of his closet. He pulled it out. The shoulders were covered with a thin layer of fine, gray dust and it could stand to be ironed, but it might work. And, it was November so he could wear a coat some of the time, too.

Jimmy pulled the shirt from the wire hanger and returned to the mirror where he slid his arms into the sleeves. The fit was tight, but if he left it unbuttoned over the t-shirt, it covered many of the bulges and looked, to his mind, intentionally casual. He hooked his thumbs in his belt loops and assumed a casual pose.

"It could work," he murmured as he turned to the side and craned his head so he could see what he looked like from the back. It wasn't great but it wasn't awful either.

Relieved that he had at least picked out what to wear, Jimmy undressed, making sure not to look at his nearly naked reflection. Once back in his track pants and sweatshirt, he picked up the oxford and studied it. No time to get it professionally laundered nor was there the money to justify it—not even for Helen.

Helen.

Jimmy closed his eyes and wondered yet again how he could have let it get this far. If only she hadn't contacted him in the first place, he reasoned and then stopped himself from the justification.

It's your own fault, he thought angrily. *You did this to yourself and you have no one else to blame.*

Jimmy opened his eyes. His right eyelid twitched. Stress. He sighed and threw the shirt onto the bed with the pile of clothing he was taking to the Laundromat to wash before his trip. All of this was his fault. He knew that. He also knew there was a special place in hell for people like him—people who lied and manipulated innocent people. He shook his head slowly and then turned back to the closet for the black duffle bag he had stuffed in the corner after he had returned from the hospital. Like the shirt, it, too, was covered with a thin layer of dust.

Story of my life, he thought bitterly as he carried it back to the bed and dropped it next to the pile of dirty clothes. He started to brush away the dust with his hand before stopping and fishing a white tube sock from the laundry stack. They were dirty clothes already, he reasoned as he used it to wipe off the bag. He finished, tossed it back on top of the oxford, and then unzipped the bag. Inside were two pairs of jockey shorts and one of the bracelets they had attached to his wrist when he had been a patient. It was green. What had green meant? Go?

Jimmy had hated the hospital and everything about it. The interruptions. The smell. The desperation. Even now, a year later, the sight of the plastic bracelet made him wince. He wondered suddenly if he had hidden any pills in the recesses of the bag and had to stop himself from checking.

The pull was still strong and he had to close his eyes, breathe deeply, and swallow several times before he felt in control again. It was surprising how he could go for months without thinking about getting high and then have such a strong, almost overwhelming desire. He wondered if it would always be like that.

Think about what Diane said. Do something to take your mind off of it. Engage your body; distract your mind. He looked down at the bed. Laundry. He had to do laundry. He scanned the room for the tan canvas bag he used to transport his clothes to and from the Laundromat. It lay crumpled in the corner next to his nightstand. He moved quickly to pick it up and stuffed his clothes into it. The detergent was already in the trunk of his Ford Escort.

Jimmy heaved the bag over one shoulder and winced at the flare of pain in his back. He needed to be careful not to reinjure himself, especially if he was going to spend the better part of a day sitting in a bus seat. He imagined how it would look if, in addition to everything else, he showed up to meet Helen hunched over like Quasimodo.

Jimmy shook his head. He wouldn't think about it, he vowed as he stood straighter, picked up his keys, and headed toward the front door. As he pulled it open, he saw himself reflected in the glass pane of the dented aluminum storm door. The image was distorted, but still accurate enough to dispel any illusions he might have created. He was still fat, he was still ugly, and he was still a liar.

Helen

"SO, I TOLD him that it was completely unacceptable. I mean, Jesus, can you believe it?"

Helen cradled the phone between her ear and shoulder. David's rants about other peoples' ineptitude had a tendency to go on much longer than necessary and more often than not, she found herself zoning out. As he continued to talk, she looked down at her list. Pack . . . check. Mail bills . . . check. Thaw lasagna for dinner . . . check. Get money . . . this she still needed to do.

"Uh huh," she said into the phone as she walked back into the living room.

She stretched up onto her toes and pulled the books she wanted off of the uppermost shelves. They were romances chosen specifically because she knew that David wouldn't even bother to give them a second glance.

"Mindless drivel," he observed one evening as she walked into the room with the hardback Danielle Steele novel.

He was watching Masterpiece Theatre at the time and, for whatever reason, tended to speak to her as if it were 1920 and he were an English gentleman.

Joke's on you, buddy, she thought as she opened the books one by one and pulled out the thin stacks of hundred dollar bills she had secreted between the pages. On the phone, David continued to talk as she carefully replaced the books, returned to the couch, and silently counted her stash. She knew to the dollar how much was there but wanted to double check anyway.

Five hundred, six hundred, seven hundred . . .

"Helen?"

She jerked and almost dropped the handset from where it was cradled between her ear and shoulder.

"Oh, God, I'm sorry, David," she said. "I didn't catch that last part. I was . . . the neighbor's dog is sniffing around the trash again and I was putting my shoes on in case I had to go out."

David made a noise of disgust. "Damn dog. If they're going to let it out into the common area, they should pay attention to it and keep it out of the trash. Did I tell you that I stepped in dog crap yesterday?"

Helen rolled her eyes and resisted the urge to sigh. "You did. But, you were saying . . . ?"

"Dinner," he said with a twinge of exasperation. "I was thinking about inviting Kevin and Jenna and Steve and Nancy over for dinner sometime next week. I wanted to make sure you could shop and cook."

Helen had to bite back the nasty response about not wanting to entertain his work friends. "That's fine."

She felt bad about the lie, but only momentarily. She had no intention of being there to cook for David next week—or ever again for that matter. Or wash his clothes. Or listen to his self-indulgent pontifications.

"Well, I've got to go," he said finally. "Not all of us get to take the day off."

"I had to use my excess vacation or—" Helen began.

"I know, or lose it," David interrupted. "Well, have a good day. I'll be home by six. Let's have supper by seven, okay? Maybe chicken? Gotta go. Talk to you later."

Helen pressed the disconnect button without answering.

"Asshole," she muttered as she tossed the phone onto the couch.

It bounced off the cushion and onto the floor. Helen stared at it, tempted to pick it up, and put it where it belonged. *No*, she told herself. Let David find it when he got home. It would be just one more thing she hadn't done to his satisfaction, but she didn't care. She'd be long gone by then.

She turned back to her stack of cash. There should be almost three thousand dollars. It wouldn't last long, but that, plus half of the money she and David had in their savings account, would be enough to get her started. It seemed only fair, she reasoned, given that she helped earn it. In fact, if she wanted to break it down, she made more money working for the insurance company than David did as a technical writer.

Maybe that was the problem with their marriage, she thought suddenly. David was used to the detail of technical writing. He thrived in the step-by-step controlled environment at work where he dictated the order of things. But she wasn't one of his projects.

She didn't want to have the flowchart of her life written out by
someone else—at least, not anymore.

It hadn't always been that way. Or, at least it hadn't seemed so
stifling. When they had first gotten together, David had seemed so
sure of everything. His organization had given her life structure.
It had. But now, it was just oppressive; which was why she was
going to run away. She was going to take control of her own life.
She was going to eat fast food for every meal if she wanted. She
was going to have more than one glass of wine with dinner. She
was going to scream and dance and fuck. She was going to make
a mess of her life and apologize to no one.

Helen glanced down at her watch. It was just after one o'clock.
She had planned her escape with a meticulousness that in different
circumstances would have made David proud. She had only a
couple of hours to finish packing her bags, run to the bank, and
get to the Greyhound bus station by three p.m. so she could buy
her ticket for the four p.m. departure.

Helen allowed herself a quick smile, feeling suddenly giddy
with the possibility of the unknown. She was running away. She
was going to ride with strangers on a bus that would shoot through
the night and deposit them in New York City where they would
all begin the next day of their lives. Some, like her, might take an
express bus to Boston. Others would stay in New York City. And
still others would go north to Maine or even Canada.

Helen folded the bills and put the wad into her pocket. Being
free only accounted for half of her excitement. Leaving David
meant that finally she could pursue her relationship with James.
She grinned at the thought. They had, up to this point, only
corresponded online and by phone and text. But by tomorrow
evening, she was going to not only meet him, but also, she hoped,
take their cyber relationship to the next level.

Maggie

"SERIOUSLY?" MAGGIE SCREAMED at the car in front of her and banged her palms on the steering wheel in frustration. "Could you go any slower?"

When it came to driving pet peeves, Maggie had no patience for two things: people who drove below the speed limit and people who didn't understand that the left hand lane was for passing only. The woman in front of her, who could barely see over the steering wheel of her twenty-year-old Volvo, was doing both.

Maggie flashed her headlights.

Nothing.

She growled in frustration.

It wasn't that she insisted on driving fast—though she did always set the Lexus's cruise control at four miles over the speed limit. The fact of the matter was Maggie simply didn't like having cars in front of her. They blocked her view of the open road and for some reason she couldn't articulate, that made her angry.

"Move!" Maggie yelled and was about to flash her lights again when her cell phone rang. Without looking at the display, she pushed the hands-free button on the steering wheel. "This is Maggie."

"It's me," Betty Jo said, as always, skipping over the niceties. "I thought you would want to know that Benny called looking for you."

Maggie frowned. Her brother rarely called unless he needed something and had nowhere else to turn.

"Did you give him my new cell number?"

"Of course," Betty Jo said with a note of indignation. "But he didn't seem like he was going to call you so I thought I'd let you know . . . so you could call him."

Maggie sighed. Dealing with Ben's drama was the last thing she needed on top of preparing for her presentation and psyching herself up for a confrontation with Sarah. His timing, as always, was impeccable.

"I'm sure he's fine."

Betty Jo made a non-committal noise but said nothing.

"Really," Maggie insisted.

"You just might not want to wait for him to call you is all I'm saying," Betty Jo said.

"Did he sound desperate?" Maggie asked.

Betty Jo sighed. "He sounded like Benny."

Maggie nodded. The description was enough. Though there had never been any overt animosity between Maggie and Ben, his relationship with their parents had been strained since he had gone away to college and refused to major in mortuary sciences or take over Anthony & Son. The argument had been ongoing. Franklin pushed and Ben pulled away until it all came to a head in 2001. Ben was home for Easter and Maggie, who was in her senior year of high school, had just made the decision to enroll in the Mortuary Sciences program at Ivy Tech Community College in Indianapolis. She had hoped her announcement would relieve the tension. Instead, it had the opposite effect.

"Well, at least one of my children sees the value in what I do," Franklin had said. "Maybe I should change the sign out front. Anthony & Daughter."

Ben, who was hunched over his plate, shoved a forkful of sweet potato in his mouth and shrugged. "Maybe you should."

Franklin dropped his fork and knife onto his plate with a clatter. Maggie looked quickly down at her dinner. The gravy had broken and bubbles of fat from the drippings gleamed in the light of the chandelier. She hoped her mother wouldn't notice.

"It amazes me how you continue to go out of your way to disparage the business that puts a roof over your head and provides the food you eat." Franklin's voice was tight with anger. "All I have ever wanted is to pass along my father's legacy. It's a shame your sister has to pick up your slack."

"Really?" Ben stood suddenly, his chair falling backward with a loud bang. "That's your concern? Has it ever occurred to you that I hate what you do—that I have always been embarrassed by you?" He snorted. "When people ask me at school what my childhood was like, I have to lie because it freaks people out to know that I grew up in a house filled with dead bodies."

"It's an honorable—" Franklin began.

"It's disgusting," Ben interrupted. "*You* are disgusting. And you know what I'm talking about."

Maggie glanced from her father to her brother and then back. Franklin's face turned a deep crimson at Ben's last statement and Maggie realized on some level that it wasn't anger that caused the flush, but shame. She looked again at her brother. His chest rose and fell in quick, heavy breaths.

"I'm done," he said and turned to their mother. "I'm sorry, Mom, but I can't be here."

Jackie nodded without looking up from her plate and in that instant, Maggie understood that she was aware of Franklin's infidelity. Maggie blinked and looked again at her father, who stared blankly at the center of the table where the half-carved ham sat on her mother's "special" silver platter. The muscles of his jaws jumped and twitched as he clenched and unclenched his teeth.

"I'm done," Ben repeated and then turned and walked out of the room.

Maggie hadn't realized just how serious he had been until he dropped out of school and disappeared from their lives.

For several years, Ben had wandered aimlessly around the East Coast working odd jobs. The last time Maggie had seen him had been four years earlier when their parents had died while on vacation in India. He came home for the funeral, stayed long enough to sign his half of the funeral home over to Maggie, and then left in the middle of the night. Last Maggie had heard he was working on a fishing boat someplace in Louisiana.

"So?" Betty Jo's tone made it clear what she expected.

"I'll call him," Maggie said finally. "I'm sure I'll have plenty of time on the bus. Did he leave a number?"

"No, but I looked at the caller ID and it's the same one he had before."

"All right," Maggie said as she flashed her lights at the car in front of her again. In her rear view mirror she could see the line of cars stacked up behind her. "Anything else?"

"Nothing I can't handle," Betty Jo said. "Travel safe."

Maggie was about to reply when the line went dead.

"Okay," she said sarcastically as she pushed the disconnect button on the steering wheel. "Nice talking to you, too." Though she was used to the abruptness of Betty Jo's phone calls, at times her shortness irritated her.

She was ready to take out her aggression on the woman in front of her by honking her horn and flashing her lights. After several seconds, the right turn signal of the Volvo blinked.

"Finally," Maggie muttered as she accelerated dramatically.

As she sped past the Volvo, she turned her head to stare down the offending driver. The woman was at least eighty years old with white hair and thick glasses. Suddenly, Maggie felt bad about her behavior. The woman turned to meet her gaze and Maggie smiled apologetically and raised her hand in a "thank you" wave. The smile died on her lips as the woman jerked her chin and extended her middle finger.

Maggie blinked in surprise. "Right," she said softly as she pushed harder on the accelerator and shot past the Volvo.

To make a point, she signaled and merged into the right hand lane in front of the elderly woman, allowing the cars behind her to pass and hurry on.

The passing lane cleared and she signaled, then eased the Lexus into the left hand lane and slowed until she was again alongside the Volvo. The older woman turned to look at her, her expression wary. Maggie pulled her lips into a brilliant smile, and before she could stop herself, raised her right hand with the middle finger extended.

"Take that you old biddy," she muttered in satisfaction.

It was childish and passive-aggressive behavior, she knew, but she didn't care. She was sick of being polite and socially appropriate. If she truly was going to make changes, it might as well start now. Without waiting to see if her slight had its intended impact, she pressed her foot firmly on the accelerator and roared away. She didn't have time for this crap.

Bug

BUG SAT ON the edge of his bed and studied the tiled floor between his feet. The design was the same as what they had at school, he noticed. It was even the same, nameless color. He wondered if all unhappy places had ugly floors. The school did. His mother's house did. The shelter obviously did.

"Sam?"

The voice shook him from his reverie. He looked up. His bangs hung in front of his eyes and he didn't bother to brush them aside. He could still see the woman standing in the doorway.

"How are you doing?"

Gail's voice was soft. In fact, everything about Gail seemed soft—her voice, her sweaters, even her hands when she occasionally touched his hair or arm. He liked Gail. She was pretty. In some ways, she reminded him of Grandma Jean, though, much, much younger.

Bug shrugged and dropped his gaze to the edge of the bed. The comforter was worn from too many washings. Gail stepped into the room and sat on the bed across from his. She had come to the school early to take him back to the shelter so he could have some private time, without the other boys around, to pack up his few belongings and prepare for the trip to Boston.

"Are you nervous about going to live with your aunt?" Gail asked. "You shouldn't be. She seems like a really nice woman."

Bug nodded but still didn't look up.

"She's a teacher," Gail continued. "At a college. That's pretty cool. Think of all the things you'll learn."

"I don't know her," Bug said softly. "I just saw her that one time."

"I know, sweetie." Gail sat down next to him. The addition of her weight on the bed caused the mattress to dip and Bug had no choice but to lean into her sideways hug. "But I think you're going to like staying with her."

"What about Rhonda?" Bug asked. "What's going to happen to her?"

Gail sighed deeply. "Well, she's going to spend some time in the hospital and the doctors are going to try to help her get healthy again. And then she'll go through a program to help her find a job or get training for a job."

"Is she going to come say goodbye?" Bug asked. "Before I leave?"

Gail was silent for several seconds.

"Sweetie, she can't." Gail hesitated. "The place where she is . . . she has to stay there. She can't leave." She leaned away and looked at Bug. She gently brushed the hair from in front of his eyes. "Your mom has some problems with alcohol and drugs. But you know that, don't you?"

Bug nodded, even though it wasn't really a question. He wanted to tell her it wasn't Rhonda's fault—that she couldn't help it. But he knew from past experiences that trying to explain didn't make any difference.

"And sometimes, when people are addicted to drugs and alcohol, it takes over their minds," Gail continued. "They can't think about anything else. And they'll do anything to get them. Even if it means breaking the law. That's what happened with your mom."

"Rhonda," Bug said. "She doesn't like it when I call her mom."

"Okay," Gail said and squeezed his shoulder. "Rhonda. And when she has done all the things she needs to and shown us that she's better, we'll see if you can go live with her again."

Bug stared at the tile for several seconds before looking up to see Gail watching him.

"So . . ." Gail looked around the room.

Bug followed her gaze. He knew what she was seeing. After two months in the shelter, his quarter of the room had never looked occupied and now, with his few belongings packed in the nylon duffle bag on the floor at the foot of his bed, it looked as if no one had been in the space for months.

She sighed. "Are you all ready to go tomorrow?"

Bug nodded.

"Well, the bus leaves at nine o'clock so we should plan to leave here by seven-thirty," Gail said. "That way we'll have plenty of time to get there, pick up your tickets, and get you settled in. Are you sure you're comfortable doing this by yourself?"

"We always took buses," Bug said.

"Well, you won't be alone," Gail said. "There is a representative from the bus line that will make sure you get to the right bus when you transfer in New York City. Then, when you get to Boston, your Aunt Sarah and a woman named Tara will be there. She's a social worker like me and she'll help your Aunt Sarah get you settled and then, in a couple of days, check in to see how you're doing."

"Will I ever see you again?" Bug asked. He glanced shyly up at her. "Can I write you?"

Gail smiled. "Of course you can write. I'd like to know how you're doing. You can tell me all about Boston. I've never been there." She gave Bug's shoulder another squeeze. "I'm actually kind of jealous. Boston is so much cooler than Philly."

Bug smiled weakly.

"Maybe your aunt will take you to see the USS Constitution," Gail said. "Do you know what that is?"

Bug shook his head.

"The USS Constitution is the world's oldest naval ship that still sails," Gail said. "It was named by George Washington in honor of the US Constitution and nicknamed Old Ironsides after bullets bounced off its sides during the war of 1812. It's really cool. And there's the Freedom Trail and the harbor where they had the Boston Tea Party. There's so much to see and do. You're going to love it there. And I'll bet you're going to love your aunt."

Bug's smile faltered at the mention of his aunt.

"It's going to be fine, Sam," Gail said reassuringly as she gave him a final hug and stood. "You're going to be so busy you're not going to have time to think about all of us stuck back here." She glanced down at her Mickey Mouse watch. "You've got a little time before the rest of the boys get back. You want to come out and use the computer or hang out here and read?"

"Read," Bug said and gestured toward the dog-eared Hardy Boys mystery. "I want to get it done before I leave."

"You know what?" Gail leaned down conspiratorially. "If you don't, it's okay for you to take it." She smiled and walked the short distance to the doorway.

He didn't answer her, and she turned to look back at him.

"Thanks," Bug mumbled. "But some other boy might need it."

Gail frowned and nodded slowly. She seemed to be waiting for Bug to say something else. "So, I'll see you later?" It was both a question and a statement.

Bug nodded. "Seven o'clock," he said softly. He tried not to sound miserable.

Gail studied him, her expression unreadable.

"Sam," she began and then stopped.

Bug knew that tone; it was pity. He inhaled deeply and forced himself to meet her eyes. The only way to make her feel better was to lie. He smiled and gave her a quick nod.

"I know," he said. "It's all going to be okay."

Jimmy

RED. BROWN. WHITE. Black. Red. Brown. White. Black.

Jimmy leaned back against the bank of washers that ran through the middle of the room and watched his clothes as they tumbled against each other in the dryer. He never really minded taking his clothes to the Laundromat; the smell of laundry soap and bleach was comforting. It reminded him of when he was in the paramedic program and, because of the rigorous schedule, he and his study group would meet on Sundays to do laundry and run flashcards. "Doing double duty," they would say. The memory made him smile.

As grueling as the program had been, Jimmy had enjoyed it. He liked the camaraderie and the fact that all of them were experiencing the same thing and working together as a group. Never before had he had so many friends. Typically, his inherent shyness made it hard for him to meet people. But in The Program, as they liked to call it, students were thrown together for a purpose and they had become, for at least two years, close—almost like family. It had been the happiest time of Jimmy's life.

And then they graduated.

Jimmy had tried to keep in touch. And at first, so did the rest of the group. But jobs and families and life got in the way. Get-togethers became impromptu lunches, which became promises to meet for coffee—promises that never came to fruition. They had all moved on—including Elizabeth. Just the thought of her name made Jimmy wince.

He had seen Elizabeth during paramedic school orientation and had fallen instantly in love. At best, most people would have described her as cute with her mousy brown hair that was curly to the point of frizzy, pale blue eyes, and dusting of freckles across the bridge of her nose. But to Jimmy, she had been mesmerizing. He watched her from his seat in the back of the room, her body hunched over her notebook, her Bic ballpoint pen never stopping as she scribbled notes in a small, precise script. He liked that about her. She took notes with purpose, not looking anywhere but at the instructors and her notebook.

Jimmy had been elated when they were assigned to the same study group, though it still took him almost a month to work up the courage to speak to her about anything unrelated to class work. He probably wouldn't have spoken to her at all except for a chance encounter. He had been walking through campus on his way to the library when he had seen Elizabeth sitting on a bench in the outside commons area. Her hair fell across her face as she scrutinized the bulky anatomy textbook and he stopped to watch her. He wasn't expecting her to look up and when she did and caught him staring, he felt himself blush. Elizabeth blinked uncomfortably and waited several seconds before raising her hand in a wave.

"It's now or never, Jimbo," Jimmy muttered to himself.

He raised his meaty hand in response, took a deep breath, and walked toward her. She watched his approach almost cautiously.

"Hi," he said as he drew near. He could hear the tremor in his voice and cleared his throat.

"Hi," Elizabeth said. She was still hunched over her textbook as if she were scared he was going to steal it. Her expression and tone suggested wariness.

Jimmy shoved his hands into the pockets of his black, uniform cargo pants and tried to appear nonchalant.

He jerked his chin toward the textbook. "Ready for Jaskowski's test?"

Elizabeth nodded. "I think so. I've looked over everything I can think of that he might ask."

Jimmy grinned. "If anybody's ready, it's you. You're the smartest one in our class."

"I just take the most notes," Elizabeth said wryly, seeming to relax somewhat. She smiled. "I don't know as it's the same thing."

"I think it is," Jimmy said quickly. "I always like hearing you talk in study group."

He cringed. He sounded like a thirteen-year-old boy with a crush on his teacher. Elizabeth nodded again. The wariness had returned.

Jimmy rocked forward on the balls of his feet.

"I'm going over to the library," he finally said, after what felt like at least a minute. "I was going to do some research on pneumothoraxes. I found the discussion the other day really interesting."

Elizabeth, who had been idly studying the detailed picture of the lung in her textbook, looked up in sudden interest. "Me, too. I was especially interested in some of the new techniques for stabilization en route."

Jimmy grinned. "You're . . . uh . . . you're welcome to come with me." He tried to casually incline his head in the direction of the library. "I mean, if you want to." He felt his face flush again.

Elizabeth nodded slowly and closed the book. "Yeah. I'd like that. I think it would be good to focus on something else for a little bit. After a while you just need to give your head a break."

Rather than speak and look stupid again, Jimmy simply bobbed his head and watched as Elizabeth packed her book, her ballpoint pen, and the highlighter into her bag, and then stood.

In retrospect, it hadn't been a particularly auspicious first date—not that Elizabeth called it that. Only Jimmy considered it a date. But it had been the first time the two of them were alone together. Jimmy felt sick when he thought about the last time—the night of the graduation ceremony. The entire group had gone out to celebrate at Chewy's, the bar where they had previously gone to commiserate.

"We are done!" Jimmy had crowed and lifted his bottle of Budweiser in a toast. He turned to take in the group and waited until everyone was looking at him. "To us!"

"To us!" the group had echoed and clinked their glasses and bottles.

It had been perfect. They had drank and laughed and the fellowship was more intoxicating than the beer.

"Can you believe it's over?" Jimmy asked Elizabeth after he had consumed several beers and a shot of tequila. He squeezed her shoulder. "We're full-fledged paramedics."

"I know. It's hard to believe all that work and stress and now . . . poof. Done." She took a sip of her beer, made a face, and set the glass back on the table. "I'm not a beer drinker."

Jimmy looked at the bar and then back at Elizabeth. "Do you want something else? A mixed drink? Something sweet?"

She shook her head. "Not really. It's actually about time for me to head out. I've got to start packing in the morning and there are so many details to take care of."

Jimmy frowned.

"Why are you packing?" he asked quickly and then cleared his throat. "Are you taking a trip?"

Elizabeth nodded slowly and leaned closer so she could speak without the entire table hearing their conversation. "Yeah. I didn't want to make a big deal about it, but I'm moving to Albuquerque to be closer to my family."

"But you're not certified there," Jimmy said quickly. "Shouldn't you wait until you've taken the test to make sure you'll get certification in New Mexico?"

To their right, one of their classmates was making another toast. Elizabeth smiled slightly at the drunken revelry and leaned toward Jimmy so he could hear her.

"I graduated at the top of our class," she said and her expression became serious. "I'm not bragging, but," she shrugged, "I think I'll be able to pass the certification exam."

Jimmy reached out again and this time touched her forearm, his eyes wide with concern that she had misinterpreted what he had said.

"No. No. Of course you'll pass. I just meant that it's so sudden and I guess I thought you'd do like the rest of us and get a job here." He swallowed. "I didn't expect you to leave, you know?" He faltered and Elizabeth raised her eyebrows as if to encourage him to continue. "I just . . . wanted to take you to dinner. To celebrate."

"That's sweet," Elizabeth said. "But I'm probably not going to have much time. I'm hoping to leave in a couple of days."

"I could help you pack. I could get a pizza and some beer." Jimmy remembered suddenly that Elizabeth didn't like beer. "Or wine coolers. I could get some wine coolers and come over and help load the truck." He could hear the desperation in his voice and hated himself. "Do you need someone to ride out with you?"

Elizabeth's brow furrowed into a slight frown and she sat back, shaking her head slowly. "I'm just using a U-haul. I don't have all that much stuff, really." She twisted and unhooked her purse from the back of the chair. "And I had better get going." She stood and several of the people at the table looked up.

"You're not leaving, are you?" Derek asked from the other end of the table.

"I need to get going," she said as she pulled the purse strap over her head and settled it across her chest. "I'm sure I don't need to tell you all to have fun tonight."

She smiled as everyone waved and cheered their good nights.

"Let me walk you out," Jimmy said and stood as she turned to leave.

"That's okay," she said. "I'm fine and besides—"

"I want to," he insisted. "Please?"

She gave a short, brief nod and then walked toward the door.

Jimmy followed, ignoring the catcalls from their classmates. Neither spoke as they stepped outside and headed down the sidewalk toward the parking lot next to the bar. Elizabeth pulled the key fob from her purse and pressed a button. The lights on the Honda flashed. "I'm going to miss talking to you," Jimmy said as they neared the car.

"There's always e-mail. And phone." Elizabeth leaned to open the car door, but Jimmy reached down and pulled up the handle before she had a chance. She smiled politely. "Thanks."

"My pleasure," Jimmy said as he stared at her, wanting desperately to pull her into his arms and kiss her.

She stared down at the ground. He waited for Elizabeth to give him some sign as to what to do. The silence was awkward. Jimmy leaned forward and raised his hands to her face and pulled her lips to his.

Elizabeth jerked backward at the contact. "Jesus! What are you doing?" Her eyes were wide, her expression startled.

"I was . . ." Jimmy stammered. "I thought you wanted . . ."

"No," Elizabeth said. Her expression changed from one of surprise to fear.

"I'm sorry," Jimmy said. "I read it all wrong. I thought you were interested."

"What gave you that idea?" Elizabeth wiped at her mouth with the heel of her hand.

Jimmy blinked several times and pushed his hair back from his forehead. He blushed in embarrassment. "I'm sorry. I really like you and I thought . . ." He spread his hands in supplication. "I didn't mean to make you feel uncomfortable."

Elizabeth slipped into the car and pulled the door closed with a loud bang. Jimmy could hear the electric locks engaging as she pushed a button on the inside. The realization of what that sound meant made him feel even more mortified.

Elizabeth lowered her window a couple of inches. "I've got to go, Jimmy. Take care of yourself."

She started the car.

Jimmy leaned down and spoke into the open section of window. The inside of her car smelled like patchouli. "I didn't mean to overstep. I just—"

"It's fine," Elizabeth said as she put the car into gear.

"Can I call you sometime?" Jimmy asked. "I'm still available to help with the move."

Elizabeth stared out the front window, her hands on the steering wheel, her jaw set. Finally, she sighed and tipped her head upward so that she was looking at Jimmy through the open portion of the window.

"Look, Jimmy," she said. "I don't want you to take this the wrong way, but I'd really prefer if you didn't contact me. I know you like me. I've known it for a while. But I don't feel the same way and I think to stay in touch would just be kind of weird."

Jimmy opened his mouth to disagree and then stopped. What could he say? He nodded twice, shoved his hands in his pockets, and stepped back from the car. Elizabeth's brake lights blinked off as she took her foot off the brake and eased slowly forward.

"Take care," she said as she pulled away.

Jimmy watched until the tail lights of her car disappeared around the corner before he bent forward and cursed.

Why was it, he wondered as he watched the washer begin the final spin cycle, that he always did the wrong thing? Elizabeth hadn't been interested in him. Deep down he should have known that; no girl was ever interested in him. What was it about him that made them uncomfortable? *If only they could see the real me. If only—*

"Excuse me."

Jimmy blinked out of his thoughts and turned to look blankly at the elderly lady who stood next to him. Her white eyebrows were coarse and wing-shaped. Jimmy noticed that she had several wiry gray hairs growing out of the center of her chin.

"I'm sorry, what?" he asked.

"I asked if you had a spare quarter," she said. "I'm twenty-five cents short."

"Sure," Jimmy said as he pushed himself forward so he could slide his hand more easily into the pocket of his track pants.

The coins clinked together as his fingers brushed against them and he was momentarily reminded of his father and his habit of jingling the change in his pockets. *I need to make amends with Dad*, he thought as his fingers closed around the coins and he withdrew his hand.

"Help yourself," he said to the woman as he extended his hand, palm up. In addition to the quarters, a piece of grayish lint lay in his meaty palm.

"Thank you," the woman said as she delicately took one of the coins.

Her skin was thin and papery; her veins prominent. Jimmy wondered how quickly he could hook her to an IV.

"You're welcome," he said automatically as he stared at her arm and calculated how likely it would be for her vein to roll or collapse. He decided that he could do it in thirty seconds.

"Is something wrong?" she asked.

Jimmy raised his eyes to meet hers only to realize she was studying him with a strange expression. "No. Why?"

She frowned slightly and shook her head. "You just had a strange look on your face."

"Sorry. I was just thinking about . . ." To tell the woman he had been calculating how quickly he could stick a needle into her vein would likely upset her. Normal people didn't do that. He shrugged and tried to grin good-naturedly. "I was just thinking about how you meet the most interesting people at the Laundromat."

The elderly woman studied him, her gaze shrewd. "That you do." She turned and began a slow shuffle back toward the bank of machines, the quarter still pinched between her fingertips. "That you do."

Helen

HELEN PULLED THE Toyota Camry into the narrow parking space and looked to make sure there was at least six inches on either side of the car. It was a tight fit with barely enough room to open the door and slide out without causing damage to her car or one of the others. She couldn't tell if cars were getting bigger or if parking stalls were getting smaller.

"Probably both," she murmured as she pushed the gear shift into park and turned off the engine.

She pressed her body back into the seat, straightened her spine, and closed her eyes. This was it. She was doing it. She could feel her heart thudding loudly in her chest. She inhaled deeply and concentrated on slowing its rhythm. After several seconds, she opened her eyes and grinned giddily at the futile attempt. How could she calm herself when at last she was breaking all of her carefully constructed rules?

But that's the thing, she reminded herself. They weren't her rules; they were David's. And as of this moment, they no longer applied. From now on, she was going to lead *her* life and do what *she* wanted.

She remembered the moment she made the decision to leave him. It had been after a conversation with James. He had been talking about how he wanted to trek to Everest Base Camp and suggested they both put it on their bucket lists. It wasn't something Helen had ever considered, but at the mention of it, she suddenly knew she wanted to do it. She also knew that it was a pipe dream. The reality was that her life would never change unless she stopped settling for what was safe and familiar. And it was at that moment she knew that if she ever wanted to live an authentic life, she needed to step outside of what she had become. She needed to leave.

She had told no one of her decision but her friend, Emma. They had met four years earlier through work and she was the one person with whom Helen shared her innermost thoughts—well, most of them. There were some things that not even Emma could know. They were both at work, talking on the phone, when Helen shared her decision.

"You're joking."

Helen heard the "pssssst" and crack of Emma opening a can of Diet Coke and then the soft noise of her swallowing.

"I just can't do it anymore. I hate who he's made me become." Helen shook her head. "Actually, I hate who I have allowed myself to become."

Emma was silent and Helen pictured her sitting at her desk, her papers spread out in front of her, her black Mont Blanc loosely clutched in her left hand. It was what Helen called her "thinking pose." Helen heard the thump of Emma's pen being tossed onto a pile of papers and then her deep sigh.

"As your lawyer, I have to tell you that you need to seriously think this through," she said at last.

Helen smiled and leaned back in her chair. "You're not my lawyer, Em."

"Well, I am *a* lawyer. And I'm also your friend. And as such, I have to caution you against this. I'm not talking about leaving David; he's an ass and you should have done it a long time ago. But quitting your job? Starting over? It's risky. Can't you just transfer to another office? What about New York? Or you could come here."

"I appreciate your concern. Really. But this is something I have to do. I can't just keep trudging through life. I need a complete change. I want to start over. I need to take a risk."

Emma laughed softly. "That sounds funny coming from a woman who investigates accidents for a living."

"Not for much longer," Helen said.

"You should come here and stay with me," Emma said. "It would be good for both of us. And since David doesn't even know I exist, you can disappear for a while."

It was something Helen had considered, but wasn't sure how to broach. The fact that Emma lived in the same town as James made her the perfect backup plan. The only problem was she hadn't told Emma about James. Not yet. She wanted to. She wanted the luxury of a confidante—needed it, in fact. But Emma had strict rules about what was appropriate and what wasn't. And infidelity wasn't. Even before her partner ended their seven-year relationship for a woman she met at a conference, Emma hadn't condoned infidelity. Now, she was adamant.

"I don't know," Helen said.

"Well, I do," Emma said. "This place is lonely without Sarah and it would be nice to have a friend. Besides, you're quitting your job. Staying here is free and it would give me a chance to dust off my Boston Brahmin hostess skills." She laughed softly.

"I don't know what that means," Helen said.

"I was just being self-deprecating," Emma said. "But seriously, why not? Do you have a better offer?"

Helen considered the invitation. Having a backup plan wasn't a bad idea. And, if things with James went as well as she thought they would, she would have a home base while they explored their relationship. She thought about how she would explain him to Emma. She would have to lie about how and when they met.

It was a good idea. And despite her desire to start fresh, it always made good sense to have a plan B. She wouldn't commit to a specific date, though. Better to go to Boston, meet James, and *then* contact Emma. Helen shook her head. Keeping track of her lies and half-truths was exhausting.

"Honestly, I don't know for sure what I'm going to do, but I *do know* that even if it's just for a visit, Boston is in my future. Would it be okay to play it by ear?"

"Of course," Emma said. "Just know you have a safe place to land if you need it. I don't know what I would have done without you this last year."

Helen waited through the silence.

"It's strange, isn't it?" Emma sighed.

"What?"

"Just where we've ended up—how much we've changed in the past four years. You and David. Me and Sarah. Love bit us both in the ass but we keep moving forward."

"Like there's an alternative?"

"I guess that's true." She paused. "Listen, I've got to go do a deposition, but promise me you'll think about it?"

"I will," Helen said. "I'll let you know more when I have more details."

"Okay," Emma said. And then she was gone.

Helen pulled the phone from her ear. The screen was smudged with makeup from where it had been pressed against her cheek.

She considered fishing around in her purse for a tissue but instead used the underside of her blouse.

Could she live with Emma? They were so different, such unlikely friends—Emma with her old money Bostonian propriety and Helen with her second generation Polish parents. And, to be honest, at first Helen hadn't liked Emma. She was too polished with her expensive suits and her effortlessly perfect hair. Day after day, she sat impassively at the conference table as they discussed the Air India crash and the company's obligations for payout and possible lawsuits. She capped and uncapped her pen, scribbled notes, and drank one Diet Coke after the other. It had only been one night after work when the team had gone out for a drink that the two of them had talked—and then only because Emma instigated it.

Helen had been standing at the bar, waiting for the bartender to bring her glass of Chardonnay when she sensed someone beside her. She turned to see Emma, purse over her shoulder, a credit card elegantly pinched between her fore and middle fingers.

"What can I get you?" the bartender asked as he carefully placed Helen's wine on the white beverage napkin in front of her.

Emma looked around him to the rows of liquor bottles. "I'll have a double Lagavulin. Neat." She handed him the card, tipped her head slightly in the direction of Helen's wine, and smiled politely. "And put both of them on the card, please."

She said nothing as she watched him leave.

"Thank you," Helen said. "You didn't have to buy my drink."

Emma looked sidelong at her with the same polite smile she had given the bartender. "I wanted to. Actually, I wanted to talk to you."

"Oh." Helen blinked. "Well . . ." She turned to look at their coworkers who were crowded around two tables that had been shoved together. Their conversation was loud as they talked over each other. She gestured instead at the bar stools in front of them. "Do you want to sit here?"

Emma glanced at the table and then back at Helen. "Yes."

She slid elegantly onto the stool just as the bartender returned with her drink and the folder with the credit card slip. Emma nodded in thanks, picked up the drink, and then turned her body so she was facing Helen.

"So, why don't you like me?" She gazed steadily at Helen as she raised the tumbler to her lips and took a sip.

Helen felt her face flush. She shook her head. "I don't know what you mean."

"Umm." Emma arched a perfect eyebrow and set the glass back on the bar. "I'm not offended. Just curious." She gave Helen a small, closed-lipped smile and seemed to wait for her to speak. When she didn't, she leaned forward and said in a low voice, "Is it because I'm a lesbian?"

"Oh my god, no." Helen sat back so quickly, she almost lost her balance.

Emma laughed and caught her arm. "I'm sorry. Sometimes I can't resist trying to get a reaction out of people—especially if I don't think they like me."

Helen blinked several times and tried to smile good-naturedly. "Why do you care if I like you or not?"

"I'm not sure." Emma's smile faded. She picked up her glass. "But I'm not wrong, am I?"

Helen frowned. "I don't know as it's a case of not liking you. I think it's more that you . . ." She shook her head and tried to think about what it was about Emma that was off-putting. "I think you intimidate me. You're so," she waved a hand up and down in front of Emma, "well packaged."

"Ah." Emma nodded and took another sip of her drink. She held the scotch in her mouth for several seconds before swallowing. She stared down into the tumbler as she spoke. "Looks can be deceiving." She looked up and met Helen's gaze.

Helen tipped her head slightly to the side. "This is a strange conversation."

"It is. Still." Emma smiled the genuine smile again and Helen found herself softening. "I'm not sure why it feels so important to me, but I'd like for us to become friends."

And they had. In fact, Emma had become her best friend even though she never even told David of her existence. Not only would he not have approved of her lifestyle, but also he would have thought she was pretentious. Her money and manners would have intimidated him. But, if she were honest, that wasn't the real reason she hid her friendship. The truth was, Helen wanted Emma all for herself. She wanted a person who was hers only. And Emma was. And now, so was James.

At the thought of his name, Helen's grin widened. He was the one responsible for all of this—or if nothing else, the impetus. James, with his dark curly hair, handsome face, and lean runner's body, was the one who showed her that she could seize the life she wanted. He'd done it.

There was nothing he wanted that he didn't go after. Despite being from a poor family, he put himself through medical school. And rather than make a lot of money in private practice, he opted to work in the ER where he was able to help people on a daily basis. He liked good food, good wine, and he lived each day to the fullest. He ran. He climbed mountains. He parasailed. And, he loved her. The thought still made her flush with excitement.

James Reilly loved her.

It was almost too good to be true. She hadn't been looking to fall in love. She had just been doing her job. It had been a routine investigation on an insurance claim. A man had died while parasailing. She had been researching the activity. It had simply been happenstance that she read James's comments in a threaded discussion. Even now she couldn't say exactly what it was about his posts, but something about the way he wrote, the warmth in his words as he talked about the experience of floating, dipping, and gliding through the air, compelled her to search him out.

She knew even as she clicked on the link to his Facebook page, that it was unprofessional. But she couldn't stop herself—just as she couldn't stop herself from looking at his pictures and reading his posts. And then she contacted him. It had all been under the guise of her job, of course, but the conversation had flowed. And before she knew it, they had become intimate.

Helen swallowed as she remembered the first time their correspondence had been more than just casual. She had been sitting at her desk at work. They had been instant messaging each other all afternoon. James was in his office at the hospital. Things had been quiet in the ER and so he was taking a break. The conversation had started out innocent enough with just a little flirtation.

So, how are things in the world of insurance? Anything interesting going on?

She had grinned as she typed her reply.

Not really. How's your day going?

She glanced out the doorway of her floor-to-ceiling cubicle to
see if anyone was in the walkway as she waited for his reply.

All's quiet here. A kid came in with a broken arm about
an hour ago. But other than that, not much else going
on. What are you up to?

Helen's fingers raced over the keyboard.

Not much. Just the usual. I'm just waiting until the
workday is over so I can get out of here. I have a massage
scheduled for 6 and I can't wait! I have some kinks that
really need to be worked out.

She wasn't trying to be provocative, but there was a part of
her that hoped James would reply with something less-than-
appropriate. They had exchanged pictures and knew enough about
each other to recognize that they both were fairly attractive. And,
from the subtle flirting in which they had been engaging in the
past couple of weeks, she was pretty sure the attraction to each
other was mutual. She wasn't disappointed with his reply.

Too bad I'm not there. Massages are great. I'm told I
give great back rubs. Great body rubs, too.

Helen blinked as an image flashed into her mind of his hands
on her body, his tanned skin a sharp contrast to her lighter
complexion. She closed her eyes for several seconds, enjoying the
thought of his hands moving across her thighs and—
"Helen, do you know where the Lockhart file is?"
Helen's eyes flew open and she sat rigidly upright. Her
supervisor, Greg, stood in the doorway, a foam stress toy in the
shape of a football clutched in one hand, a ballpoint pen in the
other.
"I'm sorry, Greg," Helen said quickly, embarrassed to have
been caught mid-fantasy. "You wanted the . . . ?"

"Lockhart file," he said and squeezed the foam toy rhythmically. "The scuba death? In South Florida?"

"Right." Helen scanned the papers and file folders on her desk. Her instant messenger alert pinged. She glanced at the screen. It was James.

> The key is plenty of oil and really using your thumbs to stimulate the muscle.

Greg stepped into her cubicle and moved to stand next to her desk.

"I . . . uh . . . don't think I have it." Helen prayed he wouldn't step around the desk where he could see her computer screen. "I think it's in Susan's inbox."

Her instant messenger pinged again.

> Are you there?

Greg's eyes flicked to her computer. He frowned slightly and continued to squeeze his stress toy. Helen smiled innocently up at him and waited for him to reply.

"Okay. I'll go ask her." He turned to leave and then snapped his fingers and spun back around to face her. "When you get a second, could you come by my office? I have a new claim I'd like you to look into."

Helen nodded and forced herself to smile. "I'll come by later this afternoon."

Rather than reply, Greg tipped his head slightly to the side and studied her. Helen tried not to flinch at the scrutiny.

"Are you doing something different with your hair? You look . . ." He shrugged. "Different."

Helen relaxed. She wasn't in trouble. She grinned. "I am. Thanks for noticing."

"Looks good." He smiled and, with a final squeeze of his football, turned and walked out of her cubicle.

When he was out of sight, Helen let the smile disappear and inhaled deeply. There were strict rules about personal e-mail at work and given the nature of James's last couple of messages, she would have in the very least been reprimanded had Greg seen the interaction. She glanced down at the screen just as another message appeared.

I didn't scare you off, did I? I was just joking around.

Helen shook her head slightly. She needed to end the correspondence. The fact that she was communicating with James at work was the least of her transgressions. Add to it the fact that she only corresponded with James while she was at work so David couldn't find out and, more importantly, that she hadn't told James she was married, and it was clear that she was breaking some pretty major rules. She raised her fingers to the keyboard and considered what to write.

"Just tell him the truth," she muttered after several seconds of staring at the screen. "That, in itself, should be enough to scare him off."

My boss just came into my office.

She hit send. She was buying time and she knew it.
"Come on, Helen. Just do it." As she prepared herself to type the truth, James sent another message.

Whew! I thought maybe I had gone too far.

Helen studied the words and reconsidered her response.

Not too far at all. In fact . . .

The words appeared almost by their own volition. Helen punched the "enter" key, sucked her lower lip gently between her teeth, and waited for his response.

So, it's mutual?

She exhaled the breath she hadn't realized she was holding. "Fish or cut bait," she told herself.

Yes. It's mutual.

She waited through what seemed like an interminable silence.

> Okay . . . so since we're being honest, is it too weird to say that I think I like you more than just flirting? I'm not trying to rush and I know we live in different states, but I find you very . . . interesting? Fun? Sexy as hell?

Helen flushed with pleasure even as she felt the tingle of apprehension at what she was doing.

> Not too weird at all. I feel the same way. There's something about you that I can't seem to get out of my system. How's THAT for creepy. I promise you I'm not a psycho.

> *Grin* I know you're not psycho. You forget, I'm a doctor. I'm trained to recognize the symptoms.

Helen tapped her fingers nervously on the desk. She needed to tell James the truth. As exciting at the exchange was, it was unfair to continue to lie to him, even if it was a lie by omission. She raised her eyes to the screen when the alert pinged again.

> So, where do we go from here?

Ultimately, they had continued to communicate online. And later, over the phone. And finally, they had agreed to meet. It had been, Helen realized as she studied her reflection in the rearview mirror, inevitable that she would end up here, sitting in her car at the bus terminal in downtown Chicago. She glanced down at the watch David had given her for their wedding anniversary along with a card that jokingly suggested it would help her be on time. It was almost three o'clock. She had an hour in which to buy her ticket, get some candy for the road, and wait until time to board.

Helen looked around the interior of the car once more. This would be the last time she would see it. Eventually, when the divorce came through, she would get her share of the house and their jointly owned possessions. But for now, all she wanted to be responsible for were her bags and herself.

She pulled her phone out of her purse and texted James.

> At the bus station. We leave at 4. Can you believe that
> in a little over 24 hours I'll finally be in your arms? I
> love you.

They had agreed that since she wouldn't have the opportunity
to charge her phone while on the bus and since he was on call,
they would only text occasionally during her trip. Ironically, it
would be the longest time they would be out of communication
since they first began to correspond. As she waited for his reply,
she used the edge of her shirt to wipe at the remaining smudges
on the screen.

> Travel safely. I will meet you in the lobby of your hotel.
> There is something I need to do first thing. There's
> something I need to tell you.

Helen smiled. She imagined that he wanted to kiss her. Maybe
he wanted to make love to her. Maybe he wanted to . . . No. It was
too soon for that. But maybe . . . They both had shared that this was
"it." She shook her head as if to dispel the idea. Whatever it was,
she would know soon enough. But, she thought as she reached for
the door handle, if she didn't get moving, she would miss her ride.

Maggie

MAGGIE STARED AIMLESSLY at the darkness on the other side of the windowpane and tried once again to force herself to focus on her presentation. Writing never came easily for her and her nervousness about finding and opening herself up to Sarah only made it that much more difficult to concentrate.

She glanced down at the open laptop. The pipes on the screen saver snaked and twisted maniacally as it waited for her to do something—anything. She raised her fingers to the keyboard and then sighed as she realized she didn't know what she wanted to say. She looked around the bus instead. She had chosen to leave so late on a Wednesday afternoon with the hopes that there would be fewer passengers traveling from Indianapolis and she hadn't been disappointed. The bus was less than half full.

"I like it when there aren't so many people." The elderly woman on the other side of the aisle voiced Maggie's thoughts. "Gives you room to spread out." She looked pointedly at Maggie's open computer. "You, too?"

Maggie nodded and gestured at her laptop. "I'm hoping to get some work done."

The woman tipped her head slightly back and smiled, the beam from the overhead reading light catching the dirt and smudges on her glasses. Maggie resisted the urge to offer her a tissue.

"You girls today. Always rushing around doing things. Lots of papers and phone calls." The woman shook her head in disgust. "My granddaughter works for some big company in Indianapolis. Always too busy to come home. Always too busy."

Maggie smiled but didn't respond. No sense in trying to point out that staying at home and raising children wasn't really an option for most women anymore.

"So, what do you do?" the woman asked when she realized Maggie wasn't going to reply.

"I'm a funeral director." Maggie braced herself for the usual reaction—what she called the Eww-face.

Instead, the woman smiled. "That's a hard job, I can imagine.

My husband, Billy, died six months ago in a hunting accident. The people at the home were so kind." She leaned forward. "Of course they tried to charge me an arm and a leg, but I stuck to the plan Billy bought us in '76. It was the bicentennial and he looked at me and said, 'Eddie.' That's what people call me. My real name is Edith, but growing up my brothers called me Eddie and it just stuck. So anyway, he said, 'Eddie, we're not getting any younger. I think we need to start planning for what comes next.' So, that very next day he goes out and gets life insurance policies and funeral insurance."

Maggie sighed inwardly, knowing this was not going to be a short story and wondered how she could extricate herself from the conversation. Thankfully, her phone vibrated. She glanced down at the number. It was Ben.

"I'm sorry." She smiled apologetically and held up the phone. "I don't mean to interrupt, but I really have to take this."

The woman looked suspiciously at the phone and then shrugged.

Maggie tapped the green answer icon. "Hello?"

"Hi, Mags." The voice on the other end of the line was deep and familiar.

Maggie was always surprised how much Ben sounded like their father and for a moment, she felt a poignant sense of loss. Even though Ben hadn't been close to Franklin, Maggie had.

"Hey, Ben. What's up? I was beginning to worry. I haven't heard from you in so long."

"I've been keeping myself busy." He laughed.

Maggie glanced at Eddie and noted that she appeared to be listening with interest to her end of the conversation. Without trying to appear obvious, Maggie turned her body so she was facing the window. It didn't afford much more privacy, but it was better than nothing.

"Still working on the fishing boat?" she asked, her voice intentionally low.

Ben laughed again. "Nah. I'm in Mendocino now working as part of this organic cooperative. We grow everything and share whatever we have. It's entirely off the grid. Solar panels . . . a well . . . totally contained waste management system."

Maggie resisted rolling her eyes. "It sounds like a cult."

"Commune," Ben corrected. "And it's not like that. It's more like . . . oh, I don't know. It's like friends pulling together."

"Well, do me a favor and if they offer you Kool-Aid, don't drink it." Maggie regretted the words the moment they left her lips.

Ben made a noise that was a cross between irritation and disgust. "So, how's the dead body business?" His tone was equally cutting. "Embalm anyone we know, lately?"

"Ben—"

"I know, I know." Ben sighed. "Sorry. Old habits."

"Me, too," Maggie said softly.

Neither spoke for several seconds.

Finally, Ben cleared his throat. "So, you're probably wondering why I called."

Maggie picked at a loose thread on the cuff of her blouse and waited for him to continue.

"It's a long story but . . . I need to borrow some money." He paused, and then added more softly, "Mags, I'm going to be a dad."

Maggie blinked in shock. "You're what?"

"I've been seeing this woman at the cooperative," Ben continued. "Her name's Ellen and *we're* going to have a baby."

"Oh, Benny," Maggie said. "How did you let this happen?"

"I wanted it to happen," Ben said. "I'm ready to settle down."

"Really." Maggie couldn't stop the snort of disbelief. "You're ready to settle down and be a family man, but you want me to loan you money?" She sighed. "What happened to the money you got from the buyout?"

"I used it for living expenses and to buy into the co-op," he said.

"You had to buy in to this commune?" Maggie said louder than intended. She glanced at Eddie, who was openly eavesdropping, and then turned back toward the window. "What kind of ridiculous Ponzi scheme is this place?"

"It's not like that," Ben said. "It's an open way of life. We honor the earth and each other. We show respect and—"

"Whatever," Maggie said, in a dismissive tone that she knew sounded like their father's.

Ben sighed. "So, will you help me out or not?"

Maggie ran her fingers through her hair and then down to the back of her neck. She rubbed at the tight muscles and shook her head. They both knew she would give him the money. That was their dynamic and it always played out the same way.

"When is she due?" she asked finally.

"Six months." The relief was evident in his voice.

"There are going to be some strings this time," she said. "I'm on a bus right now, but if you call me next week, we can make the arrangements."

"I'll call next week. Thanks."

After they said their good-byes, Maggie stared at the phone's dark screen.

"Families," Eddie said.

Maggie raised her eyes to meet her gaze.

Eddie shook her head. "Can't live with 'em, can't kill 'em." She smiled suddenly and leaned forward. She waved her gnarled hand, beckoning Maggie to come closer. "But, if you do kill 'em . . ." Her tone was conspiratorial and she winked dramatically. "Make it look like an accident."

Bug

BUG CLOSED THE book propped up against his knees and shut his eyes. The ending, as with all of the Hardy Boys books, had been predictable. But that was part of why he liked them. He knew that regardless of the mystery, regardless of the danger faced by Frank and Joe, they never lost their nerve and they always came out on top. It wasn't like real life. In real life, when bad things happened, they rarely got better. If anything, they got worse.

In the hallway, he could hear the voices of the other boys who shared the room with him. From the sound of it, they were talking about dinner.

"I love franks and beans," Calvin said as he walked into the room and headed over to the bed closest to the window. Behind him trailed Tony and Sid.

"Beans, beans, the musical fruit," Tony sang with a grin. "The more you eat 'em . . ."

"The more you toot." Sid cocked his hip to the side and let out a loud fart. "Ha! Whadidja think, Talbott? Like that? Yeah! Eat it, sucker." He cocked his hip to the other side and farted again.

For not the first time, Bug wished he didn't have to share a room with Sid. He liked Calvin, a wiry African American who carried himself with a calculated, hunched indifference. And Tony, a slow, rather dim-witted Hispanic boy, was harmless enough. He did whatever Calvin told him to do. He was a follower. But there was something about Sid that made Bug uncomfortable. He was always loud and pushy. And gross. Like with the whole farting thing.

"Knock it off, Sid," Calvin said as he flung himself onto his bed and tucked his hands behind his head. "You're stinkin' up the place, man." He screwed up his face in disgust. "Jesus. Open the fuckin' window."

Sid bent over and gave one more fart in Bug's direction and then ambled over to the window. The panes were fogged with the heat of the room. He tried to raise the window. It wouldn't budge, and he pounded on the swollen wood with the heel of his hand. He grabbed the handle and tried again. It was still stuck.

"Fuck it." He turned to Calvin and shrugged. "Won't open. Want me to break it?"

Calvin frowned and shook his head. "No, dude. Just sit down. And stop farting."

Sid grunted and shuffled over to his bed, flopped down, and began to pick his nose.

"Whatcha reading?" Calvin asked.

Bug blinked and turned his attention back to Calvin who had turned his head so his chin rested on his bent forearm. Bug thought he seemed genuinely interested in the title.

He held up the closed book so the cover was facing Calvin. "Hardy Boys. *The Secret Warning*."

Calvin nodded. "It's one of the old ones, right?"

The makeshift library at the shelter had a variety of musty, outdated books, most of which had been donated by people who wanted them out of their houses, but didn't have the heart to throw them away. *A lot like us*, Bug thought. He nodded.

"What did you think?" Calvin turned his body slightly so he was partially facing Bug.

Bug considered how to respond. Calvin had never been mean to him. If anything, he had always gone out of his way to be nice. But people acted differently when their friends were around. Bug knew enough to be cautious.

"Good," Bug said finally. "Kind of out of date."

Calvin smirked. "Yeah. I always wonder how they get the money to do all that stuff. And how do they get out of school?"

"It's part of the American Teens Against Crimes, man," Sid volunteered. "It's like top secret government shit. They get out of school to take on missions 'cause it's like black ops stuff."

"That's in the newer ones," Calvin said. "We're talking about the old ones—the ones with the old cars and shit where they were sneaking around behind their dad's back."

Sid shrugged. "Those are lame. 'Sides . . . they don't help me get ready for the ATAC, like the new ones." He grinned. "I'm gonna be all up in that shit when I'm old enough."

Calvin frowned, glanced quickly at Bug, and then back at Sid. "Man, you know that's made up, right? There's no ATAC." His tone was gentle.

Sid shook his head emphatically. "No, man, it's real. I've got a cousin who knows a guy who's in it."

Tony watched the exchange with interest, his gaze darting back and forth between Calvin and Sid.

"Man, you're cousin is feeding you a line," Calvin said. "The ATAC isn't real. Do you really think the government is going to use kids to solve crimes like that?"

Bug nodded in agreement with Calvin's statement.

Sid jerked his head to glare at Bug. "You a bobblehead, Talbott?" He swung his feet to the floor and stood. His face was a dark red, though from embarrassment or anger, Bug wasn't sure. He took a step toward Bug.

"Leave him alone, Sid." Calvin, too, stood but didn't move toward them.

"Why?" Sid kept his gaze on Bug's face. His voice held a note of defiance.

"Because I said so." Calvin took a step toward Sid. "He's leaving tomorrow. It's not worth the trouble you'd get into from Fugly."

Sid snickered as he always did at the name they used for Mrs. Johnson, the portly director of the shelter. "I suppose you're right. Guess it's your lucky day, Talbott." He turned and flopped back down on the bed. The metal frame squeaked.

"You *are* leaving tomorrow, aren't you?" Calvin asked Bug.

Bug nodded. "I'm going to Boston to stay with my aunt. She's gonna watch me until my mom . . ." He shrugged and Calvin nodded in understanding.

Each of them was in the shelter until they were shipped off to relatives, until their respective parents or caregivers had worked through whatever problems made them unfit guardians, or until they could be placed in a foster home.

"She cool?"

Bug considered how to answer the question. He could lie and say she was or he could tell the truth and admit that he had no idea. He shrugged again. "I don't know. I don't know her really, at all. She sends birthday and Christmas cards but I've only met her once. She seems nice."

"I'm sure it'll all be good." Calvin rubbed at his ear with the side of his forefinger—a gesture Bug had come to realize meant that he was thinking. He walked to the edge of Bug's bed and turned so his back was to Sid and Tony. "You ever been placed before?" he asked in a low voice.

"Not really," Bug said. "Just with my grandma. She took me when Rh—my mom . . . you know."

Calvin nodded.

"Okay, so, even though it's different when it's family, it's still not . . . right?" He crossed his arms. Bug could see the knobs of his elbows poking out on either side of his narrow chest. "Just keep your head down and do what she wants. Don't give her any reason to kick you back."

"I don't think she would," Bug said. "She seems really nice and she teaches college there so she's around kids a lot. My grandma always said nice things about her."

Calvin shook his head. "It don't matter. People get weird when they have to take care of somebody else's kid. She's gonna wish you weren't there." He raised his eyebrows. "You gotta make her glad you are. Trust me. I know what happens if you don't."

"Is that what happened to you?" Bug forced himself to hold Calvin's gaze.

"Lots of shit happened to me. I'm just tellin' you this because it's your first time and . . ." Calvin shrugged. "Just, if you want to stay there, make her like you and do what she wants."

Bug nodded and lowered his gaze to the floor. Calvin's left shoe was bound up with duct tape. He knew that Calvin had other, nicer shoes, but he refused to wear them, preferring instead the damaged ones he had brought with him.

"Hey, what are you guys whispering about?" Sid asked suspiciously.

Bug looked up to see Sid watching them.

Calvin turned and walked back to his bed. "Nothing that's any of your business."

He lay back down and returned to his previous position. He waited until Sid started talking to Tony before turning his head back to Bug.

"Just remember what I told you," he said. "Don't give her a reason to send you back because whether you know it or not, she's looking for one."

Jimmy

JIMMY STUDIED HIS face in the bathroom mirror. He looked nothing like any of the pictures he'd sent Helen.

"What the hell have you done?" he asked his reflection.

At first, it hadn't seemed like that much of a deception. Dr. Hamblin was the type of guy women wanted to date and men wanted to be. He was handsome, successful, and adventuresome. The women in the ER swooned when he walked by. And in the beginning, Jimmy hadn't felt all that guilty for borrowing some of his Facebook pictures. They were just pictures for God's sake. Lots of people used fake profile pictures. In fact, most people probably did. That was the point of the Internet, wasn't it? Its anonymity allowed you to be whomever you wanted, or at least the person you would be had you not been limited by genetics, health, or appearance.

That had been his rationale. And he had kept his interactions surface level. He got close to no one. No harm, no foul—that was until Helen contacted him and wanted information about parasailing. She had seen some of his posts on a discussion thread and contacted him. She was, she'd explained, an insurance claims investigator and doing research on parasailing. Could he answer a few questions?

He'd hesitated before responding and even when he did answer her questions, it was only after he had Googled the answers or parroted what someone who knew what they were talking about had written. And he bought time by asking Helen questions about herself and her interests.

It had actually been kind of fun at first. But after a while, he had begun to like her—had begun to more than like her. And then he became scared of losing her. So, instead of just using Dr. Hamblin's pictures, Jimmy tried to add to his allure by using his career and other hobbies as well. As a paramedic, he knew enough about emergency medicine to fake being a doctor as long as the person he was talking to didn't know much about the medical field. And Helen didn't.

Jimmy turned his face to the side and studied his profile. It didn't help that he looked almost jaundiced in the fluorescent lighting of the bathroom. He frowned a little and studied the plane of flesh that ran straight from his chin to his neck. It wasn't, he acknowledged, flattering. He pulled at the skin, trying to tighten it.

Better, he thought. But he couldn't go around pulling at his face. He released the flesh and tipped his head slightly back. He could see a hint of a jaw line. *Maybe if I let my beard grow . . .* He shook his head. It was hopeless. In less than twenty-four hours, Helen was going to find out that the man she had been complimenting and about whom she had been fantasizing wasn't a dark-haired, chiseled prince, but in fact, a toad. Jimmy closed his eyes and sighed. How had it all gone so wrong?

"It's because you lied," he murmured as he opened his eyes and forced himself to meet his own, recriminating gaze.

He was guilty of catfishing. He hadn't realized at first there was a name for what he was doing. The term made sense, though. Catfish were bottom-feeders, and wasn't that what he was? A bottom-feeder? The lowest common denominator? He felt the familiar tightness in his chest. There was only one way out of this. He needed to call Helen now and tell her not to come. He needed to tell her the truth. Wherever she was, she could get off the bus and go home.

He walked back into the bedroom, picked up his cell phone, and flipped it open.

You have 1 new text.

Jimmy stared at the screen for several moments before clicking on the message. It was from Helen, of course. No one else ever texted him. It had come in several hours before and he was just now seeing it.

At the bus station. We leave at 4. Can you believe that in a little over 24 hours I'll finally be in your arms? I love you.

Jimmy blinked. If he were any kind of stand-up guy, he would end this now, before she arrived in Boston. Yes, she would be hurt. And yes, she would be angry. But at least she wouldn't be waiting for a man who didn't exist. He considered his options. His inclination was to lie.

He rubbed the fleshy part of his thumb over the buttons as he thought about what to say. Maybe something like: I hate to do this but I have been called into the ER to cover. He shook his head. Helen thought he lived in Boston. So what if he had to work? She would just tell him they would see each other when he got off his shift. No, he should be clear that she shouldn't come. He began to type.

> Don't come. There's something I have to tell you.

Jimmy considered the message. It sounded cryptic. And, if he was going to write something like that, shouldn't he just be honest and just type the words?

> Helen, please don't come. I lied to you. I'm not who I pretended to be.

It was the truth. And maybe, just maybe, if he were honest, Helen could look past the lies. She said she loved him. And what he had shown her was his authentic self—or at least who he wanted to be. Maybe if he were truthful, she would still give him a chance to salvage their relationship.

"Don't be a pussy. Do it." Jimmy took a deep breath and forced himself to type out the words even as he reminded himself that if she loved him—truly loved him for who he was—she would overlook the lies. Right?

Wrong.

She wouldn't come if she knew the truth. He'd never hear from her again. He needed to see her just once. And maybe, if they saw each other, she would give him a chance. Maybe he could still salvage this. Quickly, he deleted the note and typed instead:

> Travel safely. I'll meet you in the lobby of your hotel. There is something we need to do first thing. There is something I need to tell you.

He hit "send" and sighed. It was done. There was nothing he could do to change the wheels set in motion. All he could do now was plan what he was going to do next.

He tossed the phone onto the bed and looked down at his open duffle bag. Inside were already a couple of pairs of underwear, socks, and the clothes he would wear when he went to meet Helen. Next to the duffle were his warm-up pants and shirt for the bus trip. He would probably need some warmer clothes, too. Boston in November was cool. He went to the closet where he had carefully stacked his collection of sweatshirts. Two plus the one he was going to wear on the trip should be enough.

It was seven-thirty by the time he finished packing and zipped closed the duffle bag for the final time. Carefully, so as not to hurt his back, he lifted it from the bed and carried it to the front door. He was ready for his five a.m. departure for the bus station. He looked around the tiny apartment. He should eat and then go to bed, though he suspected sleep would be elusive. Times like this he most felt the urge to disappear into the foggy calm of oxycodone. Just the thought of it made his scalp tingle.

Jimmy closed his eyes. *Slow, deep breaths,* he reminded himself. Think about what Diane said: do something else to distract yourself. In his head, he could hear his counselor's pack-a-day rasp telling him to slow down and center himself.

"When it gets bad, take yourself out of the game," she had said at their last session. "Go for a walk around the block. Call somebody. Read a book. Do something to get your mind off of it. Addictions can be controlled."

Jimmy had looked at her hands as she spoke. Something about Diane intimidated him and he generally found it easier to look anywhere but at her face.

He could tell she had, at one time, been attractive. Even now with her graying brown hair and hazel eyes, he could imagine the younger Diane. But decades of hearing other people's problems, too many cigarettes, and lack of exercise were beginning to take a toll. Some days she looked every bit of her, what Jimmy guessed to be, about fifty years. But not on her hands. Never her hands. Small palmed with long, tapered fingers and neatly trimmed nails, they still looked young and powerful. He had wondered more than once if she played piano. He could imagine her fingers poised elegantly above the keys.

"—but you have to want it." The change in Diane's tone jerked Jimmy back to the conversation.

"It's just so hard." Jimmy closed his eyes and inhaled slowly. "The craving . . ." He shook his head and exhaled. "It's so strong."

"It is . . . I know."

Something about the way she said the words made Jimmy open his eyes. Rather than looking at him, Diane now was the one studying her hands. She rubbed the thumb of her right hand along the waxy, yellow nicotine stain on the inside of her middle finger.

"Sometimes the desire can be almost overwhelming." Her voice was so low that Jimmy had to lean forward to hear her. "But you have to keep your sights set on the bigger picture . . . turning your life around . . . making a difference . . . making amends."

She looked up and blinked as if in surprise to find him there.

"You know, don't you?" Jimmy asked even though he thought he already knew the answer. "Not just from this job, but . . . you *know*."

A faint smile appeared and she shook her head sadly. "I've been doing this for a long time, Jimmy. I've seen a lot of people go through what you're going through. It's different for everyone, but the one constant is the need. I'm not just talking about the need to get high, but the need to feel okay for just a little while."

Jimmy watched Diane in fascination. It was the first time she had shown him anything other than what she called her tough love style of counseling.

"But here's the thing, Jimmy." She raised her gaze and her expression resumed its usual hard set. "The pills don't ever make anything okay. It's just an illusion." Her voice rattled with phlegm and she cleared her throat. "You want to get past this, then you need to learn to be okay with yourself." She sat up straighter and looked him up and down. "You need to let go of the fat kid baggage. You need to recognize your worth as a person. So what if you're shy. So what if you're not in with the popular crowd."

"But, how?" Jimmy tried not to sound whiney or desperate. "How do I do that?"

"By respecting yourself." She waved her hand up and down. "Sit up straight. Take some pride in your appearance." She cleared her throat again. "You know how they say to dress for the job you want, not for the job you have? Well, the same applies here except it's not just about clothes. It's about self-respect. Present the man you want to be. You've got to get over what happened with your father. You can't let your crappy childhood dictate the rest of your life."

Jimmy snorted. "Easier said than done."

"It is. But it's also possible. The question I guess I have is if you really want to get past it." Diane paused and stared hard at him.

Despite his best efforts not to, Jimmy squirmed under the scrutiny.

"Why wouldn't I?" he asked finally, when the silence became too much.

Diane sat back in her chair. "You tell me."

Jimmy frowned. He hated it when she did this—when she turned his words back against him. "I don't . . ." He tried to figure out what Diane wanted to hear. He shook his head. "I don't know what you mean."

"Yes, you do." Diane continued to watch him.

"No, I—"

"You do, Jimmy." Diane leaned quickly forward and several strands of hair slipped out of the hammered silver barrette she always wore clipped low on her neck, but just above the collar of her blouse. "Consider this . . . maybe it's easier to have an excuse for not changing your behavior. 'I had a bad childhood' . . . 'My father was a drunk who beat me' . . . 'I was the fat kid no one liked.' Don't you get tired of hauling all the excuses around? Wouldn't it be nice to just let all of that go?"

Jimmy jerked his head in a tight nod.

"Everything you do over the course of every day is within your control." She reached out as if she was going to touch him and he tensed. "But you have to be the one to make the decision, Jimmy. *You* have to be the one to choose not to hide behind the safety of the past."

Jimmy swallowed. "But what if it's not the safety of the past? What if it's my punishment?"

Diane sat back, her expression shifting from one of confrontation to interest. She tipped her head slightly to the left and raised an eyebrow. "What do you mean?"

Jimmy felt the rush of heat suffuse his face and chest. He

hadn't told Diane about Helen. He had rationalized it at first as not something real and therefore, not worth mentioning. And then later, when it became far too real, he was too embarrassed and guilty to confess the truth. Despite everything else, he wanted Diane to like him.

He shrugged.

"No," Diane said. Her hazel eyes were piercing in their intensity. "You don't get to do that. Explain what you mean."

Jimmy inhaled deeply and then slowly let the breath out. He stared fixedly at the button on Diane's blouse just above the scratched, decorative buckle of her belt. Like her barrette, it too was hammered silver.

"What if the things that happen to me—the situations I create—are really just punishment for the things I did . . . the things I . . . do?" He met Diane's gaze for less than a second before looking back down.

"Explain what you mean," Diane said.

Jimmy rubbed his hands together and felt the scratch of a hangnail on the outside edge of his left thumb. He reached instinctively for the clippers he always carried in the pocket of this warm-up pants before remembering he had attached them to his key ring.

"Jimmy?" Diane was still waiting for an answer.

He considered telling her about Helen. If he was ever going to admit it, now was the time. He opened his mouth to speak and then closed it. "Like my dad," he said instead. "Maybe the reason why all of this happened was because I never forgave him. I could have moved in and taken care of him. I mean, I'm a trained medical professional. But instead, I got power of attorney, put him in that shitty nursing facility and left him there to rot. I haven't been to see him. Not once. Maybe all of this is my punishment for not doing the right thing."

"Like he did for you?"

Jimmy blinked but didn't respond.

"You have done nothing wrong," Diane continued. "In regard to your father, you made the decision that was best for you. And now, you're taking each day as it comes. You're working the program, you're coming here, and you're working at being the best version of yourself. But, Jimmy, you need to let go of those things you've made amends for and not accept responsibility for what's not yours." She was silent for several seconds. "Have you been going to meetings?"

Jimmy nodded even though it was a lie. There were just some rules he couldn't bring himself to break and as ironic as it was, lying to other addicts was one of them. If he went to a meeting and spoke, he would have to admit what he had been doing. Honesty was the bedrock of the program. It didn't matter whether it was Narcotics Anonymous, Alcoholics Anonymous, or any of the others he probably should join; to be there meant he had to tell the truth. And he couldn't. Not in good conscience. He didn't even carry his sobriety chip.

"Good." Diane seemed about to say more but the small alarm clock on the side table beeped, signaling the end of their session. She stretched to the side and pushed the small button that silenced it. "Our time is up. But before we wrap this up, I want to reiterate that all of this is in your control. It may not seem like it sometimes, but it is. It's there every time you make the decision not to use. It's there every time you make the decision to let go of the guilt of things that are in the past."

"She's right," Jimmy reminded himself as he stood in his apartment, his eyes still closed as he recalled the conversation. "I'm in control. This will pass."

He balled his hands, which hung at his sides, into fists and pinched his eyes more tightly shut. *I'm in control. I'm in control. I'm in control.* He stood that way, reciting the mantra, until the weakness passed. He opened his eyes and glanced at the clock. Only five minutes had passed since he had placed his bags by the door. Distraction, he reminded himself. Dinner. He went to the refrigerator and opened the freezer. It was empty aside from several Lean Cuisines and a frozen pizza. Neither sounded appealing but with no money and no other options, it was that or nothing.

Jimmy pulled out the frozen pizza. It was going to be a long night.

Helen

Helen felt the vibration of her cell phone and knew without looking that it was David calling. Again. She had been on the road for almost four hours and already he had called seventeen times. She closed her eyes and leaned her head back against the seat's headrest. She imagined David's reaction when he came home and found her gone. She had left the letter in an envelope on the kitchen island, David's name scrawled messily on the front.

She imagined him calling out for her as he came through the front door. When she didn't answer, he would go into the kitchen. He would see the envelope propped up against the fruit bowl. Knowing David, he would get a knife from the drawer and carefully slice open the envelope to access the single folded sheet of paper inside.

Helen had been surprised to realize that writing the letter had been the hardest part. She had sat at the kitchen counter for more than thirty minutes, trying to figure out how to explain to David the reasons why she was leaving. Snatches of the letter came back to her as she opened her eyes and rolled her head slightly to look out the window.

. . . have become someone I don't like . . .

. . . want more out of life than this . . .

. . . need to figure out who I am and what I want . . .

. . . want to take a chance . . .

. . . don't try to find me. I'll contact you when I'm ready . . .

Helen pressed her lips together as the bus sped down I-90, the Indiana farmland a blur of tans and brown. As far as she could tell, they were about thirty minutes outside of South Bend. She felt her phone pulse with the alert that she had a voice message. It was the fifth message David had left in addition to several texts. Eventually, she knew she would have to look at them. But at the moment, she didn't have the energy or the desire.

Where had their relationship gone wrong? Helen knew there had been problems before the miscarriages, but it just seemed like after they had accepted the fact that they couldn't get pregnant, everything changed. It was as if David blamed her because her body, for whatever reason, couldn't carry a baby to term. She exhaled softly through her nose. She had wanted a baby more than anything. Admitting that she would never be able to get pregnant or be a mother was one of the hardest things she had ever had to accept.

Perhaps it was better this way. At least now there was no child to worry about. And, if she were honest, she wasn't sure what kind of father David would have been anyway. His exacting standards and desire to control everything and everyone made him far too rigid for the messiness of a child. It made him far too rigid for the messiness of her. He hadn't always been like that. Or had he? She tried to remember when she had first noticed David's true nature. It had become obvious after they were married. But, had she seen signs of it before?

Helen turned her head and stared at the plushy, blue fabric and faux leather of the back of the seat in front of her. She had, she admitted, probably seen it on their fifth date. It had been a rainy day and traffic on Wabash had moved at little more than a crawl as her taxi from the main offices in The Loop navigated the congestion. Despite having paid the cabbie and jumped out of the taxi several blocks from the Italian restaurant where they were meeting, she had arrived about ten minutes late. David was waiting in the bar.

"I'm so sorry," she said in a rush as she slipped out of her trench coat and gave him a quick hug. "The traffic was a mess." She laughed. "I finally said, screw it and walked the last three blocks."

Rather than laugh with her, David smiled tightly and wiped at the droplets of water that had fallen from her hair onto his shoulder.

"You're all wet." He scowled slightly before returning his attention to her. "You should have just waited in the taxi."

Helen frowned. "But that would have made me later."

David seemed to consider her words before nodding slowly. "I suppose you're right." He turned to the bar and indicated the stool in which he'd been sitting. "When you were so late, I took the liberty of ordering you a drink."

Helen looked at the bar. A glass of white wine, the outside

cloudy with condensation, sat in the middle of a white paper cocktail napkin. She smiled even though she preferred red.

"Thanks." She slid onto the stool and picked up the glass. "After the day I've had, I could probably use the whole bottle."

David frowned again and lifted his own glass—a red, Helen noted with just a twinge of irritation. "That's a little excessive, don't you think?" He took a small sip and placed the glass neatly on his own beverage napkin.

"Only if I were serious," Helen said. Her tone was sharper than she had intended and she tried to soften her words with a grin.

David smiled stiffly.

"So . . . are we on the list?" Helen looked around the bar. Men and women, many of whom appeared to be co-workers having a happy hour, stood in groups or at tables talking and laughing loudly.

David nodded and his expression again became serious. "We *had* a table. But they won't seat you until your entire party is here. Since you were late, I had to give it away."

Helen fought back a sharp retort. "Well, I'm here now and hopefully it won't be long."

Rather than reply, David glanced down at his watch. He looked at the hostess stand and then back down at the time. "I should go check and make sure they haven't overlooked us. They might have forgotten that I said we'd be in here." He patted Helen lightly on the arm before striding toward the front of the restaurant.

Helen picked up her glass, took a large swallow, and grimaced at the sweetness. It was a Riesling. She looked up to see the bartender watching her.

"Doing okay?" He grinned and gestured to the wine. "Want something else?"

Helen glanced at David, who was talking to the hostess and then back at the bartender. The light shone off the pomade holding his dark curls into place. He grinned conspiratorially.

"Could you?" Helen asked.

The bartender nodded. "What would you like?"

Helen looked at the wine and sighed. "I don't want to hurt his feelings so I should probably stick with white." She shifted her gaze to the bartender who pulled the rag off his shoulder and wiped at the glossy wood. According to the silver tag on his shirt, his name was Josh. "How about something tart? Sauvignon Blanc?"

"Coming right up," he said as he grabbed the glass of Riesling, emptied it into the bar sink, and selected a fresh glass. Helen glanced back at the hostess stand. David appeared to be finishing his conversation. As he turned in her direction and headed back to the bar, the bartender quickly filled her glass.

"How much do I owe you?" she asked softly, hoping he would answer in kind.

He grinned, revealing a row of unnaturally white teeth, the canines pointed and prominent in a way that made him look sexy and dangerous. "On the house."

She smiled her thanks as David arrived at her side.

"They are clearing our table now," he said as he picked up his glass of wine. He raised it in the direction of the bartender. "Please transfer the tab to the table."

"What about a tip?" Helen murmured.

David frowned. "All he did was pour some wine. It's not like he waited on us."

"David." Helen frowned. "He gets paid next to nothing and survives on tips. I think you can afford to give him a couple of dollars."

"If it's so important to you, then why don't you leave him a tip?" David said. "It wouldn't have even been an issue if you'd been on time."

Helen blinked. "That's what this is about isn't it?" She snorted softly, opened her purse, and pulled out her wallet.

She had two twenties, a ten, and a five. Without hesitation, she pulled the ten dollar bill out of her wallet and laid it on the bar.

"Thanks, Josh. You were great." She smiled up at him and he gave her a quick wink. "And as for dinner . . ." She turned to David. "I've actually lost my appetite. I think I'm going to just go home."

David opened his mouth to protest but before he could speak, Helen held up her hand. He blinked twice, brought his lips together, and scowled.

"I'm tired and I think this is just not a good night for us to interact with each other." She gulped down her wine in several large swallows and carefully replaced the glass. "Call me when you're in a better mood."

She had walked away without looking back or waiting for a response.

David had called the next day to apologize. He'd had a bad day, he explained. Work had been crazy and what with the rain and his irritation at the world in general, he'd taken it out on her. He was sorry. And she had forgiven him, just as she had the next time. And the time after that. She had believed him every time he said he was trying to be more patient. Eventually, she had married him.

"And now I'm here," she murmured.

She stared out the window. Though it was dark, she could tell that the farmland had been replaced by suburbs. She glanced down at her watch. It was just after seven o'clock. They were supposed to have a ten minute layover in South Bend.

The thought of getting up, stretching, and perhaps texting James made her smile. Of course, that also meant seeing the texts from David. She sighed. She wasn't in the mood to think any more about David. She knew she would have to deal with him eventually, but not now. Before she could change her mind, she pulled out her phone and punched in the code to unlock it.

Without looking at her texts, she deleted the contents of her inbox. She didn't want to deal with the recriminations or with David's accusations. She considered blocking his number, but given that he was on the account, knew it would likely do no good. He could go into their account and remove the block. He could probably disconnect her number if he wanted.

Her stomach dropped at the realization that he had access to her phone records. He could easily find out where she was and who she was with. She began to text James to warn him but then stopped. She couldn't tell him about David. James didn't even know she was married. It was one of the things she intended to tell him in Boston.

"Fuck," she muttered.

The gray-haired man sitting next to her frowned in disapproval.

"Sorry. I just realized something that . . ." Helen dropped her head into her hands. She rubbed at her temples. "Sorry."

The man studied her for several seconds before nodding sympathetically. "I've had those kinds of days, myself. Anything you want to talk about?"

Helen raised her eyes to meet his gaze. There was something

grandfatherly about him that made her want to confide in him—to ask if he had a Werther's. His smile was kind. She looked down at her lap and shrugged.

"I'm running away from my life." She looked slowly up to gauge his response.

He nodded but didn't speak.

"I married the wrong man and then fell in love with the right one. And now I'm going to be with him but . . ." She faltered. "He doesn't know I'm married. And I'm worried that my husband will figure out who he is and contact him before I can."

The man inhaled slowly and pursed his lips. "Well, you are in a pickle, aren't you?" He shook his head and exhaled. "What are you going to do?"

Helen held her hands up helplessly and then dropped them back into her lap. "I don't know." She shrugged. "Nothing, I suppose. I guess I'll just tell James the truth when I get there. To be honest, he doesn't know that I'm doing more than just coming to meet him in person. He thinks this is just a visit." She laughed ruefully. "I don't even know why I'm telling you this. I don't even know your name."

"I'm William. William Francis." He extended his hand. It was warm and dry.

Even his touch is comforting, Helen thought as she shook it.

"Helen Whitman," she said. "Thanks for listening."

William smiled. "It's what I do—or actually what I did. I was a Presbyterian pastor for forty years."

"Great." Helen grimaced. "I just confessed my infidelity and lies to a pastor. You must think I'm a horrible person."

William shook his head. "Not really. You'd be amazed at the things I've heard over the years." He chuckled. "Your confession pales in comparison to some of the doozies I've heard." He paused and seemed to consider what to say next. "Not that you've asked for it, but if you don't mind some advice . . ."

Helen nodded.

"I've counseled a lot of people about a lot of things. And the one commonality, regardless of anything else, is fear."

Helen blinked in surprise. "I'm not sure I know what you mean."

"Everything goes back to fear," William said. "Fear of being found out. Fear of being abandoned. Fear of the unknown."

"And for me?" Helen wasn't sure she wanted to know the answer.

William raised his eyebrows. "You tell me."

"There are too many to list. Probably at the top is fear of being controlled—of being boxed in by a life I didn't realize I was choosing." Helen sighed. "I'm scared of being stuck where I am now. I just want out." She was about to say more but the bus decelerated and made its exit off of I-90 onto a smaller highway.

Helen looked out the window and saw a sign indicating the exit for the airport and bus station. William leaned forward to look out the window as well.

"Looks like we're almost there," he said as he looked down at his watch. He tapped the beveled face with his finger. "And, we're right on time." He pulled the sleeve of his sweater down over the watch and looked up at Helen. "So, I take it you're not getting off here."

Helen shook her head. "I stay on this bus all the way to New York City. Then I switch to the express to Boston."

"Beantown. And that's where this man lives?" He paused for several seconds as the bus turned off the highway and headed toward the South Bend Airport. "My advice is to face your fears, tell the truth, and live the life you want to lead." He pointed at Helen as he spoke the last few words.

The bus made a final turn and pulled into the bus station loading and unloading area.

Overhead, the speakers crackled. "Welcome to South Bend, Indiana," the driver said quickly, the words almost unintelligible. "If you are connecting with another coach, your checked baggage is not automatically transferred. If this is your final destination, welcome to South Bend. For those of you continuing on, this will be a ten minute stop."

The bus rolled to a gentle stop and around them, the other passengers began shifting and talking louder. William stood and pulled a thick, brown wool jacket from the overhead storage. Rather than put it on, he looped it over his arm and leaned down.

"One last thing," he said with a gentle smile. "Just remember, it's always darkest before the dawn. This will work out. It may not be the way you'd like, but in the end, everything works out according to God's plan. You need to trust in that." He shrugged. "And besides, what's the alternative?"

Maggie

MAGGIE BLINKED AS she realized she had been staring blankly at the back of the seat in front of her for several minutes. Almost as a reflex, she tapped the touchpad of her laptop to keep the current screen active. She needed to work on her presentation but she couldn't stop thinking about her conversation with Ben. He had sounded different—less angry. And he had apologized for his snide comment about the business. That, too, was new.

Maybe this relationship with Ellen and the prospect of becoming a father had changed how he viewed family and the decisions parents had to make for their children. Maybe he had finally forgiven Franklin, though for what exactly, Maggie was never entirely clear. Was it for his infidelity? Was it for his insistence that Ben take over the business? Was it for something that Maggie didn't know about?

She used to be close to Ben. They used to talk to each other. They used to tell each other everything. Or at least they had until the summer before he left for college. She was fifteen and just becoming aware of her attraction to girls. He was biding his time until he could get out from under Franklin's thumb. There was tension in their home, but it was contained. And then he had walked in on Franklin and Betty Jo.

"They were . . . too close," he had told her several days later.

"I don't understand," Maggie had said.

They were sitting on the top row of the aluminum bleachers overlooking the deserted baseball field. After several days of angry silence, Maggie had insisted Ben join her for her daily run.

They had left at dawn and set off down 4th Street toward Elm. The moist air still held the coolness of the night before, and they ran most of the three-mile loop without speaking, their only conversation the soft huffs of breath as their feet slapped out a steady rhythm on the cracked sidewalks. As they neared the softball fields in Shields Park, Ben eased to a walk and gestured toward the faded aluminum bleachers along the third-base side of the field. Still without talking, they climbed to the top tier and sat facing each other.

"Dad and Betty Jo are fucking." Though his words were spoken in a normal tone, they seemed almost too loud for the soft morning.

Maggie blinked and leaned slightly forward. "What?"

"Dad and Betty Jo," he said. "I walked in on them. They pulled apart, but I could tell. They were too close."

"I don't understand." Maggie shook her head. "What exactly did you see?"

Ben raised his arm in front of him, tipped his head, and wiped the sweat from his forehead against the shoulder of his t-shirt before turning to her. "I was looking for Dad. I needed to talk to him about signing some paperwork for school. You were at the pool." He jerked his head in the direction of the fenced-in public pool where Maggie and her friends spent their afternoons. "Mom was at the grocery store. They probably thought they were safe since you guys were gone and I never go into that part of the house if I can help it."

Ben glanced sideways at Maggie and she nodded for him to continue.

"So, I walked into the office. Betty Jo wasn't at her desk but Dad's office door was closed, so I figured he was in there working." He shook his head. "I probably should have knocked but I just opened the door and there they were."

"There they were what?"

Ben sneered, his upper lip curled slightly in disgust. "They were standing over by the filing cabinets. Betty Jo had her hand inside his pants. Her blouse was open and he was feeling her up."

Maggie jerked slightly backward in shock. "Oh my god, what did they do? What did you do?" She gasped as another thought occurred to her. "Do you think Mom knows?"

"They tried to break apart, but Betty Jo's hand got stuck. They both had these stupid looks on their faces." He lifted his shoulders in a small shrug. "I don't know if Mom knows or not."

"Did Dad try to talk to you about it?" Maggie asked. "I mean, did he try to explain or something?"

"Oh yeah." Ben snorted softly through his nose. "He tried to explain all right." He sat up straighter and adopted the tone their father used to comfort and soothe families who had just lost a loved one. "'You're too young to understand, son. It's complicated. Let's just keep this between us.'"

He leaned forward and rested his forearms on his knees. His back was arched in such a way that Maggie could see the knobs of his vertebra through his thin t-shirt. He stared across the ball field.

"And this is the life he wants me to lead," he said softly. "Working for him. Living here in this shitty town. Watching him cheat on Mom. Pretending to be this great guy in front of everyone in town." He shook his head and gave a humorless laugh. "No way. I'm not going to ruin my life just because he's a miserable hypocrite."

Maggie placed her hand on his back and rubbed small circles like their mother did when she comforted them. She could feel the heat of Ben's body beneath the damp, coolness of his shirt. "So, what are you going to do?"

He shrugged and then, after several seconds of silence, turned and looked sideways at her. His expression was serious. "I'm getting out of here and never coming back. I don't care if I have to work at McDonalds. I'm never going to be like him."

In retrospect, Maggie could see that's exactly what Ben did. She wondered what she would have done—how she would have felt—if she had been the one to walk in on their father. Would she have been angry? Would she have run away, too? There was no question that the family dynamics had impacted how she lived her life. Unlike her father, she didn't mix business and pleasure. She was disciplined. She had her professional life and, when she could sneak away to the anonymity of Indianapolis or an out-of-town conference, her private life.

But was that even really a life? She told herself that being a workaholic and needing to maintain a certain reputation were the reasons for her one-night stands and inability to commit. But deep down, she knew it was more than that. More and more, she was beginning to wonder if she used these rationales as excuses not to get close to anyone. Her parents' marriage had been . . . what? A sham? A partnership? And she saw daily the pain that came with caring about people—the pain that came with investing in a relationship and then losing it. Maybe, in her own way, she was just as damaged as Ben.

She had asked him once, why he didn't settle down—why he didn't stay in one place or have relationships that lasted more than a couple of months. It had been the night after their parents' funeral. Everyone had finally left and it was just the two of them. They had taken one of the bottles of wine left over from the reception out to the landscaped area that had been their mother's garden. The solar lights glowed softly along the path that led to the wrought iron bench that was next to the koi pond. It had been their mother's favorite place to sit in the evenings and had seemed fitting somehow to sit there now and watch the dusk fade into night.

Ben had been in the process of lighting a joint when she asked the question. He sucked deeply, held the smoke in his lungs, and then slowly exhaled. Despite the heat of late May, they were still in their funeral clothes. Maggie kicked off her black leather pumps and extended her stocking feet out in front of her. Without asking if she even wanted a hit, Ben handed her the joint, loosened his tie, and leaned back into the seat. Maggie grinned and tried to remember the last time she got stoned. It must have been college. She raised the joint to her lips, sucked the smoke deeply into her lungs, and waited for his answer.

"I haven't found the place where I fit," he said finally. "I've traveled all over and met lots of great people, but at the end of the day, it's just not where I'm supposed to be." He lifted the wineglass he had set on the paving stones next to the bench and took a sip. "I don't know as I'll ever fit in." He reached out for the joint and made a "gimme" motion with his fingers. Maggie exhaled slowly and took another hit before handing it back.

She held the smoke in her lungs and leaned down for her own wineglass. "Are you happy?" She knew she asked it as much for herself as for him.

"No." The end of the joint glowed brightly and then dimmed. After several seconds, she heard him exhale. "But I'm not unhappy either. I'm just . . . I don't know. Waiting."

Maggie shifted so she faced him. She rested her elbow on the back of the bench and leaned her head against the fleshy part of her palm. "For what?"

Ben laughed softly. "I don't know . . . completion. Maybe I'm waiting for all those things that I lack to magically appear and make everything right."

"So, what's missing? What do you think you lack?" Maggie was truly curious to know the answer.

Ben was silent as he seemed to think about it.

"Connection," he said in a hollow voice. "Most of the time, I feel completely untethered, completely disconnected from my own life." He sighed. "I have been trying so hard to find meaning—to find authenticity. But at the end of the day, it's never the right fit and I run away. I used to think I was running to something. Now I'm not so sure."

Maggie nodded. Though their circumstances were different, what they were experiencing boiled down to the same thing. Both of them longed for security and commitment even as they ran—or in Maggie's case—pushed it as far away as possible.

"What about you?" Ben asked.

"Huh?"

"What about you? What's missing for you? Now that Dad is dead, are you going to tell people you're a dyke?"

Maggie felt her mouth drop open and she squinted into the darkness to try to see his face.

Ben laughed. "What? You think I didn't know? I could see it when you were a kid. All mooning over Claire Danes and Sarah whatshername, the Vampire Slayer? And then when you were all twenty-four-seven with Rachel Gleason? Come on."

Maggie took a large swallow of wine. Her hand shook so she rested the glass on her thigh. "Do you think Mom and Dad knew?"

She heard the rustle of clothing and guessed Ben had shrugged. She heard a soft rasp and then a click as Ben spun the spark wheel of the lighter. He held the flame to the tip of the joint and sucked deeply. Even after he had released the button and extinguished the flame, Maggie could still see the yellow and green aftereffects.

"I don't think they could see past their own shit. Dad was too busy being Mr. Chamber of Commerce and Mom . . ." He paused for several seconds. "Mom was too busy pretending everything was all right and showing everyone in Seymour that we were the perfect family."

Maggie stared into the darkness. The rhythmic sound of the frogs and cicadas suddenly seemed too loud. The cacophony was almost claustrophobic. Her parents were dead. And after Ben left for wherever he was going next, she would be alone.

"What ever happened with Rachel, anyway?"

The question caught Maggie off guard and for a moment, her mind seemed to go blank. Then came the rush of memories— unbidden flashes of color and emotion so palpable that it almost took her breath away: Rachel, her head thrown back in laughter, the vein on her neck prominent and fascinating . . . The two of them speeding down deserted gravel roads on humid summer nights, the tape deck blaring Melissa Etheridge, their hair flying wildly around their faces . . . The hours they had spent exploring each other's bodies with a wonder and reverence that Maggie knew now came only with that first love . . . Rachel's face creased in anger, her words sharp and cutting, as she demanded that Maggie make a decision. And then it was done.

"She ended it," Maggie said softly. "I couldn't . . . I wasn't able to . . ." She sighed. "Fuck it." She raised the wine glass to her lips and took a deep drink. She held the wine in her mouth for several seconds, embracing the astringent prickle on the back of her tongue. She swallowed, licked her lips, and then rubbed at the corners with the side of her forefinger. "Doesn't matter anyway. Love is for idiots."

They had sat in silence, then, drinking and smoking, both lost in their own worlds. That was the last time they had connected so intimately, Maggie realized. As soon as she had bought out his half of the funeral home, he kissed her good bye, climbed into his battered pickup, and set off in search of . . . whatever he was looking for.

They had talked occasionally, in the four years since, but never like they had that night. But maybe, with his decision to marry Ellen and the fact that they were going to have a baby, maybe that would change. Maybe he had finally found that connection. And maybe, she thought as she again tapped on her laptop touchpad, if she could find Sarah and tell her the truth, maybe she could finally find it, too.

Bug

BUG TURNED ONTO his side, hugged the lower half of the pillow, and brought his knees up to his chest. It was his last night in Philadelphia—his last night in the same city as Rhonda. He knew she wasn't able to come say goodbye, but a part of him had hoped that somehow, magically, she would appear. But deep down, he suspected that even if she could have come, she wouldn't have. Rhonda probably didn't even know he was leaving tomorrow. If he were honest, he knew that she probably didn't care. Rhonda didn't care about much anymore except for getting high. It had always been bad, but after his father died, it got a lot worse.

Bug didn't really remember Anton Lewis. He had a sense of the man from flashes of memory and from pictures Rhonda kept around the house, but often, Bug wasn't sure if they were real or if they were just manufactured. He had been three when his father was killed in Malcolm X Park, just a few blocks from the house he shared with Rhonda, a two-story row house on Addison that had been in Anton's family for decades. It had belonged to Anton's mother, Ruby, who insisted that Rhonda live there so she could know her grandson.

"Thank god she died so soon after I moved in," Rhonda would say whenever she talked about Nana Ruby. "The bitch hated me for being white—for having a white baby. Can you believe it? Hated me for being white? It was reverse discrimination."

Bug was never quite sure what to think about Nana Ruby or if Rhonda's description of her was accurate. She had died while he was still a baby, but the pictures he had seen of her were of a very large, very black woman with kind eyes. It was clear that Anton had been her son. Even though he had been lean and wiry, they looked a lot alike in the face. Bug had spent a lot of time studying the pictures in the hopes of seeing himself in either his father's or grandmother's face. But he looked nothing like them. He was lean like his father but in every other way, he looked like his mother's side of the family with his pale skin, straight, reddish-brown hair, and green eyes.

"You actually look more like Sarah than you do me," Rhonda had said more than once. "If I hadn't shot you out of my cooch, I would've wondered if you were even really mine."

She always laughed when she said this but Bug could tell it wasn't a real laugh. It was too sharp, too brittle. It was true, though. When he lived in Harrisburg with his other grandmother, Grandma Jean, he had looked through the photo albums and at the framed pictures on the walls. He looked a lot like his Aunt Sarah.

He had been six when he went to live with Grandma Jean. Bug knew it was partially because Rhonda wanted to be high more than she wanted to take care of him. But he thought she also did it because she loved him. She wanted him to be safe and cared for. At least, he wanted to believe that. He wanted to believe the best about Rhonda. And, regardless of her motives, living with Grandma Jean had been the best years of his life. She had been kind to him in ways that Rhonda was incapable. She made him meals, tucked him into bed at night, and made sure that he knew he was loved.

He hadn't been sure at first if she had wanted him living with her. Rhonda had made the decision without discussing it with him. He had come home from school to find his clothes, shoes, and books stuffed into a bulging white trash bag with a bright red plastic drawstring. He hadn't even taken off his jacket before she hauled the bag off the couch and slung it over her shoulder.

"Daryl, you ready?"

Bug frowned, unsure who she was talking to, until a short, stocky black man with a shaved head and a face like a pug stepped out of the kitchen. His eyes were large and so dark brown they looked almost black.

He squinted at Bug, as if he couldn't see well. "This him?"

Rhonda gave him a look that suggested he was stupid. "Yeah, it's him. Who else would it be?"

Daryl shrugged. "I didn't know. He's just so . . . white. He don't look much like Anton." He stepped closer and leaned forward to look more closely at Bug. His aftershave smelled like the bags of cedar they put in the hamster cage at school.

Rhonda laughed, the sound dry and harsh. "He's got my good looks, cantcha tell?" She turned back to Bug. "Daryl is going to drive you and me to your grandma's house. I got a new job opportunity and can't do that and take care of you. It won't be for long. Maybe a couple of months."

Bug nodded. He had learned not to respond with more than a nod to anything Rhonda said for fear of how she would react. He looked around her to Daryl, who smiled, his teeth small, even, and shockingly white against his dark skin. The smile did nothing to make him look less menacing. If anything, it made him look more dangerous.

"We need to leave now, though. I got to start tomorrow." Rhonda gestured toward the door with her free hand.

Outside, Bug watched as Daryl took the trash bag from Rhonda and put it into the trunk of his Honda Accord. He waited to see where he was supposed to sit. Rhonda went around the front, opened the passenger's door, and climbed inside. Bug reached for the door handle, but Daryl beat him to it. He pulled it open and Bug climbed inside. The interior smelled like Pine-Sol.

"Buckle up," Daryl said. "I don't want to get hauled in for something like a seat belt violation."

Bug pulled the seat belt across his body and clicked the buckle. Rhonda turned her body to do the same in the front. As she pushed the tongue into the buckle, she looked back at him and smiled—a real smile. And in that moment, despite her deteriorating teeth and sallow face, he saw what she could have been had she chosen a different life.

Bug blinked and forced himself to push down the tears he felt behind his eyes. Rhonda studied him for several seconds until Daryl started the car with a loud *vroom* and the moment was gone.

They drove through the city and to the turnpike where Daryl pulled up to the kiosk for a ticket. Once they were on the highway, he turned on the radio. Bug was surprised that the music was jazz. The rhythm was unpredictable, but somehow smooth. And soothing. He craned his neck to look out the window. All he could see were trees and other cars and after a while, even those seemed to run together in a blur of gray and evergreen. At some point, he must have fallen asleep because when he opened his eyes, they were getting off the turnpike.

"You're going to want to turn right onto 283. And then stay on that until you see the exit for Capital Beltway." Rhonda turned off the radio.

Daryl looked at Rhonda. He shook his head and made a low clicking sound. "Woman, don't you know better than to touch a man's radio?"

Rhonda laughed.

Bug had been to Grandma Jean's house only twice before, and almost didn't realize where they were when Daryl pulled up in front of a small, red brick row house divided into three residences. Grandma Jean's was, he remembered, the middle one. The steps were painted tan with a dark brown carpet that ran up the middle of the stairs to the brown front door.

"Nice place," Daryl said as he put the car into park and turned off the engine.

Rhonda made a noise, unfastened her seat belt, and turned to Bug. "You be good while you're here, okay? Do what she tells you and don't cause trouble. Got it?"

Bug nodded and, seemingly satisfied with his answer, Rhonda turned and opened the passenger door.

Bug unbuckled his seat belt, grabbed the handle to his own door, and pushed it open. The crisp fall air was a relief after the thick, oily aroma of the pine tree air freshener. He tried not to be obvious as he breathed deeply.

Rhonda came around the front of the car and grabbed Bug's hand. Without speaking, they climbed the six steps to the front porch. Rhonda pulled open the screen door and, rather than ringing the bell or knocking, pushed open the front door and stepped inside. Behind them, Daryl bounded up the stairs two at a time, the trash bag full of Bug's things clutched in his right hand.

"Ma!" Rhonda gestured for Bug and Daryl to enter behind here. "Ma, we're here!" She walked across the small entry into the open living room.

Bug could hear Grandma Jean moving around upstairs.

"Be right down."

Bug looked around the small first floor. It was almost all open. To his left were wooden steps that led upstairs. In front of him was the living room with a long, gold-and-brown patterned couch. In front of the big front window was a worn brown recliner. Next to the red brick fireplace sat a rocking chair. A faded quilt was draped over the armrest. Everything, he realized, was so clean. The lemony scent of furniture polish hung in the air.

Bug looked past the two half walls that separated the living room from the kitchen. The decoration there, too, was brown and gold, although the kitchen wallpaper looked like a yellow-and-gold diamond pattern. A wooden table covered with a pale yellow tablecloth stood at an angle in the corner with two of the four chairs pushed up against the wall.

"Hey, Ma."

Bug turned to see Grandma Jean standing at the foot of the stairs. Behind her, the front door was still open. She glanced at Daryl and then at Rhonda. She frowned, looked toward the interior wall next to the stairs where the ornate cuckoo clock softly ticked.

"You're three hours late."

"Yeah, sorry." Rhonda gestured in Bug's direction. "Bug had school." She laughed. "I don't know what they do in first grade but, you know, he was there." She shrugged.

Grandma Jean shook her head and then turned her attention to Bug. She broke into a smile. "Hey, Sammy Boy. You get bigger every time I see you." She held open her arms. "Come give me a hug."

Bug hesitated and then stepped forward. Grandma Jean wrapped her arms around him. She smelled like cinnamon and vanilla.

"Hi, Grandma," he said, his words muffled by the cloth of her Philadelphia Eagles sweatshirt. He relaxed into the hug and only let go when she gave him a quick, gentle squeeze. She continued to look at him as he took a step back.

"So, we need to be getting back to Philly," Rhonda said. "I got this new job and I want to relax tonight before I have to start work."

Grandma Jean looked up at her daughter, made a soft noise, and nodded. "I expect that's right." She returned her attention to Bug. "I think we'll be just fine."

And, Bug remembered, they had been. As soon as Rhonda and Daryl had left, Grandma Jean took him up the narrow steps to the second floor where she walked to one of the closed doors and threw it open.

"You can have your pick. This one was Sarah's and this one," she stepped to one of the other doors, "was your mother's."

Bug walked to the adjacent doorways and looked inside both

rooms. To his surprise, Grandma Jean had done little to change either of them from when he imagined his mother and aunt had lived there.

"I know," she said as if she could read his mind. "I keep thinking I want to turn one into a sewing room and one into a guest bedroom, but I never have guests and I don't sew much anymore." She shrugged. "Oprah says knitting is in. All the stars are doing it. Even Julia Roberts. So, now I knit."

Bug looked into Aunt Sarah's room. The walls were covered with posters. One was a movie poster of Indiana Jones. The rest were of women with guitars. Rock stars, he supposed by their clothing. On the desk and shelves were stones, fossils, and the skeleton of some small animal. The room was neat and orderly.

He stepped to the side and looked into his mother's room. In contrast to Sarah's browns and tans, his mother's room was decorated with reds, pinks, and oranges. The colors seemed to leap out at him and his heart beat faster.

"We would change the bedspread and pillows for whichever one you choose," Grandma Jean said. "We could even repaint. God knows it could probably use it."

Bug turned and looked at the other two closed doors. "Which is your room?"

Grandma Jean pointed to the door farthest from them. "The door is usually open, but I didn't get a chance to tidy it today so I closed it."

Bug nodded slowly. When Rhonda's door was shut, it meant one of two things: there was a man inside with her or she was passed out. Noises usually indicated which. But either way, the closed door meant to stay out. And he did.

"You can always come in." Grandma Jean walked to the door and pushed it open. Inside was a double bed without sheets and a laundry basket on the floor. "I was about to remake the bed when you all showed up." She smiled. "If it's ever closed, it just means that I'm changing clothes. And that never takes long." She gestured at her sweatshirt and cotton pants. "I've got nobody to impress. But, back to you and which room you think you'd like."

Bug turned and, without thinking, pointed toward Sarah's room. "I like the rocks and the posters."

Grandma Jean laughed. "The one of Indiana Jones or the ones of Melissa Etheridge and the Indigo Girls?"

Bug shrugged. "Both. But Indiana Jones the best."

"Good choice." She glanced at her wristwatch. "I'll bet you're hungry. How would you like some spaghetti?"

Bug's mouth watered at the thought of that meal. It had been the first between him and his grandmother. She had made homemade spaghetti and meatballs and encouraged him to use as much of the dry cheese in the green container as he wanted.

"We need to get some meat on those bones," she said with a grin to let him know she was teasing. "You look like a scarecrow."

Bug came to realize that for Grandma Jean, feeding him— feeding anyone from the neighborhood that stopped by, for that matter—was her way of showing love. And for three years, he felt that love. He came to rely on it. But then she died.

No one had known she had cancer. Bug knew she got tired easily and that she didn't eat much. And he recognized that her skin and the white parts of her eyes were a strange color of yellow, but, then, so were his mother's. He now knew the name for that. It was called jaundice. He had heard the paramedics say it a couple of times when they were working on her and had later looked it up in the battered Funk & Wagnall's dictionary Grandma Jean used for her crossword puzzles.

He had been in the kitchen pouring milk into a bowl of Cheerios when, from upstairs, he heard what sounded like a plate breaking and then a loud thump. He had waited for several seconds, anticipating Grandma Jean's voice calling down that she was all right but she needed him to please bring her the broom and a trash bag. When the summons didn't come, he slid back the chair and hurried up the narrow stairs.

"Grandma?" He stood outside the partially open door to her bedroom. "Grandma Jean?"

At first, he thought she wasn't even in the room. He turned and looked down the hallway to the bathroom. The door was fully open and he could tell no one was in there. He turned back to her bedroom, raised his hand, and hesitantly pushed open the painted white door. The hinges groaned faintly.

He hesitated and then crept inside. Grandma Jean lay next to the bed on her right side, her robe open and her nightgown up past her knees. He stared for a moment, his breath suddenly shallow and tight. He resisted the strange urge to pull her nightgown down where it belonged and instead, turned and raced downstairs to call for help.

He now knew that the thing that had killed his grandmother was pancreatic cancer.

"She didn't tell anyone," his Aunt Sarah had told Rhonda two nights after Grandma had been hospitalized.

He was in his bedroom, supposedly sleeping. Sarah had come from Boston immediately. His mother, although closer in proximity, showed up a day later looking tired and unwashed.

"She shoulda, you know?" Rhonda's voice was rough and scratchy. Bug knew it was from the cigarettes. "She's taking care of my boy. What if something had happened and he got hurt?"

Sarah didn't respond. One of them must have shifted because the chair squeaked. Bug imagined them sitting at the discolored Formica kitchen table where he and Grandma Jean ate all their meals.

There was silence for what felt like a long time, punctuated only by the sound of Rhonda sucking deeply on her cigarette. Bug could already smell the smoke and knew that if Grandma Jean had been there she would have made Rhonda stop. She hated the smell of cigarette smoke. He tried to imagine what Aunt Sarah and Rhonda were doing. Were they looking at each other? At the table? At nothing?

"Doctors are sayin' she's not gonna make it, aren't they?" Rhonda finally said.

Her voice was strained as she spoke through a smoky exhale. Bug imagined her pinching the butt between her stained thumb and forefinger and then crushing it down into the saucer she was using for an ashtray.

"The prognosis isn't good," Sarah said. "They only give her a week at most. She let it go untreated for too long."

Rhonda cleared her throat. One of them, Bug guessed his mother, pushed back her chair. The metal legs scraped across the cheap linoleum in a low moan. Grandma Jean hated that sound.

"So, what's the will look like?"

Bug could hear the hopefulness in Rhonda's voice.

"You've got to be kidding me." Though Sarah didn't raise her voice, Bug could hear the anger in her words. "She's not even dead and you're asking about what you'll get? Jesus, Rho."

"I've got my boy to think of," Rhonda said. "We got needs and if we need to find somebody to sell this place, I'd like to do it as soon as we can. I'm not like you. I don't have some rich lawyer to take care of me. I got no extra money to be paying bills here. If Anton's house hadn't been paid for, I couldn't even afford that."

"I refuse to have this conversation with you while our mother is lying in a hospital bed dying." Sarah spat the words. "And as for *your boy*, has it even occurred to you that he saw his grandmother—the woman who has been caring for him for the past three years—collapse in front of him? Have you even considered comforting him?"

Bug heard Rhonda snort.

"Don't tell me how to take care of my son. What do you know about it anyway? You're just some rich-bitch-dyke who can never have kids of your own because you're too frigid and—"

Bug heard a slap. It was the sound of the color red, though not for blood. It was red for the stinging burn that came after. More than once he'd been on the receiving end of those slaps when Rhonda was high or drunk. It felt strange, knowing she was the recipient for once.

Part of him had wanted to go out and defend her. She was his mother and it was his duty. But a larger part of him hadn't wanted to stand up for her. He had been glad she had gotten what she deserved.

In the bed next to him, Calvin shifted his position and mumbled something about dogs. Bug scrunched up his eyes in the hopes of keeping the tears from forming. Did Rhonda know somehow that deep inside he hated her as much as he loved her? Was that why she ignored him or shipped him away? He knew the answer. He had always known the answer.

It's because she doesn't want you; she never wanted you. No one, he knew, had ever wanted him except Grandma Jean and now she was gone. He was alone. At the thought, Bug pulled himself into a tighter ball, hugged the pillow as tightly as he could to his chest, and, for the first time since Grandma Jean's funeral, cried.

Jimmy

JIMMY THREW BACK the covers and swung his legs over the side of the bed. As hard as he tried, sleep was proving to be elusive. He had gone to bed early with the hopes that he could get some rest before leaving for the bus station but he realized within the first hour that he was too keyed up to sleep. Instead, he had tossed and turned, unable to get comfortable and even less able to stop the same negative thoughts from running over and over through his head.

He leaned forward, rested his elbows on his knees, and dropped his face into his hands. His head felt heavy and thick. He rubbed roughly at his forehead and temples. There was no way he could go through with this. It was stupid to think he could ever apologize enough, that Helen would ever forgive him, and, on the off chance she did forgive him, she would ever be able to trust him.

It's your punishment.

Despite what Diane had said about letting go of the guilt, Jimmy knew the universe had a way of repaying good with good—or in his case, bad with bad. He felt the familiar pressure of anxiety building in his chest and forced himself to breathe slowly and deeply. *It will pass*, he reminded himself. It wasn't a heart attack. He wasn't going to die. Ride it out. Let it go.

Jimmy stood and shook first his head, then his upper body and arms, and finally, his legs. *Let it go.* This time he heard the words in Diane's voice rather than his own.

At least I have her. But even that wasn't true. Diane was required to be in his life. It was her job. And who was he kidding to think that she might actually care about him? She didn't even really know him. She knew about his addiction, of course. And she knew about his issues regarding his father. But she didn't know about Helen. She had no idea he had simply replaced one unhealthy behavior with another.

He walked to the window and pulled open the blind. The street outside was dark aside from the dim glow of the single streetlight that did little to illuminate more than a rounded patch of sidewalk.

He leaned his forehead against the cool glass and closed his eyes. It felt comforting against his heated skin and he turned his face to the left so his cheek and right temple were in contact with it. Not for the first time, he wished he lived in a better neighborhood so he could safely go outside for a walk around the block.

This part of Harrisburg would never have been his choice if left to his own devices. But the dilapidated, red brick townhouses and condos that made up the bulk of Section 8 housing around 13th and State Streets were all he could afford. And, he reminded himself, it could be worse. He knew from personal experience it could be a lot worse.

Somewhere down the block, a dog barked and he thought longingly of Boomer. Jimmy opened his eyes and stared down at the deserted street. During the summers, people were outside at all hours, talking, drinking and, as the night wore on, fighting. This neighborhood, he knew, had one of the highest crime rates in the city—especially violent crime. Part of it had to do with the under-educated and immigrant population of poor Puerto Ricans and Haitians, but most of it had to do with the underlying powerlessness of the residents, many of whom, if they even had jobs, worked in fast food or as cashiers.

Jimmy glanced back at the alarm clock on the nightstand by the bed. It was only midnight. Even if he were to magically fall asleep now, he would only get a few hours of rest before he had to get up and get ready to leave. Maybe he should just stay awake and then try to sleep on the bus. He could go downstairs and play Xbox until it was time to leave. That was better than lying in bed staring at the ceiling or looking out the window. He wished, not for the first time, that he could just take a sleeping pill—just something to knock him out for a few hours. But he couldn't risk it. Even a couple of Benadryl would be playing with fire.

He probably should have known he had the type of personality that would lend itself to addiction. Growing up with an alcoholic father should have prepared him to recognize the signs. But his addiction to painkillers happened so slowly, he didn't realize how badly he needed them until it was too late.

It was funny how things happened—how certain decisions made on the spur of the moment changed everything. If only he hadn't agreed to sub so that Ramirez could go to his son's school play. If only it hadn't been on the back of his own very busy shift during which he had no chance to sleep. If only he hadn't been so jittery from all the coffee and the adrenaline of the call. If only . . . if only . . . if only.

It had been a routine call. He and Roberta had just returned from transporting a man from a nursing facility to the hospital when they were dispatched to one of the older residential areas in the Allison Hill neighborhood. The patient was an unresponsive elderly woman who had collapsed in her home. Her grandson had called 9-1-1. They had arrived at the same time as the police and the fire department's first responders. The boy, Sam, had let them in and then led them up the narrow stairs to the second floor bedroom. Jimmy and his partner, Roberta, entered the room first. Mrs. Talbott lay on her right side, her robe open and her nightgown up past her knees.

"Why don't you guys get started with her and I'll see what I can find out from the grandson," Roberta said.

Jimmy nodded and squatted down next to the elderly woman. "Mrs. Talbott? Mrs. Talbott, my name is Jimmy. Can you hear me?" He looked up at the two EMTs. "She's non-responsive but her airway is clear."

He pinched the skin on the back of her hand to check her level of consciousness. Nothing. He looked down at her hand. The skin he had pinched was still tented.

"She's pretty dehydrated. Let's get an IV started . . . 500 ml bag of normal saline . . . get her started on oxygen and . . ." Jimmy scanned her body. Even though she was laying on her right side, he could tell that the leg underneath her body looked slightly longer and the toes were turned awkwardly outward. "It looks like a possible hip fracture. Where's the scoop stretcher?"

The taller of the two EMTs stepped forward with the yellow stretcher. The other EMT moved to Mrs. Talbott's head and Jimmy went to her feet. Together, they separated the vertical blades of the stretcher that was split down the middle and placed on either side of the woman.

"Okay, let's get a pillow between her knees to stabilize her hip and . . . now . . . let's bring the sides in."

As gently as possible, the three slid the angled halves together under the patient. Even though he heard the click of the securing clips engage, Jimmy looked at both men. "Are the clips secured?"

Both nodded.

"Good. Let's finish taking her vitals."

Jimmy pulled his penlight out of the breast pocket of his uniform and shone the light into first one and then the other eye.

"Pupils are equal and reactive to light," he said. "But her eyes look jaundiced."

Jimmy looked down at her hands. The nail beds were slightly yellowed, as well. He glanced up to see Roberta standing next to him.

"I wasn't able to get much from the grandson." She bent forward, her arms straight, her palms braced on her knees. "He said that he didn't think she took any medications and that she didn't ever go to the hospital for anything. He did say she was tired all the time and hadn't been eating."

"Makes sense. She's dehydrated and jaundiced." Jimmy glanced back at the boy, who now stood between the dresser and the door, his eyes wide and frightened as he watched them work on his grandmother. "I think she's a lot sicker than the kid knows," he said in a low voice.

"Yeah." Roberta stood to her full height. "Are we ready to move her down to the cot?"

Jimmy looked at the EMTs who nodded.

"Okay, then." Roberta turned to the police officer. "Can you take Sam downstairs and then spot us?" She looked at Jimmy and the first responders. "Let's do a four-person carry. Given how narrow those stairs are, how about one on each corner? Jimmy and I will take her head. On my count. One . . . two . . . three."

In one smooth movement, they lifted the stretcher and walked in unison to the doorway. The EMTs went first, careful to keep the stretcher level as they descended. Roberta and Jimmy followed.

Halfway down the stairs Jimmy misjudged the depth of the next step and caught the edge with his heel instead of landing with his full foot. Though he tried to catch himself, his weight was too far back and his feet slid out from under him. He fell backward, his corner of the stretcher tipping dangerously. His lower back hit the edge of the step, followed by his shoulders, neck, and head. He was vaguely aware that Roberta had grabbed his corner of the stretcher.

"Keep her steady," she said. "Jimmy? You okay?"

"Fuck," he groaned. "I think I fucked up my back."

"Okay, don't move," she said and then, to the EMTs. "Let's get her out to the cot and then we'll deal with him."

Jimmy waited until they had maneuvered the stretcher down the stairs before he tried to move. He grimaced in pain as he forced himself to first sit and then used the railing to pull himself into a standing position. His skin tingled with the rush of adrenaline.

He felt light-headed and closed his eyes for several seconds. He opened them and saw the grandson at the foot of the stairs staring up at him. The police officer who had taken over Jimmy's corner of the stretcher must have left him alone in the living room. The boy's dark green eyes were wide within his thin, pale face and Jimmy felt sorry for him. He seemed like a good kid and had been calm throughout what must have been a terrifying experience.

"Your grandma's going to be okay," Jimmy said.

"No she won't." The words were flat and emotionless.

Jimmy thought about the jaundiced skin and eyes . . . the weight loss . . . the injury to her hip. The boy was probably right. His grandmother was likely very sick. He tried to smile reassuringly, however.

"They're going to get her to the hospital and get her fixed up good as new," he said as he eased down the stairs one at a time. "Your name's Sam, right?"

He could feel the pain not just in his back but also in his neck and head. At the bottom of the stairs, he raised his hand and gingerly touched the tender place where he had hit the back of his head. A goose egg was already forming.

"Yes," Sam said. "Can I go with her to the hospital?"

The pleading note in the boy's voice was heartbreaking. Jimmy shook his head and immediately regretted it. He closed his eyes against the light-headedness and grasped the banister. "Probably not. The police officer will stay here with you until your mom or someone can pick you up."

"My mom lives in Philly," Sam said, dully. "She doesn't want me."

"So, you live with your grandma?"

Sam nodded. "Since I was six."

Jimmy studied him and tried to guess his age. It was hard because he was so small and skinny. "How old are you now?"

"Nine."

Jimmy did the math. Sam had been living here for three years. He wondered how the grandmother had hidden her illness.

"Will I have to go live with Rhonda?"

Jimmy looked up.

Sam's eyebrows were drawn into a frown, his lips pressed together in a thin line. Despite his age, he looked heartbreakingly old and beaten down. Jimmy wondered what he had seen and experienced that caused such sadness. He was about to ask who Rhonda was when the police officer and the shorter of the two EMTs came back into the house.

"Colin went with your partner to the hospital," the EMT said as he approached Jimmy. His name tag caught the light. *M. Houston.* "She also called in the incident so you're officially benched. Your supervisor is on his way. How are you doing?"

"I'm fine." Jimmy waved his hand. "Just fell wrong. How's the patient?"

Houston glanced back at Sam and gestured for the police officer to take him back into the living room. He waited until they were alone before answering. "The same. It doesn't look good."

"Did she . . . when I fell, was there any additional injury?" Jimmy hated asking but he needed to know.

Houston raised his shoulders in a small shrug and shook his head. "She's still unresponsive so it's hard to say." He cocked his head and studied Jimmy intently. "Man, you really don't look so good. I think I should look you over."

Jimmy opened his mouth to answer and then heard the slam of a car door outside. Houston stepped back and craned his neck to look out the front door. "Looks like they're here." He turned, went to the door, and opened it. Stu Mendel stepped inside, gave a general nod of hello, and then walked to Jimmy.

"Why are you standing?" He turned to Houston. "Why isn't he at the very least sitting?"

Houston held up his hands. "I went to help load the patient and when I came back, he was up."

Stu turned back to Jimmy. "Reilly, you know the protocol."

Jimmy looked down at the floor and stiffly shifted his weight to his right leg. The flare of pain in his back made him gasp.

"Okay, first things first," Stu said. "You're clearly injured. Is it your back?"

Jimmy nodded, his gaze still trained on the floor.

Stu sighed. "Did you hit your head when you fell?"

Jimmy briefly considered lying before realizing the truth would probably come out anyway. He looked up and saw Stu watching him. "Yeah."

Stu pressed his lips together and turned to Houston and the police officer. "I'll need both of you to fill out an incident report. And you . . ." He looked at Jimmy. "We need to get you to the doctor and get the paperwork started."

"I don't think it's a big deal," Jimmy said quickly. "Just a few bumps and bruises."

"Well, let's just let the doctor make that call, okay?"

Jimmy had filled out the incident report on the way to the outpatient center where the worker's compensation doctor put him on leave for further tests and sent him home with a prescription for muscle relaxants and pain pills. It had been the beginning of the end.

At first, he really had taken them for the pain. But after a while, he had grown to like the comforting fog that smoothed the edges of his consciousness. The feeling was deliciously warm. A wonderful place to be. But to stay there took increasingly higher doses.

Jimmy winced at the memory of going to different doctors and emergency rooms to get prescriptions that he filled at pharmacies all around the city. He had been a slave to the addiction. The nagging hunger was all he could think about when he wasn't high. And when he *was* high, he didn't think at all. Not about his loneliness. Or his lack of career. Or about his crappy, pathetic life.

Now, all he did was think—think and play Xbox.

Helen

HELEN STARED BLANKLY at the Chicago Tribune crossword puzzle. She had been sporadically working on it for about an hour and had only managed to solve one-third of the clues. She twisted her wrist and glanced down at her watch. She really should try to get some sleep, even though the chances of that happening were slim. She wasn't the best of sleepers generally and to try to do it on a bus wasn't likely to be successful. Still, if she didn't want to look like a zombie when she met James for the first time, she needed to give it a shot.

She carefully folded the newspaper and slipped it between the pages of the book she had brought with her. The story, set in 1930s Chicago, had been one she had wanted to read for some time. But each time she had tried to focus, she found herself blindly skimming over the words, thinking instead about how she was going to explain to James that she had misrepresented herself—about *why* she had misrepresented herself. She placed her hands over the book, closed her eyes, and tried to relax back into the seat despite the uncomfortable, upright position.

She tried to clear her mind, but her thoughts quickly returned to the conversation she knew she had to have with James. The objective side of her brain knew it was important she broach the subject right away and admit what she had done. She would explain that she had been lost in her marriage long before she had met him and that knowing him and seeing his approach to life had made her realize just how unhappy she had been. It had shown her she didn't have to settle—that she deserved to be loved for who she was as opposed to what someone else expected her to be.

It was easy to point to David as the problem, but that, she knew, was a cop out. Her trajectory had been established long before she had even met him. She had always wanted more than what was allowed a girl in her rigid Catholic family. Despite the sexual revolution of the 1970s, life in the Kaczmarek household had remained traditionalist Catholic with most of her time away from her all-girls school spent at St. John Cantius Church. And

that fact alone had made her stereotypically rebellious. Drinking
. . . smoking . . . sex . . . she had done it all. And the more her
parents, conservative second-generation Poles, had tried to rein
her in, the wilder she had become.

Eyes still closed, she exhaled softly.

Karl and Evelyn Kaczmarek had been good parents. They were
hardworking, devout, and, though she hadn't been able to see it at
the time, kind. They had put up with all of her crap and then some.
She shuddered to think what would have happened if they had
known the true extent of her rebelliousness—if they had known
about the abortion.

She had been about to graduate high school and was set to
go to DePaul in the fall when she realized she was pregnant. She
hadn't told anyone but Alan. Just the thought of his name made
her feel the familiar shame. She had used him to get back at her
parents. He had checked all the boxes of what they didn't want
for their daughter, beginning with the fact that he was Jewish all
the way to his chosen career of being a stand-up comedian like
Jerry Seinfeld. There was nothing about him of which her parents
approved and naturally, she was instantly attracted to him.

The more her parents tried to stop her from seeing Alan, the
more determined she was to disobey. At first they simply met at
Clark Park after they each got out of school. Helen told her parents
she was at the library or studying with friends so they would have
time to disappear into the woods to make out or, as later became
the case, have sex. At the time, Helen would have said they were
making love but now, in retrospect, she knew it had been just sex.
And then she got pregnant.

Helen had been surprised at how easy it had been to get the
abortion—not in terms of securing the procedure, because that
had been difficult. What surprised her was the lack of spiritual
guilt she felt at defying the concepts under which she had lived
her entire life. The pregnancy had been a problem and she had
simply . . . taken care of it. She knew she should have felt bad for
terminating the pregnancy, but she hadn't—or at least she hadn't
at the time. All she had felt was relief. The regret came later, when
she was older, married to David and actually wanted to have a
baby and couldn't.

A part of her always wondered if her inability to carry a baby to term was in some way a punishment for her lack of guilt and for being so cavalier in doing what many considered murder and an offense against God. And though she had convinced herself she didn't care, she knew deep down that a part of her did. She knew what she had done was grounds for excommunication. But more terrifying than going to hell was the fear of losing her parents. She knew her mother suspected something, though she might not know exactly what. After years of trying to guilt her into embracing her faith, Evelyn finally had come right out and confronted her.

It had been a Sunday morning about a year into her marriage to David. Helen had slept in and was having her first cup of coffee when she heard a knock at the front door. At the time, they were living in David's apartment, a drafty, two-bedroom, third-floor walk-up in the West Loop. It wasn't the type of place she would have chosen on her own, but David preferred it because it wasn't too expensive and it was already his space. As had become her habit, Helen found it easier to give in rather than fight for something different.

Helen looked through the peephole and saw her mother standing on the other side of the door, the strap of her purse looped over her shoulder, the bag clutched close to her side. She was wearing a light spring jacket over one of her "good" Sunday dresses.

Helen turned the bolt that released the dead bolt and twisted the worn door knob.

"Hi, Mama," she said as she pulled open the door. "What are you doing here? I figured you'd be at church."

"I'm going to the High Mass at twelve-thirty." Evelyn stepped into the apartment and pulled Helen into a quick hug before thrusting her away, tipping her head back, and examining her critically through the lower part of her bifocals. "You're too thin, Sloneczka." She stepped back and dropped her arms. "And you look tired."

"Mama, I'm fine." Helen smiled. "I just got up."

She turned and gestured with her head for Evelyn to follow her into the living room. She scooped up the television remote control from the coffee table and muted the weekend news program.

She turned back to her mother. "Would you like some coffee? It's a fresh pot."

Evelyn shook her head and went to the couch. It was one of the few pieces of furniture that Helen had been allowed to bring with her into the marriage. She sat rigidly on the edge of the cushion, her knees together, her purse squarely in her lap. Helen felt the familiar knot of anxiety in her chest as she realized there was a purpose to this visit.

"Where is David?" Evelyn asked. She looked around the room and then in the direction of the kitchen as if she expected him magically to appear.

"He's with his brother," Helen said. "They have this new thing where they run along Lakefront Trail on Sunday mornings."

Evelyn nodded absently.

"Mama, are you okay?" Helen walked to the couch, put her coffee cup on the low table, and sat down next to her mother. She grasped Evelyn's wrist and tipped her head to meet her eyes.

Evelyn pressed her lips together in a semblance of a smile and nodded. "I'm fine. But we need to talk."

Helen's stomach sank. Nothing good ever followed the statement, "we need to talk." She leaned slightly back and sat up straighter. "Okay . . ."

Evelyn pushed her glasses up and put her hand on top of Helen's. "Sloneczka, I'm worried because I can tell you've fallen away from the church." She lifted her hand and gestured at Helen's pajamas. "When was the last time you went to Mass?"

Rather than answer, Helen gave her mother's wrist a quick squeeze and picked up her coffee cup. She took a sip and then rested it on her knee. "It's been awhile. Probably Christmas, when I went with you and Daddy." She looked up to meet her mother's gaze.

"Why?"

Helen blinked and looked back down at her coffee. Even though she had always resented the rigidity of the Catholic faith, both in church and at school, a part of her couldn't escape its teachings. There was no atoning for what she had done. In the eyes of the church, she had committed murder. She was going to hell anyway, which was how she justified going to Mass on holidays and taking Communion when she had no choice but to join her parents.

Evelyn cleared her throat. She was waiting for an answer.

"It's just not as important to me as it is to you and Daddy," Helen said finally. "It's . . ." She shrugged.

"I know it's more than that."

Though the words were spoken softly, their impact was the same as if Evelyn had screamed them. Helen flinched. Her heart thudded loudly in her chest.

"A mother knows things." Evelyn paused and took a deep breath. "I know that you're troubled, Sloneczka. I've known it for a long time." She touched Helen's leg. "I know that you're scared to confess what's on your heart, but God can only help you if you tell him what's wrong."

"Mama—"

"If you would just go to confession," Evelyn said. "God can forgive."

Helen blinked back the tears forming behind her eyes and quickly looked back down at her lap. Her throat felt thick and she cleared it. "Not this."

That was the closest Helen had ever come to admitting the truth. She could feel her mother's stare and, after several seconds, forced herself to look up. Evelyn seemed lost in thought, her eyes focused on Helen's shoulder, her eyebrows pulled together in a small frown. Helen wished she'd say something.

"Mama?"

Evelyn jerked slightly as if she had been startled and met Helen's gaze. Her expression was a combination of worry, disappointment, and sadness. She nodded slowly. "I will pray for you, Helen." She stood. "I need to go if I'm going to make Tridentine."

"Mama . . ." Helen could hear the entreaty quality to the word. She jumped to her feet and grasped her mother's hand. "I . . ." She faltered, unsure what she wanted to say, given that whatever words she chose could never be taken back. She looked pleadingly into Evelyn's eyes. "I'm sorry if I've disappointed you. I love you."

Evelyn had smiled then, Helen remembered. It had been a sad smile that said more than words ever could. And then Evelyn had hugged her. Tightly. And kissed her on both cheeks. That was the last time they had discussed it. It had been, in fact, the last time they had ever discussed anything of importance.

Helen wondered what her parents would say when they found out she had left David. Ignoring what was either unspoken or in the past was one thing. But a divorce? There was no way to pretend that wasn't happening. Her excommunication was unavoidable, as was their condemnation.

Helen opened her eyes and looked down at her watch. It was only a little past midnight. She had no doubt that it was going to be a long night.

Thursday Morning
November 13, 2014

Maggie

MAGGIE STRETCHED AWKWARDLY and waited for the other passengers to file down the aisle toward the front of the bus. They had a fifteen minute layover in Harrisburg, Pennsylvania, and, despite the chill of the pre-dawn, she wanted more than anything to stretch her legs and, if only for a few minutes, breathe fresh air. Behind her, she could hear Eddie shuffling along, muttering to herself. She had no intention of spending these precious moments of freedom with the elderly woman and promised herself the minute she stepped off the bus, she would escape into the darkness.

At the head of the line, a heavyset woman with tightly-permed hair was struggling to pull a Hawaiian print tote bag from the overhead shelf. Maggie closed her eyes and willed herself to remain calm. Finally the line moved again and Maggie stepped out of the coach and onto the sidewalk.

Despite the tinge of bus exhaust and the oily smell of diesel, the crisp morning air was refreshing. Maggie inhaled greedily and held the fresh air in her lungs for several seconds before exhaling in a slow, moist cloud. She stood taller and pulled her stomach in, enjoying the feel of her spine as it lengthened.

The depot was illuminated by globed, antique-looking streetlights and Maggie walked briskly out of the unloading area and up the short stretch of sidewalk to the corner. Across the street, in front of what appeared to be the tallest building in vicinity, was a grassy area. She glanced at the illuminated numbers on the face of her watch. There was still ten minutes before they were scheduled to depart.

She walked slowly around the small park, occasionally stopping to roll her shoulders to loosen the tight muscles in her neck and back. The thought of settling back into the narrow bus seat wasn't appealing, but given her inability to handle air travel, buses and trains were her only option if she wanted to use her time efficiently, though, truth be told, this trip hadn't been her most productive.

Between the phone call from Ben and her anxiety about

showing up unannounced on Sarah's doorstep, concentrating on her presentation had been next to impossible. She hated the idea of just winging it, but if she didn't get her act together, that could actually happen. Of course, given that the basis of their relationship had been built on a series of coincidences and lies, just appearing on Sarah's doorstep would be in keeping with how things had progressed so far.

Though Maggie considered herself too pragmatic to think in terms of bumper stickers or catchphrases, she heard them daily as a funeral director. Eulogies rarely failed to include the dearly departed's outlook on life: Steve "lived life to the fullest" . . . Elizabeth knew that "for every door that closed, God opened a window" . . . Rachel always wrote in the front of her notebooks, "Dance as if no one were watching, sing as if no one was listening, love as if you had never been hurt, live as if it were your last day on earth."

As morbid as it was, Maggie liked to imagine her own funeral. She had it planned, of course, but it was nothing elaborate. Just enough that the people of Seymour would feel like she had done her family's legacy justice. She had a nice casket, tasteful flowers, and a selection of music that included some traditional and expected hymns in addition to a couple of more contemporary songs. As much as it had pained her to forego *The Big Chill* homage and include The Rolling Stones' "You Can't Always Get What You Want," she knew that few in town would find the humor—or, in reality, the truth—in it.

But it was the truth, wasn't it? She had never gotten what she wanted. She said that, though, she wasn't sure she ever really knew what exactly that was. She knew there was something missing. She was often aware of "its" absence, particularly in the mornings right after she took that first deep breath but still hovered in the hazy purgatory between sleep and awake. Memories of Rachel crept unbidden into her thoughts during those unguarded moments.

The loss of a first love was always hard. She knew that. But despite her best efforts, even though she had been the one to end it, Maggie still couldn't seem to let go. Her guilt for what she put Rachel through by living a lie, by denying their love, by shutting her out, still haunted her.

Rachel had been the great love of her life. It didn't matter that it was a high school romance. It didn't matter that it was the only real relationship she had ever had—ever allowed herself to have. Rachel had been "it." And Maggie had been too young and too scared to handle it. She knew that now. Of course, knowing was only part of the equation. Getting past it was the harder part. Impossible, in fact. So, rather than allow herself to feel vulnerable, she convinced herself that hiding her lifestyle was necessary for the reputation of the business. Anonymous sex satisfied her physical needs and relieved of the burden of emotional attachment. And it had worked—until Sarah.

Maggie remembered the night they met. She had been in Seattle at a conference and as she usually did when away from home, she had made a beeline for the nearest lesbian bar. The pulsing beat of the music had assaulted her the moment she stepped inside the bar. The outside had been innocuous, but inside, the pinkish interior and the strings of white Christmas lights gave the bar an unexpected intimacy. The atmosphere and almost sweet smell of years of spilled beer was almost like a trigger that left her public life at the door.

She grinned, and, as always, paused to enjoy the feeling of anonymity. Here, she wasn't the small-town, workaholic, female funeral director. Here, she was no one. And here, no one knew or cared what she did or with whom. All she needed to do now was to get a drink and choose who she wanted to take back to her hotel.

She threaded her way to the bar through the clusters of women who stood talking and flirting, past the separate dance floor where various combinations of women rocked and grinded to the pulsing beat. The place was busy for a Thursday night and it took a few minutes to catch the eye of the bartender, a young, tattooed woman with a pierced eyebrow.

"What can I do for you?" Her flirtatious tone was more than a little practiced.

"Dirty Ketel One martini, dry, up, with a couple of olives," Maggie said loudly so she could be heard over the music and chatter.

The bartender gave Maggie a second, more interested look, and grinned. This time, her flirtation was more genuine.

"I can do that. How dirty would you like it?"

Maggie returned the grin.

"Fairly dirty," she said. "But not filthy."

"Done." The bartender stepped back to the well, grabbed a slightly battered cocktail shaker, and reached into the ice bin for the scoop.

While she waited for her drink, Maggie studied the other patrons. She could tell immediately that it was a typical lesbian bar scene. Women danced, laughed, and flirted all around her. Lapses of judgment were occurring on the dance floor and in dark corners. Mini-dramas were being subtly and overtly played out and through it all ran a tightly-strung thread of sexual tension.

She smiled and turned back to the bar to find the bartender placing a heavy-looking martini glass with three skewered olives in it on the cocktail napkin in front of her. In her right hand, was the shaker. She gave it a couple of final vigorous shakes and removed the top.

"I already washed the glass with vermouth." She poured the drink into the glass through a strainer. "Like what you see?" She jerked her head toward the dance floor but Maggie could tell that wasn't what she meant.

Maggie looked her up and down. She was cute and just a little dangerous looking. She wasn't what Maggie was looking for tonight, but still, flirting was fun and so she went with it.

"I do," Maggie said. "Is it always this busy on a Thursday night?"

The bartender nodded. "Usually, yeah. Seattle's got a pretty active scene." She ignored the women trying to get her attention for drinks and leaned closer. "I could show you around the city if you'd like."

Maggie tipped her head slightly to the side. "What makes you think I'm not from here?"

"Believe me. I can tell locals and you're not from anywhere near here." The bartender studied Maggie. "I'm guessing . . . Midwest? Here on business. Away from the husband and kids for a few days? Cutting loose?"

Maggie smiled, enjoying the opportunity to be someone else. "You're good. Omaha. Married twelve years. Three kids. I work for a company that manages call centers. I'm here for a company meeting."

"And you had 'experiences' in college that you never quite

forgot," the bartender continued. "So when you're away from the hubby you like to play."

Maggie nodded.

"Jesus, Chloe." One of the women waiting for a drink held up her empty Budweiser bottle. "Stop hitting on the soccer mom and get us some drinks."

Chloe shrugged.

"I've got to work, but if you're still around when we close, maybe we could . . . ?" She gave what Maggie was coming to recognize as her slow, practiced, pick-up grin.

"Maybe. What do I owe you?" Maggie gestured at the drink.

"On me," Chloe said with a suggestive wink before turning to the loud cluster of women trying to get her attention.

"I'd be careful with that one if I were you."

Maggie turned her head to her left. A slender woman with auburn, shoulder-length hair sat on the stool next to her. She pulled the red cocktail straw from her drink and used it to point in Chloe's direction.

"I can guarantee you she's been with just about every woman in here," she said. "Or at least, every good-looking woman."

Maggie glanced at Chloe and then back at the woman next to her. Something about her seemed almost familiar, though she knew they had never met. Her dark green eyes were framed by thick lashes. She wasn't conventionally beautiful, but there was something very striking about her.

Maggie raised an eyebrow. "What about you?"

The woman smiled. "Have I slept with every good-looking woman in here?" she asked and then looked pointedly at Maggie. "Clearly I haven't."

Maggie felt herself blush. "Have you slept with her?" She inclined her head toward Chloe who was joking with a group of women as she pried the caps off of several bottles of beer.

The woman glanced at Chloe before shaking her head. "Not my type."

Maggie nodded and raised her martini to her lips. It was deliciously cold and very dry. Chloe might be a player but she made a very good drink. She closed her eyes and sighed in appreciation.

"Long day?" the woman asked.

"As a matter of fact, yes. I'm here for a meeting and it was deathly dull." Maggie smiled inwardly at her choice of words. "And you?"

"And me," the woman repeated slowly. "Not a lot to tell. I'm a teacher and tonight I'm here avoiding a stack of essays that need grading."

"Going out on a school night," Maggie said. "Rebel, eh?"

The woman shrugged. "This week is a little different. But we were talking about you. What do you do?"

"I work for a company that oversees call centers." Maggie decided to continue her lie. "We're based in Omaha."

"Nebraska," the woman said thoughtfully and pushed her bangs back from in front of her right eye and behind her ear. "Is it true that per capita, there are more call centers in Kansas City and Omaha than anywhere else in the US because people from those cities have no discernible accent?"

Maggie stared at her, unsure how to respond. Clearly this woman knew more about the subject than she did. She took another sip from her drink to buy time and then, after she swallowed, nodded.

"Yep," she said finally. "It's true. Where did you hear that?"

The woman grinned. "I know a little about linguistics. So, your job sounds . . . interesting."

Maggie laughed at the sarcasm. "About as much as grading essays."

"Touché." The woman raised her glass to her lips, drank deeply, and then set it back on the bar. She wiped at the corners of her mouth with her middle finger and thumb. "So, how long are you in town?"

"I leave tomorrow," Maggie lied. "We've been meeting all week so after tomorrow we all head back to our little corners of the country."

"And you're taking advantage of your last night in Seattle?"

Maggie nodded.

"With the bartender?"

"Unless I get a better offer." Maggie waited to see what the woman would do.

The woman studied her for several seconds before leaning forward so her mouth was near Maggie's ear.

"Would you like to dance?" she asked, her breath tickling Maggie's neck.

The music, Maggie noticed, had slowed though it was no less loud.

"Yes," she said.

The woman slipped off of her bar stool. They stood eye to eye and Maggie noticed again her thick lashes.

"You have great eyes," she blurted without thinking.

The woman smiled and looked genuinely pleased. "Thanks. My name is Sarah."

Maggie considered giving her a fake name. Typically she told women her name was Millie because it sounded enough like her real name that she remembered to answer when they used it.

"Maggie," she said before she could stop herself.

Sarah took her hand and led her to the middle of the throng on the dance floor. She turned and pulled Maggie toward her.

Maggie blinked at the sudden contact. Sarah was leaner than Maggie had realized, but strong. And she was warm. Maggie could feel the heat of her through their clothing.

Neither spoke as they moved against each other in time to the music. Maggie inhaled her scent, a combination of rosemary-mint shampoo and a sweet, almost woodsy cologne that reminded her somewhat of pipe tobacco. She inhaled deeply and held the breath in her lungs.

"You okay?" Sarah murmured in her ear, her breath soft on Maggie's cheek. She moved her hand from Maggie's shoulder and tucked her hair gently behind her ear, exposing Maggie's neck.

The gesture, though simple, caused Maggie's heart to beat faster and she knew without a doubt that Sarah was the one she would be taking back to the hotel. She leaned closer.

"Would you like to get out of here?" she asked in a low, intentionally husky voice.

Sarah smiled against her cheek and then pulled back and looked thoughtfully into Maggie's eyes. Maggie stopped dancing and returned the gaze. Had she read it wrong?

"You don't have—" she began.

"Yes," Sarah said. "Are you paid up at the bar?"

Maggie had nodded and just like that, they had turned toward the entrance. Outside, they had walked in silence the two blocks to Broadway where they hailed a cab. The anticipation as they sat in the back of the taxi, side by side but not touching during the fifteen-block trip back to Maggie's hotel, had been deliciously excruciating, she remembered. And by the time they had made it back to her room . . .

She blinked and looked down at her watch. More than ten minutes had passed and the bus was scheduled to leave at six-thirty. She turned toward the bus station and saw that the last of the passengers were boarding. She sighed, shoved her chilled hands inside the pockets of her trench coat, and hurried back to the bus. At the end of the line was a heavyset man with a military buzz cut. He shuffled his feet back and forth as they waited and the movement of the synthetic material of his warm-up pants made a soft "shushing" sound.

As she waited, Maggie looked up at the bus windows. Eddie was already in her seat, her overhead reading light on, her head bent forward as she studied something in her lap. She thought again about Eddie's advice about making a death look like an accident and wondered if she was just talking or if she had, in fact, murdered her husband. Maggie had seen a couple of homicides in her career and wondered, fleetingly, if Eddie's mortician had noticed anything out of the ordinary.

She snorted softly. "She was just talking," she muttered and hoped it was true.

The man ahead of her glanced back. His brown eyes were small and dark in the fluorescent lighting.

"Sorry?" His voice was softer and warmer than she had expected.

Maggie shook her head and grinned. "Nothing. Sorry. I was just talking to myself. I didn't mean to say it out loud."

The man seemed to think about this and then nodded. He gestured at the bus. "Where are you headed?"

Maggie hesitated, unsure if she wanted to have an extended conversation with this stranger. But if he was on the bus all the way to New York City, he would know anyway. She shrugged internally.

"New York City," she said.

The line inched forward. The man stepped closer toward the bus, the legs of his warm-up pants "shushing."

He faced her again. "Me, too. And then on to Boston. I'm meeting someone." He thrust his chest out a little. "A woman."

Maggie shifted uncomfortably. As had been the case with Eddie, this was more information than she wanted to know.

"We met online. She's pretty great." The man shrugged.

The woman in front of him stepped up onto the coach. Maggie tipped her head forward and raised her eyebrows to indicate that he could board. The man turned and grasped the silver handle mounted to the side of the bus. As he pulled himself forward and stepped up, he grunted in pain. Maggie realized he must have some kind of injury.

She waited until he reached the top of the steps before boarding. He limped slowly down the aisle. Beads of perspiration on the back of his neck glistened in the overhead bus lighting. He finally reached the seat behind hers, lowered himself heavily down, and exhaled loudly. His face was flushed and shiny.

"Nice to stretch your legs?" Eddie asked as Maggie struggled to pull off her coat within the confines of the aisle. Around them, people were settling themselves in for the next stage of the journey. Maggie tossed her coat on top of her briefcase and slid into her seat.

"It was." Maggie smiled politely and picked up her phone. She had a new text message from Amber. She tapped on the screen.

> Hey. About to start on Mr. Simpson. Just wanted to let you know everything here is fairly quiet. There are two intakes scheduled for later today. One's from the nursing home and the other is from a car accident. Other than that, nada. Good luck with your presentation.

"Did someone die?" Eddie asked.

Maggie looked up from the screen. Eddie was watching her with an almost hungry expression, her neck arched so she could peek at the brightly illuminated message. Maggie resisted the urge to twist the phone away so the screen was hidden.

"Just a note from work."

Eddie sat back in her seat and nodded in satisfaction. "I figured." She pulled off her glasses and rubbed at her watery eyes. "Part of life, really."

She dug at the crust in one of the corners and examined it before flicking it away and shoving the glasses back on her face.

She turned her upper body to look at the man Maggie had been talking to while waiting to board the bus.

"I'm Eddie," she said.

Maggie heard a rustling of clothing being removed or adjusted, and then the sound of the man shifting in his seat.

"James," he said and then cleared his throat. "Most folks call me Jimmy, though."

Eddie nodded. "My real name is Edith. I know all about nicknames." She paused and glanced sidelong at Maggie as if offering her the chance the share her name and join the conversation. When she didn't, Eddie turned back to Jimmy. "Where are you going, Jimmy?"

Maggie tried not to listen, but couldn't help but hear his answer.

"Boston."

"Business or pleasure?"

Maggie tried not to smile. Eddie was relentless.

"Pleasure," Jimmy said. "Well, I mean, I'm going to meet a woman. We . . . uh . . . met online and now we're going to meet in person."

Eddie nodded. "I've heard about this Internet dating. It sounds dangerous to me. In my day, you met someone and had a chance to look into their eyes. Course, that don't mean they're what they say they are. People hide their darkness in person same as they do any other way. Take my Billy. He was a drunk and a bully but you wouldn't have known it from the outside. He was sweet as pie at first. It was only after he got that ring on my finger that he showed his true colors." She nodded sagely. "How much do you know about this woman?"

Maggie heard more rustling as Jimmy shifted in his seat.

"A lot," he said. His tone was almost defiant.

Good for you, Jimmy, Maggie thought as she typed out a response to Amber.

"Well, just be careful," Eddie said. "Everybody's hiding something."

Maggie felt Eddie's gaze and lifted her eyes to see her looking pointedly at her. She knew the next words out of Eddie's mouth were for her benefit.

"And it's only a matter of time before it comes out."

Bug

BUG LAY ON his back and stared up at the ceiling. The cheap panels were partially illuminated by the glow of the streetlights. Sometimes, when he couldn't sleep, he would study the dots and connect them to form images. He liked to pretend they were stars. Tonight, though, he wasn't in the mood. Sid snored softly in the bed across from him. Usually it was annoying, but tonight, the sound was almost comforting in its familiarity. Sid's snoring was one of the things he could count on and for a moment, he thought he might actually miss it.

He wasn't sure what time it was, but from the way the night felt, he was pretty sure it was only a couple of hours before Gail loaded him into the shelter's minivan and took him to the bus station. And from there, he would travel across the country to Boston. Just the name of the place filled him with dread, though not for the reasons everyone seemed to think. It wasn't that he was scared to move. He was scared that it wasn't his last move, though nothing could be as bad as the day the social worker took him away.

The cold September morning they came to the house wasn't the first time a social worker had shown up at their door. They had been there three times before. But it was the first time Bug hadn't been able to stall them or make them believe that Rhonda was at work or would be home later.

They had caught him by surprise as he opened the door to go to school. They were standing in the doorway, the weak, early morning sunshine making them look like silhouettes. Bug had blinked and shifted to the side so he could see their faces. The man, a police officer, was a couple of inches shorter than the woman though it was obvious, despite his black uniform jacket, he was much thinner. The sunlight caught the blond stubble on his jaw. Next to him, the woman, who was very tall and boxy in her tan trench coat and red-knitted scarf, seemed to be frozen in place, her hand raised, fingers balled into a loose fist, as if she were about to knock.

"Hi," the police officer said. "You must be Sam."

Bug nodded slowly, his hand still on the knob.

The officer smiled and Bug noticed how it stretched his skin so tightly it looked like his face would crack. "I'm Officer McCully and this is Mrs. Witherspoon with the Department of Human Services. Is your mom here?" He asked the question casually, but Bug could tell it was anything but. The sound of bleeps and chatter from Officer McCully's police radio filled the silence.

"She's at work," Bug said finally.

"Really? Where does she work?" Mrs. Witherspoon asked. Her voice was much higher and softer than Bug would have imagined given her size. Her identification badge was clipped to the lapel of her coat and Bug noticed that she hadn't smiled for the photograph.

"She . . . cleans houses," Bug said. "But she has to go early so I get myself ready for school."

Mrs. Witherspoon looked over the top of Bug's head into the living room. "She cleans houses, huh?"

Bug turned and looked at the mess he was used to seeing. Though he kept his own room very clean and organized, he had given up on trying to tidy the rest of the house. Rhonda had a habit of simply leaving things wherever she happened to be when she passed out. And even though she hadn't been around for several days, the evidence of her most recent binge was still there.

Bug tried to see the scene from a stranger's point of view. The dirty paper plates stacked on the cheap, scarred coffee table. The sagging, tired-looking divan. The half-open box from South Side Pizzeria on the floor with a dried and curling slice of pizza on top. Clothes were draped over the arms of the battered recliner and, on the end table in plain view, was Rhonda's crack pipe, the glass tip brown and crusty from use.

He swallowed and turned back to face Officer McCully and Mrs. Witherspoon. He could tell from the look on their faces that they had seen it as well.

"Can we come in, Sam?"

Bug looked at Mrs. Witherspoon for several seconds before answering. "I'm not supposed to let anyone into the house if Rh— my mom isn't here."

Mrs. Witherspoon glanced at Officer McCully and nodded. Though Bug didn't know exactly what was being communicated, he could tell that whatever they had agreed upon wasn't good.

"Sam, I need you to be honest with us." Mrs. Witherspoon squatted down so she was at eye level.

Up close, Bug could see the crisscross of tiny veins on either side of her nose. Her breath smelled like stale coffee.

"How long has it been since your mother has been home? We received a report that you have been here, by yourself, for several days." She glanced up and back at Officer McCully who nodded.

"You're not in any trouble," he said. His voice was gentle. "You haven't done anything wrong. But you need to tell us the truth."

Bug's heart beat faster and despite the cold morning air, felt his face flush. "I . . . She's at work." Even as he spoke the words, he knew they sounded weak.

"Sam, how long have you been here by yourself?" Mrs. Witherspoon asked in a kind but firmer tone.

Bug swallowed again and tried to control his breathing. He opened his mouth to answer but the words wouldn't come. The police radio was the only sound for several long seconds.

Mrs. Witherspoon finally sighed, stood, and turned to Officer McCully. "I think, given the previous reports and what I'm seeing here, we have enough for protective custody without a court order. You?"

"I do." Officer McCully nodded, turned his head, and depressed the button on the radio microphone clipped to the shoulder of his uniform jacket. As he spoke into the microphone, Mrs. Witherspoon turned to Bug.

"Sam, I know you want to protect your mother, but our job is to make sure you're safe and being taken care of." She gestured to inside the house. "We don't think that's happening and so we are going to take you someplace where someone can look after you until your mom comes back."

Bug shook his head almost violently. "I can't. She's at work. Really. I have to go to school." He started to step forward onto the concrete front porch.

Mrs. Witherspoon stopped him with a gloved hand. "I need you to come inside with me so we can pack a bag with some of your things." She turned to Officer McCully who was finishing his radio conversation.

He nodded and then pushed open the door. Mrs. Witherspoon

gently but firmly ushered Bug back inside. She and Officer McCully followed.

"Where's your bedroom?" Bug heard Mrs. Witherspoon's question but didn't answer as he watched Officer McCully walk to the end table and look down at the crack pipe.

"Sam?"

Bug turned back to Mrs. Witherspoon.

"Where is your room?"

He pointed to the narrow wooden stairs. "Up there."

"Okay, let's go up and pack some of your things," she said. She looked at Officer McCully, who was pulling a notebook out of the inside of his jacket. "You'll handle things here?"

He nodded.

She turned back to Bug and indicated that they should go upstairs. "Why don't you show me your room." It wasn't a request.

Bug hadn't known what to think as he packed clothes, shoes, and his toothbrush into the plastic bag Mrs. Witherspoon had pulled out of her bag when he told her he didn't have a suitcase. He wanted to ask where they were going and how Rhonda would know how to find him when she returned, but he didn't want to give too much away. Instead, he had done what they told him to do.

From the house on Addison, he had been taken to a shelter where they had asked him questions about Rhonda, about his days, and who else in his family lived close by. When they found out that he had no one, he had been moved to this shelter where he had lived for the past two months. Rhonda, it turned out, didn't even realize he had been taken into custody until three days after Mrs. Witherspoon and Officer McCully had come to the house.

And now, after all the meetings with counselors and judges and Gail, he was going to live with his Aunt Sarah. They had spoken on the phone a couple of times and she seemed nice—nicer than Rhonda, actually. But still, he worried about Rhonda. She was in the program, but he hadn't heard from her. Was she okay? Was it working? Why didn't she seem to care that he was going away?

In the bed across from him, Sid jerked and gave a short, gurgling snort that seemed to wake him enough to change positions. Bug could hear the rustle of covers and the squeak of the metal frame as Sid turned onto his side and gave a deep sigh. The room was quiet aside from the collective sound of the boys' soft breathing.

Bug wouldn't miss the shelter. He wouldn't miss the loudness, the rambunctiousness of so many other kids. But right now, at this moment, it was better than the unknown that was yet to come.

Jimmy

JIMMY CLOSED HIS eyes and tipped his head back against the seat, thankful for the reprieve from the old woman's never-ending chatter. "What's your name? Where are you going? Why?" Her questions made him uncomfortable. They had seemed to have the same effect on the dark-haired woman who had been behind him in line and who now sat in the seat in front of him. During the interrogation, she had withdrawn into her work. He wondered briefly if she had suffered the same fate before he had boarded.

He rolled his head to the side and looked out the window. The sky had lightened and he was able to see the passing trees that flanked either side of the Pennsylvania Turnpike. He knew from the road signs that they were nearing Morgantown, which meant that Philly was only about forty-five minutes away. He also knew that somewhere, on another bus, Helen was travelling to Boston under the assumption that she was meeting a very different man—a man who had made promises Jimmy had no business making. He felt a knot of anxiety in his stomach.

In front of him, the dark-haired woman was tapping away on her laptop. Jimmy had leaned forward enough at one point to see that it was a PowerPoint presentation on something to do with women funeral directors. That had been a surprise. He had noticed her immediately when they were standing in line outside the bus because she was easily one of the prettiest women he had ever seen. And when she had taken off her jacket, he had seen that she had the body to match. But to think of her embalming bodies . . . He shook his head. That just seemed somehow wrong.

It wasn't that death upset him. When he'd worked as a paramedic, Jimmy had seen death more often than he would have liked. But it was death as it occurred—as he tried to prevent it. It wasn't a case of going someplace, collecting the body, and then preparing it for burial. The thought made him shudder.

The problem with dead bodies after they had been embalmed was that they no longer looked like people. They always looked plastic and unnatural. Jimmy frowned as he remembered his grandfather in his casket. His face and hands were really all that had been visible, but both had looked as if they'd been carved from wax—especially the hands with their too-long, thick, yellowed fingernails. He had wondered if the rest of him looked that way as well.

Jimmy grimaced at the memory and glanced back up at the nosy old woman who had asked so many questions. Eddie. She reminded him of so many of the elderly patients they had tried to resuscitate when he was still in the field—of the woman who had been on the stretcher when he had fallen down the stairs and hurt his back. She had died, though, he reminded himself, not because he had dropped her. The review commission had determined that he wasn't to blame for her death. It wasn't his fault that he lost his footing. The staircase had been so narrow and steep. It could have happened to anyone.

Jimmy studied the flap of skin along the edge of his thumbnail. He had forgotten to clip it before he left the apartment and now struggled with the desire to gnaw at it. He had broken himself of the habit in the paramedic program. He and several classmates had been practicing putting cervical collars on each other when the instructor, Dr. Gunther, had stopped them.

"Hold up," he had said and walked closer to where they were working. He leaned down and studied the placement of their hands. "First of all, the collar you're using is too short. And secondly, get the chin adjusted before you start trying to wrap the rest of it." He stood back up and Jimmy heard the crackle of his knees as he straightened. "Reilly." He tipped his head back and to the side to indicate that he wanted to talk in private.

Jimmy stood and followed him to the front of the classroom. Despite his age, which Jimmy placed somewhere near fifty, and his gray hair, Dr. Gunther had the athletic build of a baseball player. When he lectured, he tended to shift his weight from the balls to the back of his feet and then from one foot to the other, as if he wanted to be ready to leap into action at any moment.

"Your fingers." Dr. Gunther sighed and ran the knuckle of his index finger over his mustache and upper lip. "They look like bloody stumps. It's not sanitary, it's dangerous to have open cuts even with gloves and frankly," he met Jimmy's eyes, "it's disgusting to look at. Go get a manicure and for God's sake, let your fingers heal."

Jimmy felt his face and chest flush with shame. He looked down at his hands. It was a nervous habit he had struggled for years to break. He knew it looked bad, but he wasn't sure how to stop himself. Once a hangnail started, he found he simply couldn't leave it alone.

He raised his gaze and forced himself to nod. "Yes sir. I'll take care of it tonight."

And he had, though he hadn't had the money to get a manicure. Instead, he went to the school library and used the computers there to research nail and cuticle care. On his way home, he stopped at the Walgreen's and bought a cheap manicure tool set, a tub of generic cocoa butter, and a box of plastic Band-Aids. He spent the evening working on his nails and for the next two weeks, wore Band-Aids on just about every finger so he wouldn't be tempted to pick at the scabs.

His classmates had laughed and called him butter fingers, but it had worked. His fingers had healed and the clippers he carried with him became a sort of talisman—a physical touchstone that reminded him that he was able to control himself and the decisions he made. He sighed. That didn't mean he always made good decisions. He didn't. In fact, for a couple of years, he made really bad decisions—especially after the accident.

Stu had immediately taken him to the worker's compensation doctor where he had to explain what happened and how he fell. Jimmy should have known from the moment he saw Dr. Eddelston that he wasn't going to get the most attentive care. He had been sitting on the exam table, waiting and stewing as he replayed the accident over and over in his head.

He was going through it a third time when the cursory knock came on the door. Dr. Eddelston stepped quickly into the room. He was older than Jimmy had expected, with a swept-back mane of silver hair and arched, bushy eyebrows that made Jimmy think of Donald Sutherland. In one hand, Dr. Eddelston held a manila folder that Jimmy assumed contained his paperwork, and in the other, a pair of glasses that he held almost gingerly, his index finger and thumb circling the bridge and nosepiece.

"Hello," he glanced down at the folder, "James. I'm Doctor Eddelston."

Jimmy tried to smile in a way he hoped conveyed the fact

that in many regards, they were actually colleagues and he was ready to share his thoughts on the injury. "Nice to meet you." He considered extending his hand but decided that would require too much juggling on the doctor's part. Instead, he waited.

"So, you," Eddelston looked down at the file again, "took a fall." His head still tipped down, he raised his eyes. His winged eyebrows were arched upward as if to punctuate the question.

"I did," Jimmy said. "I'm a paramedic. We responded to a call regarding a non-responsive elderly woman who had—"

"I don't need to know the details," Dr. Eddelston interrupted. "You slipped and fell on the stairs, yes?"

Jimmy blinked. "Yeah, we were moving her from the second floor bedroom out to the ambulance. I was on the upper right corner and lost my footing."

"And it says here that you landed first on your lower back, then your shoulders, neck, and head. Is that correct?"

Jimmy nodded and then winced at the shooting pain in his neck.

"Uh huh . . ." Dr. Eddelston tossed the file onto the counter and pulled a penlight out of his shirt pocket and shined the light into Jimmy's eyes. "Pupils look fine," he murmured to himself, his breath smelling lightly of peppermint. "Probably no concussion though I'm guessing given your fall you have some damage to your neck and back."

"I'm thinking L4, L5, and C4 through C7," Jimmy said helpfully.

"Um." Eddelston stepped back, parted the gown, and began his examination of Jimmy's back. His hands were warm and dry on Jimmy's skin and he realized that no one had touched his bare skin since the last time he'd had a physical. He blushed at the realization that he enjoyed the sensation even though his body ached.

"Well," Eddelston said as he closed the gown and stepped back to stand at the foot of the exam table. "It's likely ruptured disks on your L4, L5, and, as you suggested, C4 through C7." He pursed his lips and frowned. "You're going to need an MRI and a CT scan to be sure. I'm guessing no need for surgery yet. We'll try rest and physical therapy. I'll give you a prescription for carisoprodol, which is a muscle relaxant and Vicodin for the pain." He turned and picked up the file, pulled a pen out of his shirt pocket, and began to write.

Jimmy should have known from the first pill that it was a mistake. The warm, tingly haze felt far too good. Was this how his father felt when he drank? Did the voices of self-doubt and condemnation quiet with each swallow? That's how it felt for Jimmy with the Vicodin. At least, it did until it stopped working as well—which was why he took it more and more frequently until every six hours became every four hours, which became every two. He complained to his doctor that the rigors of physical therapy only made the pain worse. And when that failed to get him an increase in dosage, he began to advocate for surgery.

It hadn't mattered that surgeons would cut into him and fuse his vertebrae. It hadn't mattered that there could be complications. What mattered for Jimmy was after the surgery, he would likely get oxycodone. He knew, that the six-inch incisions on his neck and lower back would be the perfect excuse for continued prescriptions. And, for a time they were. But as he needed more and more to keep his buzz, he had to resort to more creative measures.

He became the patient of a variety of doctors who treated him for pain. He visited twenty-four-hour urgent care clinics on the weekends with the excuse that he was going out of town and forgot to get a refill from his physician. He maxed out his credit cards when insurance stopped covering the cost. When he had no other options, he had forced himself to fall down the stairs with the hopes he would reinjure himself and require more surgery.

He had created the fake Facebook page during this time. It had seemed like a good idea, a way to pass the time. He was homebound and too high to do much else. And, if he were honest, he was lonely.

He didn't set out to create a fake identity. It was only after his first profile, the one that used his real picture and interests, got such little activity that he decided to cut and paste pictures from Dr. Hamblin's page. He knew enough about the medical field to impress someone who didn't know much more than what they saw on television. And then he added hobbies such as yoga, running, and extreme sports. He posted quotes from Gandhi and Mark Twain and then began to join groups. He was surprised at how quickly people, particularly women, sent him friend requests. And the way they treated him when they thought he looked like Dr. Hamblin was different than anything he had ever experienced.

Suddenly, he was popular. He was sought after. He was desirable. Just like the drugs, the attention was addictive. He became an expert at flirting. And with Google at his disposal, he could be an authority on everything from Egyptian archaeology to building furniture. Thanks to Dr. Hamblin's face, the anonymity provided by the computer, and the oxycodone, he was unstoppable. He was a golden god.

And then Helen contacted him. She had seen his posts on the parasailing page . . . wanted more information for her job . . . could she ask him some questions? Even to Jimmy's inexperienced ears the request sounded flimsy. But as he Googled the answers to her questions and they discussed things outside of parasailing, he discovered she wasn't like the other women who just wanted to snag a young, handsome doctor. She was genuine. And funny. And kind.

It became, ironically, his first *real* relationship. And, the oxycodone made it easy for him to convince himself that, despite being built on a lie, it could work. And then the bottom fell out.

Jimmy had gone to a new doctor with the usual complaint of pain. He said he had just moved to Harrisburg and, even though he knew he shouldn't have unloaded the truck all by himself, he did and had reinjured his back. He had hoped the doctor would simply offer a prescription. When he didn't, Jimmy was forced to ask.

"I'm not sure that's such a good idea, Mr. Reilly." For a moment, Jimmy forgot which doctor this was. He glanced at the identification card clipped to his white lab coat. Dr. Salam.

"I don't understand," Jimmy said and winced as he shifted on the exam table. "In the past, my old doctor just—"

"The reason I think it's not a good idea is because every time you get a prescription for an opioid, you have to sign for it. I made some inquiries and it appears that you have seen many doctors over the past year and a half. And each time, you were prescribed any variety of medications ranging from Vicodin to Percocet. There's even some Ambien." He opened the folder and read something on the top sheet. "Though it appears that oxycodone is your drug of choice."

Jimmy felt the acceleration of his heart and tried to breathe normally. He cleared his throat. "I don't know what you mean. There has to be some mistake. Maybe a mix-up in the paperwork."

Dr. Salam closed the file. "James, I'm going to level with you. You've been doctor shopping and abusing prescription medication. I have a list if you'd like to see it, of doctors all across the city who have written prescriptions and pharmacies that have filled them. What you've done is considered fraud."

Sweat broke out on Jimmy's forehead and chest. He could feel drops trickling down his back. He opened his mouth to speak and then closed it. It was there in black and white. He couldn't deny it.

"I'm sorry."

The words seemed to surprise Dr. Salam. His expression, which had been cool and professional, seemed to soften slightly. The tightness around his eyes relaxed.

"You have two choices," he said finally. "You can voluntarily go into rehab or you can try to handle this on your own. You've been red flagged and there is no way you will be able to fill another prescription. As soon as what you have now runs out, you will not be able to get any more. Also, should you choose not to get help, you could be facing criminal charges."

Jimmy closed his eyes and tried not to give in to the tears that were welling up behind his eyes. His nose and throat felt thick and he swallowed several times. He couldn't deny it any longer. He was an addict. He also knew that if he didn't get help now, he likely never would. Just from the few times he had run out of pills or tried to wean himself off, he knew he couldn't quit on his own. The symptoms of withdrawal had been excruciating. Physically, there was the sweating and vomiting. But worse was the psychological aspect. The craving. The hunger. The anxiety. The thought of oxy consumed him. All he could think about was getting more.

"James?" Dr. Salam said. "Do you understand what I'm saying?"

Jimmy opened his eyes. Dr. Salam was studying him with an expression of compassion.

Jimmy nodded. "I understand. And you're right. I need help."

Even as he spoke the words, he felt something inside himself break. This time, he was unable to stop the tears and the low, guttural sobs, when they came, were almost violent. Later, when he was required to tell and retell the story in meetings, he realized that those tears, those sobs, were about more than getting caught or admitting he was an addict. They were recognition and a release of all the hurt and loneliness, the feelings of inadequacy, the pain of his childhood. He now knew it was also when he allowed himself to begin to heal.

That said, none of it had been easy. Rehab. Therapy. Declaring bankruptcy. Making amends. All of it had taken a toll. Every single step had required him to be vulnerable. *Let go and let God.* He had hated it. But each time he took control of some aspect of his life, he felt stronger. He had dealt with just about everything. All that was left was making amends with his father and being honest with Helen.

Squaring things with Helen was, he knew, the thing that would be harder than anything else because, to tell the truth would mean losing her. And her love was the one thing he couldn't stand to give up. It was why, he guessed, even though he knew it would turn out badly, he had spent his last few dollars to buy a bus ticket to travel to a city he didn't know to meet a woman who would likely, in a few hours, hate him.

Just the thought of it made his pulse accelerate. *Control what you can.* Jimmy closed his eyes, tipped his head back against the headrest, and forced himself to slow his breathing.

"In through the nose, out through the mouth," he reminded himself softly. "Slow breaths."

He stayed that way for several minutes, breathing and clearing his mind. When he felt centered, he opened his eyes. He felt Eddie's stare before looking up and meeting her gaze. Her upper body was turned in such a way that she looked unnaturally twisted. Jimmy frowned slightly, uncomfortable with the scrutiny. Something about her questions, about the way she watched him, made him feel as if she knew he was a liar and a fake. He tipped his head slightly back and gave her a faint smile.

Eddie responded with what could pass as a sort-of smile—a tight pressing together of the lips. No teeth. No warmth. She had judged him, Jimmy knew, and he had been found wanting.

He lowered his gaze and looked down again at his hands. He rubbed the edge of his forefinger against the hangnail on his thumb. It would bother him, pick at his consciousness, unless he did something about it. He raised his thumb to his mouth and gnawed at the skin. He snorted softly. Maybe it was impossible to deny one's true nature. Or maybe he was just tired of trying. Either way, what did it matter?

Helen

HELEN RUBBED AT the grit in the corners of her eyes and thought longingly about the long, hot shower she intended to take after she checked into her hotel room. She glanced down at her watch. It was almost nine o'clock in the morning. She had fallen asleep around one a.m. somewhere after Cleveland and slept fitfully until six when the bus stopped for thirty minutes in Milesburg, Pennsylvania. She had considered getting off to stretch her legs and breathe something other than the moist, stale air inside the bus, but instead, had tugged her coat more firmly under her chin and fallen back asleep.

Now, three hours later, she felt stiff, her hands and feet uncomfortably bloated. She sniffed, wrinkled her nose, and ran her fingers through her hair. She could tell from the tangles that it must look more than a little disheveled. Her tongue felt thick in her mouth and she moved it around, hoping to generate some saliva. She felt hung over.

She rubbed again at her eyes, yawned, and looked out the window. A thin layer of frost clung to the grass that lined the edge of the highway and as they passed, it glistened in the weak sunlight. They were about two hours outside of New York City and her transfer to the express bus to Boston.

Helen rolled her head gently from side to side and massaged the back of her neck to ease the stiffness. She knew she should check her phone. James had likely tried to contact her, as had David. She could only pretend the situation was anything other than what it was for so long. She rubbed her neck harder, in ever-larger circles.

Just look and get it over with, she thought dully. With a sigh, she pulled her phone from her purse. She had turned it off after her conversation with William and left it off throughout the night. But now, it was time to face the music. She pressed the thin button at the top of the phone. As she waited for it to power up, she sighed, closed her eyes, and pinched almost savagely at the bridge of her nose. She opened them and quickly tapped in the code to unlock

the screen. She stared at the alert message. She had thirty-seven
new text messages, all from David. She clicked on the first one.

You can't do this to me. You can't do this to us.

The second was no better.

I have given you everything. How can you do this?
How can you say you want more? You'll have nothing
without me. You'll be nothing without me.

She scrolled through, deleting as she went, not bothering to
read them in their entirety until she got to the last one. It had been
sent within the last five minutes.

I looked at the cell phone bill, Helen. I know about
your new boyfriend. I had Thomas check him out. You
might be surprised at what I learned about James Reilly.

Helen's heart pounded and her pulse throbbed in her ears. Was
it possible for David to have read the texts? Could he access them
so quickly? Clearly he knew about James and whether or not he
had read their correspondence, he had guessed at the affair.

Her hand holding the cell phone trembled. David didn't like
to lose. He took pride in his control of his life. What if he flew to
Boston and was waiting there for her? She'd had no choice but
to use her credit card to make the hotel reservation. It had been a
calculated risk. What if he checked her transactions?

She took a deep breath and forced herself to slow her breathing.
*Calm down. Look at this logically. He just sent the text so he's not
on a plane.* She forced herself to look again at the screen. She
reread the words slowly and carefully.

I looked at the cell phone bill, Helen. I know about
your new boyfriend. I had Thomas check him out. You
might be surprised at what I learned about James Reilly.

Helen frowned. She had been so upset by the first part of the
text, the second part hadn't registered. David must have asked his

brother, Thomas, to use the police database to do a background check on James. Helen thought about what they could have learned. With his phone number they could get his address and from there, his driver's license . . . his medical license information . . . his credit history. They could have easily found his Facebook page and other social media sites. She thought about what information she might have posted on his page. Most of their conversation has been through e-mail, text, and later, over the phone.

What, she wondered, about James would surprise her? She knew everything, didn't she? Granted, she hadn't done any extensive background check on her own, but she hadn't needed to. She had sought James out. She had been the one to contact him.

She shook her head. David was just trying to manipulate her and make her doubt her decision. She pressed her lips together and thought about what damage control options she had available to her while stuck on a bus.

God, I could use a cup of coffee.

She could reply to David and play along with his game. She could tell him that he was right and that she was coming home. She could say it was all just a big mistake on her part, but she needed to go tell James in person that it was over. It might work. But he might still insist she come home now. Or worse yet, that he come to Boston and escort her home.

Helen frowned and rubbed at the space between her eyebrows with her index and middle fingers. She could also just continue to ignore him.

Even as she had the thought, the screen lit up with a new message. She tapped on it.

> I can't believe you would leave me for an unemployed paramedic with a drug problem. The guy can't even get a job. He owes money everywhere.

Helen frowned. David and Thomas had clearly gotten the wrong man. She smirked. It served him right. David always thought he was the smartest person in the room. The urge to show him up—to point out where he was lacking—was overwhelming. Before she could stop herself, she hit *reply*.

You always think you're so smart, David. Try "doctor" at
one of the most prestigious hospitals in Boston.

David's reply was immediate.

Doctor my ass. And he's not from Boston, Helen. Try
Harrisburg, PA.

She snorted softly. David was trying to manipulate her. James
had already explained the 717 area code. He had grown up in
between Harrisburg and Philadelphia and didn't want his family,
who was poor, to have to pay long distance charges when they
called him.
She scowled and angrily tapped out a response.

Wrong again. You don't know what you're talking about
and even if you did, I don't care. I would still be leaving
you.

She hit the send button before she could reconsider. His
response was immediate.

Maybe so. But the fact remains that you're travelling
halfway across the country to meet up with a loser, drug
addict.

Helen frowned, despite herself. There was no way David was
right about James. Thomas must have checked out the wrong man.
There was no way James was an addict. He was a doctor. He had
a job. She had chatted with him more than once while he was
at work. Or, the little voice in the back of her brain whispered,
she'd thought she had. Just because he *said* he was at work at the
hospital didn't mean he actually *was*.
All of their communication had been on his cell phone and his
personal e-mail. Helen shook her head at the thought. James had
told her he was at work and she believed him. He had no reason
to lie to her. It was just David trying to make her question herself.
Still . . . The voice refused to stop, its tone persistent and
wheedling. Despite all their conversations and the intimacy they
shared, what *did* she really know about James?

The screen on her phone dimmed. It would have been easy for him to lie. Wasn't that what she had done, after all? Hadn't she conveniently failed to mention that she was married? That she was unable to have children? That her life was a disappointing shambles? She hadn't started out intending to deceive James. It had just happened. James had been meant to be a diversion—a break from all the things about her life that were wrong. And by the time she realized what was going on, it was too late to tell the truth.

Helen felt the familiar pressure building in her chest. She hadn't had anxiety attacks like this since the last time she and David had tried to have a baby. She tried to swallow down the increasing sense of panic. In her chest, her heart beat rapidly. She bent forward and pulled her carry-on bag from beneath the seat in front of her. She hadn't needed the Xanax in months, but still carried them with her just in case. She fumbled with clumsy fingers to unscrew the cap and tap one into her palm. She considered taking two but thought better of it. She didn't need to be loopy on top of everything else. She pinched the flat, peach-colored pill between two fingers, placed it on her tongue, and, despite her dry mouth, swallowed it.

While she waited for the medication to take effect, she tried to breathe deeply and think about what was within her control. She could text David and . . . what? Ask for proof? Reiterate that it didn't matter what he said or did? Tell him to go to hell? She shook her head. Doing that would only muddy the situation and confirm that he caused her to doubt herself.

Or, the voice in her head whispered, she could call Boston Medical Center and ask to speak to Dr. Reilly. He was working today. She could say she called to tell him she couldn't wait to see him. It would be partially true. And, it would subtly settle the doubts David had raised.

Helen felt her heartbeat begin to slow. She picked up the phone, tapped on the Google icon, and typed out "Boston Medical Center ER." Within less than a second, she had the information with a hyperlink for the phone number. All she needed to do was tap the link. She swallowed. She could still feel the thrum of her pulse in her ears.

Do it. Just make the call and the worry will all be over.

Before she could reconsider, Helen tapped the link and raised the phone to her ear. It rang three times before she heard a soft click and a male voice.

"Boston Medical Center. How may I direct your call?"

Helen started. For some reason, she had been anticipating a woman on the other end of the line. She took a deep breath. "Hi. I'm calling for Dr. James Reilly. Could you transfer me to his voice mail?"

She could hear the tap of computer keys.

"I don't have anyone by that name," the operator said. "Could you verify the spelling?"

"R-E-I-L-L-Y," Helen said slowly.

"Nope, sorry," the operator said after a moment. "There is no one here by that name. I checked the staff, too. Are you sure you have the right hospital?"

Helen felt as if her heart had fallen into the pit of her stomach. She couldn't pull in air fast enough. There had to be an explanation. She knew without a doubt she had the right hospital because James had been proud of the fact that it was ranked as one of the ten best in Boston.

"Could you connect me with the ER?"

She again heard the soft tap of computer keys.

"Connecting," the operator said. And then he was gone.

"ER," a woman said.

"Hi." Helen cleared her throat. "I need to leave a message for one of your doctors?" She realized even as she said the words that they came out as a question.

"Is this an emergency?" The woman sounded distracted and Helen could hear voices in the background talking over each over.

"No, I'm just supposed to have dinner with Dr. Reilly and wanted to let him know I'll be on time."

"Dr. Reilly," the woman said, but gave no indication if she knew James.

"James Reilly," Helen clarified.

"You may have the wrong hospital, ma'am," the woman said. "We don't have a James Reilly here."

"You're sure," Helen asked.

"Yes, ma'am, I'm sure." In the background, Helen could hear the wail of a baby and a man speaking very rapid Spanish. "I'm sorry. You might want to try one of the other hospitals."

Tears stung the back of Helen's eyes. She blinked several times to keep them from coming to the surface. This couldn't be happening. David couldn't be right.

"All right," she said. Her voice sounded thin and small. She cleared her throat and tried again. "Thanks for your help."

The woman hung up without replying, the sound of the crying baby cut off in mid-wail.

Helen dropped the phone into her lap and closed her eyes. Her throat tightened as she tried unsuccessfully to hold back the tears. James had lied to her. And she had believed it. She felt sick. She was an insurance investigator for Christ's sake. She was a smart, educated woman. How could she have so blindly accepted everything James had told her without question? *Because you didn't want to*, the little voice said. *You wanted out of your life and you wanted to believe, even though some small part of you suspected something wasn't right.*

Helen snorted softly. It was true. And she had lied, too, hadn't she? She wasn't without fault. But it wasn't the same, she rationalized. She hadn't lied about who she was because the Helen she had shown James, was the most authentic version of herself. More than that, she had shared with him the woman she was going to become.

Sudden anger washed over her. How dare he? Helen glared down at her phone. She wanted to send a message to James—to tell him that she knew what he had done and that the thought of him disgusted her. She wanted to send a similar message to David.

Instead, she turned and gazed out the window. They would be in New York City soon and she would have to make a decision. She could stay in New York City for a few days and lick her wounds. She could call Emma and tell her that she would be on her doorstep in time for dinner. Or, she could go to the hotel, meet James, and confront him in person. Regardless of which option she chose, what she had written to David had been true. She was going to start a new life. And no one, not him or James or her family were going to dictate what that would be. From now on, her life was her own.

Maggie

MAGGIE STOOD WITH the rest of the passengers waiting to board the bus that would take them from Philadelphia to New York City. The cold morning air in Philly was different than what she was used to. There was a lived-in odor that she could only describe as "the city." Still, it was better than waiting inside the bus terminal with its tired interior and fluorescent lighting that screamed of desperation. That was the last thing she wanted to feel right now, though, if she were honest, the outside loading area wasn't all that much better.

She scanned the area. To her left, several Asian men and women sat on a long maroon bench, staring blankly at the pavement in front of them, their bodies bent forward over their bags and packages. Over their heads hung a long red banner with white symbols she guessed were Chinese. Boldly emblazoned in big, cartoony letters in the center was the word "Yo!"

Behind the row of angled buses in front of her was a parking lot that was bordered by a red brick apartment building, the back of which was crisscrossed with a rusty fire escape. Maggie wondered how it would feel to live in such a claustrophobic environment. Did people who live in large cities feel the stacks of lives above and below them, or were they comforted by the proximity of so many others?

Rather than think about it, Maggie chose instead to study the travelers in line ahead of her. Though a couple looked like they were going to New York City for business, the majority were bundled in tired-looking coats and jackets. She shifted the weight of the computer bag and turned to look at the people behind her. The man who had boarded in Harrisburg and who had occupied the seat behind her was farther back in the queue. Eddie had already departed on a connecting bus bound for Florida. Though Maggie had tried to tune out Eddie's conversations with anyone who would listen, she knew that there was a cousin who was a snowbird and wintered in Florida.

"Everyone has secrets." Maggie thought again about Eddie's

pronouncement. Despite her nosiness and flair for the dramatic, Eddie was right. Everyone had something they didn't want others to know. Maggie found herself studying Jimmy. He stood, head down, hands shoved into the pockets of his warm-up pants. The bright morning sun glinted off the ends of his crew cut. Slowly, rhythmically, he shifted from one foot to the other. What was he hiding? Or, more to the point, what did he think he was hiding. From the moment she had met him, she sensed his anxiety—his social awkwardness.

Maggie was generally good at reading people and anticipating their needs. It came with the job and over the years, she had become a pro. She was less skilled, however, at understanding and meeting her own needs—at least in a healthy way. She pressed her lips together. She was good at keeping people at a distance. At least, she had been until Sarah. Their night together had been different than any of Maggie's previous encounters.

She had known it as soon as she had awakened the next morning, disoriented and hung over, though not from the alcohol. It had taken her several seconds to remember where she was and why. She had looked around the unfamiliar room. Seattle. She was in Seattle for a NFDA conference. And the night before she had . . . She smiled. She had taken Sarah to bed. And it had been fabulous.

Maggie rolled onto her side and looked at the spot where Sarah had been hours before. She had fallen asleep sometime after five a.m. and Sarah had slipped out sometime after that. Maggie glanced at the alarm clock. It was just after eight o'clock.

"Shit!"

She threw back the covers and jumped out of bed. The conference started at nine and she hated being late.

She looked around for her robe before remembering she hadn't laid it out. There hadn't been the time or later, the inclination. She surveyed the room. Her shirt and bra were by the door. Her jeans were crumpled next to the bed, as were her shoes and underwear. She smiled at the disarray.

Sarah had proven to be an excellent lover. She had been aggressive, but at the same time, gentle. It had been intense and very different in comparison to Maggie's usual encounters. Usually she was the one who set the pace, who initiated the encounter. But not last night. Sarah had been the one in control—both at the bar and also in bed.

Maggie was surprised by how much she had enjoyed it. And then, Sarah left while she was asleep. She had understood the rules. Maggie, the married mother of three, was going home to Omaha and their night together was simply that. Usually, it was the way she liked it. So why did she feel so disappointed?

Though she knew there wouldn't be one, she looked around the room for a note. Nothing. She glanced at the alarm clock again and saw that five minutes had passed. She needed to get moving if she was going to get coffee before the first session started.

She walked to the bathroom and studied her naked reflection. She worked hard to keep her body in shape but her physique was nothing compared to Sarah's. She had been the perfect combination of hard planes and soft flesh. Maggie wished she could see her again. *No*, she reminded herself. *Rules are rules. No attachments and no names.*

The sound of a recorded warning to keep all bags in sight shook Maggie from her reverie. She pressed her lips together and sighed heavily through her nose as she turned back to face the bus. The driver, who had been overseeing the loading of the baggage in the undercarriage, said something to the men placing the bags in the storage space and then turned and walked to the doors of the bus. He stood with his back to the bus and raised both hands to shoulder height, palms facing outward as if fending off a mob and spoke in a loud voice.

"We'll be boarding in just a couple of minutes, folks."

Maggie glanced around, noting that most of the other passengers either hadn't heard him over the sound of the bus engines or simply weren't paying attention. The driver nodded for emphasis and then turned his attention to a small, blond-haired woman who approached from the left. She carried a nylon duffle bag in one hand. Trailing slowly behind her was a young boy in a dark blue coat that was about two sizes too large. A green, canvas backpack hung from his shoulders. He stared at the ground as the woman spoke to the driver.

He was going to be traveling alone, Maggie realized as the woman used one hand to unzip her coat and pull out a collection of identification cards clipped to a lanyard that hung around her neck. As she spoke, the driver looked at the picture of the top card, then up at her face and then down at the boy before returning his attention to the woman. He nodded at something she said and then extended his hand. The woman handed him the duffle bag and then turned to kneel in front of the boy.

He raised his eyes to meet hers as she spoke; her hands rested lightly on his shoulders. He nodded once. Even from where she stood Maggie could see he was struggling not to cry. The woman said something else and tipped her chin down, her eyes open wide, eyebrows raised for emphasis. The boy nodded solemnly. They looked at each other for several seconds before the woman pulled him into her arms. Maggie noticed that although the hug didn't appear to be unwelcome, the boy didn't fully return it.

The driver, who placed the bag in the storage area beneath the bus, returned to the pair and said something Maggie couldn't hear. The woman nodded without looking away from the boy. The driver turned and pried open the bus doors. The squeak and hiss of the hydraulic air release caught the attention of the passengers who stopped their conversations and readied themselves for boarding. The driver stepped onto the first step and turned.

The woman said something to the boy who responded and then grasped the silver handle and pulled himself up the steps, his backpack bobbing with each step until he disappeared into the bus. The woman stepped back and watched his progress. She blinked several times and wiped at the corners of her eyes with the side of her index finger.

Nothing happened for several seconds and then the driver reappeared. He stepped onto the pavement, spoke to the woman, and then turned to the line of passengers.

"We will now begin boarding," he said loudly. "Please have your tickets ready so I can see them." He gestured to the man at the head of the line, a tall, bearded black man in an Army surplus jacket, to step forward.

Maggie shifted the weight of her computer bag and, like the rest of the group, inched slowly forward until she finally stepped up to the driver and held out her ticket. He studied it for a moment before handing it back to her with a soft grunt. Without touching the handrail, Maggie stepped onto the bus.

The boy she had seen outside was sitting in the seat directly behind the partition that separated the driver from the rest of the passengers. He was no longer wearing his coat. A sticker with the name "Sam" carefully printed in black Sharpie was affixed to the right side of his hooded sweatshirt. He stared down at his hands rather than at the people filing past.

Unaccompanied minor. Maggie wished momentarily that the boy, Sam, would look up as she passed so she could smile at him. When he didn't, she continued back toward the middle of the bus. She chose the same seat number as she sat in on the other bus, removed her coat, and placed it carefully in the overhead rack. She slid into the window seat, put her bag on the seat next to her, and unzipped it. As she removed her computer, she glanced up and saw Jimmy moving slowly down the aisle. Their eyes met and for an unguarded moment, he looked as if he thought she would offer up the seat next to her. She didn't, and he seemed to nod and shifted his attention to the seat behind her.

Maggie felt her face flush as she turned her attention back to the contents of her bag. She knew the polite thing to do would have been to offer him the seat next to her. But she was tired of doing the right thing. She didn't want to have to make conversation with him or anyone. She wanted to think about what to say to Sarah after almost an entire year of not taking her calls or responding to her e-mails. That's not to say she hadn't wanted to talk to her. She had. More than once she had picked up the phone and entered the numbers. But there were rules. And one of those rules was no relationships.

Maggie sighed, abandoned the pretense of rifling through her bag, and tipped her head back and stared at the underside of the shelf above her. Surprising Sarah in Boston was a mistake. She pressed her fingertips firmly against the dull ache in her right temple. What did she hope to accomplish anyway? Commitment wasn't an option for her. Relationships were transitory. She knew better than anyone that humans were frail. Nothing lasted. She saw it every day with the loss of husbands, wives, children, parents. It was better to refrain from anything personal—nothing more than one night stands and professional friendships. It avoided the emotion. The pain. The mess. It was safe.

"And lonely," Maggie murmured and closed her eyes.

She hated the admission even though it was true. She was lonely and had been since . . . when? Certainly since before her parents died and she had taken over the funeral home. But it had started long before that. It had started with Rachel.

Maggie clenched her jaw and swallowed against the thickness in her throat. At what point, she wondered, did the grief go away? She told people every day that it would get better—that the sense of loss and emptiness would ease over time. But that was a lie. People left. People died. It was just a fact of life.

So why was she going to Boston?

It wasn't for a relationship. She shook her head. No. Sex was not a relationship. Sex was sex. And the sex with Sarah had been good. Those nights had been the only time since Rachel that Maggie had gone to bed with someone more than once. And that had been why, when it came down to it, she hadn't called. Sarah was dangerous on a number of levels. Maggie had known it the moment they had met at the WildRose. That assertion had been reinforced when they met the second time. Shocked hadn't even been a strong enough word.

It had been the end of the first day of the conference and she, like everyone else, had felt obligated to attend the cocktail mixer. She had been standing around in the corner of the hotel ballroom, watching her colleagues milling around in small groups or pairs. A few, like herself, stood by themselves, drink in hand, watching the activity, while others tapped aggressively on the screens of their smart phones. *What did we do before cell phones?* she wondered. *How else did we manage to look busy and not vulnerable or alone?*

In situations like this, she preferred to observe rather than interact. More than once, she smiled at colleagues she recognized from other conferences. She was surprised, quite honestly, how many people she seemed to know or at least seemed to know her. She glanced down at her conference badge with the name "Maggie" in 42-point font. Or perhaps, she thought with a small smile, they simply could read.

To her right, a short, slightly paunchy man with thinning blond hair caught her eye and smiled. He was familiar. Arthur? They had served on a committee together, Maggie remembered. Ardie, she thought suddenly. His name was Ardie and he was from Chicago. Details flooded back to her. He was married with a couple of kids who played soccer.

Ardie was standing with several other attendees, one of whom, based on his somewhat dramatic gestures, appeared to be holding court. *The pontificator*, Maggie thought. As if reading her mind, Ardie rolled his eyes a little and shrugged. Maggie smiled sympathetically. If she were nice, she would go rescue him.

"I don't know about you, but I think these mixers are cruel and unusual punishment."

The low-pitched voice came from her left. Maggie jerked in surprise and turned to the speaker. He was taller than her by about six inches and dressed in the dark blue pinstriped suit. In his left hand he held a clear plastic cocktail glass. No wedding ring. She raised her gaze to his face. His eyes were a dark, chocolate brown and only slightly lighter than his wavy hair.

"Evan," he said and extended his right hand.

Maggie shook it automatically.

"Maggie."

Evan sighed.

"I don't know why I even come to these things," he continued. "I usually just end up standing around by myself, getting a little drunk, and planning how long I have to stay before I can go back to my room and watch reruns of *Law and Order* on TNT."

Maggie laughed despite herself. "I know what you mean." She glanced discretely at her watch. "I've just about reached my allotted time for the night."

Evan nodded. "I wish I could say the same. But I came with one of the presenters and she's working the room." He scanned the attendees, his gaze finally landing on Ardie's group. He jerked his chin in their direction. "Uh oh. Looks like she's got a live one."

Maggie followed the direction of his gaze. Before, she had really only noticed Ardie and the pontificator. But now, she took in the other members of the group—a man wearing a suit that was slightly too short in the arms and legs, an older woman in a black suit with a polished, somewhat bored expression, and a slender woman who stood with her back to them, her auburn hair pulled back into a simple clasp. Her hair moved as she nodded in apparent agreement with something the pontificator said.

"I promised to rescue her if she got caught up in a conversation for more than ten minutes," Evan said and took a sip of his drink. He glanced down at his watch. "It's about time for me to interrupt."

As if she had heard his words, the redhead seemed to stand suddenly straighter. From behind, Maggie could tell she was looking discreetly around the room. Not seeing Evan in front of her, she turned slightly and glanced over her shoulder. Maggie gasped and stepped slightly to the side as if to hide behind Evan.

The profile was unmistakable. Evan's friend was last night's conquest. Maggie swallowed and wished she were anywhere but in this room at this moment. She watched, her heart pounding in her throat, as Sarah's gaze settled on Evan.

She gave him a look that said, "Get me out of here." From the corner of her eye, Maggie saw Evan nod. Sarah smiled and then glanced casually at Maggie. Her eyes widened in recognition and the smile disappeared from her lips. She frowned.

"That's my cue," Evan said. He looked down at Maggie and grinned. "Come with and I'll introduce you. You can be the reason why I need to pull her away from the conversation."

"Oh, no . . . I," Maggie began and considered how she could make her own exit. She stepped backward and was about to make an excuse when Sarah extricated herself from the group and turned to walk toward them.

"Hey," Evan said when she reached them. "I was just coming to rescue you."

Sarah nodded without looking at him, her gaze focused on Maggie.

"This is Maggie. She's from . . ." He waited for Maggie to fill in the blank.

Maggie was unsure if he expected her to give the name of her funeral home or where she lived. She inhaled and struggled to remain collected.

"Indiana," she said finally. "Seymour, Indiana."

"Right," Evan said and gestured at Sarah. "And this is Sarah. She teaches anthropology at Boston University and specializes in death and burial. She'll be one of the speakers tomorrow."

Sarah pressed her lips together and extended her hand.

"Sarah Talbott," she said coolly. "Nice to meet you."

Maggie grasped the proffered hand and tried not to think about how those fingers had explored her body the night before. She felt her face flush and she cleared her throat.

"Maggie Anthony," she said and forced herself to meet Sarah's gaze.

Sarah studied her for several seconds before giving the same enigmatic smile Maggie remembered from the night before.

"You look familiar," Sarah said, her tone suddenly lighter.

Maggie blinked, unsure how to respond.

Evan turned quickly to study her. "You know, you do sort of look familiar. Were you at the welcome mixer last night?"

Maggie swallowed and nodded. "For a little while, yes." Her voice sounded scratchy.

Sarah crossed her left arm across her stomach and rested the elbow of her right arm lightly on her wrist. She rubbed her lower lip thoughtfully with her right index finger.

"No, I don't think that's it. Maybe you just look like someone I know." She took her time studying Maggie, pretending to think about it. Finally, she snapped her fingers and pointed at Maggie. "That's it. You look like a friend of mine from Omaha."

She's playing with me. She knows I lied about everything and now she's playing with me.

Maggie smiled and gave a little shrug. "Well, they say everyone has a double out there somewhere. Looks like you've met mine."

"Yeah," Sarah said. "I guess I have. Maybe I should introduce you."

"Maybe," Maggie said and then, in an effort to steer the conversation in a different direction asked, "So, how do you two know each other?"

Evan grinned.

"We were engaged," Evan said just as Sarah said, "We went to college together."

Maggie raised her eyebrows slightly and looked back and forth between them.

"We were in undergrad together," Sarah explained quickly. "And we dated for a couple of years."

"But then she went off to grad school," Evan said. "And then out into the field to do research."

"But we were over by then," Sarah said quickly to Evan.

"I know," he said and nudged her. "But you still broke my heart."

Sarah narrowed her eyes, but didn't respond.

Maggie watched the exchange with interest. It was, she could tell, an ongoing issue for them. She tried to imagine them as a couple. Instead, all she could think of was Sarah pinning her against the wall of her hotel room and kissing her deeply. She blinked and realized they were both looking at her with a sense of expectation.

"I'm sorry?" she said quickly. "I didn't catch that."

"Would you like to meet up with us at the bar after this?" Evan asked.

Maggie looked blankly at Sarah. "The . . . bar?"

"The hotel bar," Sarah said pointedly. "For drinks and conversation. You know, that thing people do to get to know each other."

"Oh," Maggie said and shifted uncomfortably.

She thought about the lies she'd told the night before and the truths she might have to reveal if she accepted the invitation. Still, she considered the offer. There was something about Sarah that intrigued her. But second dates were against the rules, she reminded herself—as was information sharing. *But this isn't a date*, she reasoned. Real names had already been exchanged. Sarah knew who she was, what she did, and where she lived. Even if she wanted to sleep with her again, it was out of the question. No connections. No attachments. But even as she looked at Sarah's guarded face and Evan's pleased expression, she spoke before she could stop herself.

"Okay."

Sarah pursed her lips. Maggie could already tell that meant she was displeased.

"When?" Maggie asked.

Evan glanced down again at his watch.

"This thing's over at nine," he said and then looked at Sarah. He raised his eyebrows. "Do you need to stay for the whole thing?"

Sarah turned to look around the room. Though some people had made an appearance and then left, many still remained. "I should probably stay." She returned her attention to Evan and then Maggie. "How about we meet in the bar at nine?"

Maggie forced herself not to squirm under Sarah's gaze. Instead, she had nodded and then gestured vaguely toward Ardie. "I should go rescue him but I'll see you at nine." And before anyone could say anything further, she had stepped quickly away.

"Is this seat taken?"

Maggie's eyes snapped open to find a thin, red-headed woman in her mid-twenties standing in the aisle. The woman smiled and gestured over her shoulder at the rest of the bus. "It's filling up pretty quickly and yours looks like the best available option, if you know what I mean."

Maggie scanned the line of people standing in the narrow aisle behind her. What the woman said was true. Of all the potential seat mates, she would most likely be the most pleasant with whom to share space.

Maggie forced herself to smile warmly. "Sure."

She lifted her bag out of the seat and placed it on the floorboard between her feet. The woman slipped her large, green leather purse off her shoulder and slid into the empty seat.

"I'm Lilly," she said. She extended a slender hand in Maggie's direction. Maggie grasped it and was surprised by the strength of her grip.

"Maggie," she said. "Going to New York City?"

Lilly nodded and opened her purse. "My sister is getting married." She rummaged around before pulling out a bright green package of sugarless gum. She used her fingernail to free the red tab to remove the protective cellophane. "She and Darnell have been dating for about a year now, but she just found out she's pregnant and so they decided to tie the knot." She flipped open the paper cover and used her thumb to slide out the first foil-wrapped piece. She held the pack out to Maggie. The smell of spearmint filled the small space between them.

Maggie pulled the stick free. "Thanks."

Lilly pulled a second piece from the pack, unwrapped it, and popped it into her mouth. As she chewed, she wadded the plastic into a tight ball and then wrapped the foil around it, twisting the ends so it looked like a shiny piece of candy. She dropped both the gum and the trash into her purse and then leaned back. She turned her head and grinned again as she realized Maggie was watching her, the stick of gum still held between her thumb and forefinger.

"It's not poisoned. I just bought it." She was silent for several seconds and then sighed. "I hate the bus. But, when you're a poor college student it's the cheapest way to get from Point A to Point B." She shrugged and pulled her phone and headphones from her purse. "At least I have my music."

Maggie was about to reply but the driver's voice over the loudspeaker announced their departure. Beneath her seat, she felt the vibration and rumble of the engine as the driver pushed the accelerator and the bus backed out of the loading bay. She glanced down at her watch. It was 9:01. They were leaving right on schedule.

She turned to say as much to Lilly but stopped when she realized Lilly had already inserted her earbuds, closed her eyes, and was lost in her music. Maggie could hear the muffled, tinny sound of whatever song was being played and she frowned in annoyance. She had wanted a seat mate that wouldn't talk her ear off, yes, but still . . . She considered saying something and then stopped and laughed softly as she reminded herself, "Be careful what you wish for, for you will surely get it."

Bug

BUG STARED OUT the window as they pulled out of the bus station and onto I-95. He had traveled on buses before, but this was different. This wasn't a city bus. It was big with soft seats and thick windows. And he wasn't just going for a few stops and then getting off. He was traveling several hours. He frowned. What if he had to go to the bathroom? Did he ask the driver? He knew he had to tell the driver if he was getting off. And he knew he had to keep his name tag on at all times and never lose the envelope in his backpack with the Unaccompanied Child Form, the letter explaining his reason for travel and his identification information. But what about the bathroom?

He looked at the partition that separated him from the driver. He knew he wasn't supposed to bother him while he was driving. And he didn't have to go. Not yet. But what if he did?

Bug looked at the woman sitting next to him. She looked like she was almost as old as Grandma Jean had been before she died. He supposed he could ask her. She looked nice enough. But she was a stranger. He wasn't supposed to talk to strangers. But then, just about everyone around him was a stranger now. He was leaving a shelter full of strangers to ride on a bus with strangers to a town full of strangers to live with a woman who he didn't know. Asking about the bathroom was the least of his problems.

He was alone. He didn't even have Tasha anymore. He wondered where she was. The bus had left at nine o'clock. She would be in homeroom right now. And then there would be recess, class, and then lunch. Thursday was tater tot day.

He wondered suddenly what he would be having for lunch. He looked down at the green canvas backpack which rested on the floor next to his feet. It was stiff with newness. He ran his fingertips over the even row of zippered teeth, unable to believe that something so nice actually belonged to him. He had thought there had been a mistake when Gail pulled it out of the trunk and handed it to him.

"Um . . . I think you gave me your backpack," he had said as

Gail turned and reached back into the trunk for the battered duffle bag that contained his clothes and shoes.

"Nope." Gail turned and grinned at him. "It's yours."

Bug hesitated, hope filling his chest for several seconds before he prepared himself for the inevitable laugh that signaled it was just a joke. When Gail didn't laugh, he looked up at her through the fringe of his bangs and smiled tentatively. "For real?"

Gail nodded. "Yep." She put her hands on her hips and grinned down at him. "I put your Spiderman bag inside, along with your lunch, a puzzle book, and a surprise. But you have to promise to wait until you're on the road to open it, okay?"

Bug nodded quickly. "I promise." He looked back down at the bag and smiled. It was exactly like what the older kids carried— the kind with all sorts of pockets and clips. It was the kind of backpack that a hiker would have and one that Bug never in a million years thought he would own.

"Thank you." He tried to fill the words with as much gratitude as possible. "It's so nice." He swallowed and then looked up to see Gail watching him.

She looked sad.

Bug felt his smile fade. "I'm sorry," he said automatically.

Gail frowned and leaned slightly forward. "Why are you sorry, Sam?" She brushed the hair from in front of his eyes. "You didn't do anything wrong."

Bug shifted his feet. "I made you sad."

"No . . . no." Gail shook her head sharply. Wisps of blond hair escaped from the bun at the back of her head. She knelt on one knee in front of him, grasped his upper arms, and squeezed gently. Her breath was warm on his face as she spoke. "You didn't do anything. It's just the situation." She raised her eyebrows. "Do you understand? It's not you, Sam."

Sam forced himself to hold her gaze. He nodded but didn't speak. Gail gave his biceps another gentle squeeze. Bug blinked and then looked away.

"So," Gail said as she straightened and turned to look one last time into the trunk.

Bug, too, turned and looked. With the exception of a first aid kit, Gail's briefcase, and a battered atlas, the trunk was empty. Gail grabbed her briefcase, slung the strap over her shoulder, and then reached over their heads and pulled the lid down with a resounding slam. Despite seeing her do it, Bug jumped.

"Sorry." She grimaced. "I'm used to my Jeep."

She turned and looked at the bus terminal.

"So . . ." She sighed. "Ready?"

Bug nodded.

Gail picked up the duffle bag. Bug hooked the straps of the backpack over his shoulders and followed her toward the station. Inside the brightly-lit depot, people milled around talking softly and saying their good-byes. A security officer in a gray-and-black uniform walked slowly back and forth, his thumbs hooked under the leather of his belt, one of his forearms resting on the black metal handle of his holstered sidearm and the other on a thick leather pouch held closed by a shiny metal snap. Over by the vending machines, a young woman stood staring down at the snacks, a coin pressed between her thumb and forefinger, poised to drop it into the slot. In the corner, two teen-aged boys pretended to play one of the upright video games.

Bug followed Gail as she walked quickly to a bank of red chairs that were separated from the rest of the seats by a barrier of posts linked together with black straps like seat belts. It reminded him of the things they used to keep people in line at the welfare office where he and Rhonda used to go. Thick windows ran alongside one wall and overlooked the loading bay where buses were parked in an angled row.

Gail pulled out a manila file folder from her briefcase. They stopped and she opened it and flicked through some papers.

"You're on bus #3217." She turned and pointed to the door with a sign over it that read, "All Points North." "We'll go out that door when the time comes."

Bug bobbed his head in a nod.

Gail tipped her head in the direction of the red seats. "Wanna sit?"

Bug shrugged and was about to say "no," when a heavyset man with salt-and-pepper hair stepped into the room and began to check tickets.

"You get to board first," Gail explained. "But don't worry. When it's time, I'll walk you out and make sure you get settled." She glanced around for the station agent and gestured toward a line of interlocked molded plastic chairs. "How about you sit there while I get you checked in?"

Bug walked slowly to the chairs, slid the backpack off his shoulders and onto the floor, and then sat down. Gail had gone over to where the departure manager stood and now waited for him to finish speaking to a slender woman in tall, black boots. The man said something to the dark-haired woman and then turned to Gail. He frowned as she spoke and absently rubbed at the cleft in his chin. He glanced at Bug and then returned his attention to Gail and the handful of papers she had pulled from the file folder. He tipped his head slightly to the side as he studied them. Finally, he nodded and said something. Gail smiled, nodded, and walked back to Bug.

"All set," she said as she slid into the seat beside him. "Now I just need to . . ." Her voice trailed off as she busied herself with tidying the misaligned sheets of paper and sliding them back into the file. She slipped the folder back into her briefcase and leaned back. The chair creaked despite her slight weight.

They sat that way for several minutes, neither speaking but rather watching the other passengers until it was time for Bug to board.

Their goodbye had been brief. She had walked him out to the bus, introduced him to Lawrence, the driver, and then hugged him goodbye. At least it wasn't sad like most of his good-byes. If anything, Gail had seemed happy for him. He looked down again at the backpack. She had said there was a surprise inside. He had forgotten about it as he watched the passengers board, but now, he reached down and unzipped the bag. In addition to the smaller, grubby Spiderman backpack he used for school, he saw the brown paper bag that contained his lunch and a rectangular package that was wrapped in bright, blue tissue paper.

Bug looked at the woman sitting next to him. She was reading a book. He looked back down into the bag. Despite wanting desperately to open the package, he hesitated. This was the first wrapped gift he'd received since Grandma Jean died. He wanted to make the moment last as long as possible. He glanced again at the woman and wished she was his grandmother.

"I have a present," he said softly.

The woman finished the sentence she was reading and placed

the tip of her forefinger on the beginning of the next sentence before turning to him. "I'm sorry?"

Bug pointed down into his bag. "I have a present." He pulled out the gift. He placed it carefully in his lap. "She said I could open it once we're on the road." He looked sideways at the woman. "Do you want to open it with me?"

The woman studied him for several seconds. Her expression changed from mildly annoyed at having been interrupted to something warmer. She nodded, closed her book, and focused her full attention on Bug. "What do you think it is?"

Bug looked down and gauged the size of the package. It could be anything, but from the weight, he had a pretty good idea what it was. "I think it's a book. I hope it's a book."

Carefully, so as not to rip the paper, he picked at the tape with his thumbnail. Grandma Jean had often reused the paper and Bug took pride in almost always being able to present her with an almost perfect piece with just a little bit of tape that could be cut off or folded over onto the back. The tissue paper wasn't as forgiving as gift wrapping and the paper tore.

"It's okay," the woman said quickly. "Tissue paper rips easily."

Bug looked up.

She smiled reassuringly. "Trust me." She pointed back to the gift. "Let's see what's inside."

Bug nodded and eagerly peeled back the paper. Gail had given him two Hardy Boys mysteries. He touched the cover of the top one. They were brand new. The generosity of the backpack and the books made his chest swell with emotion.

"You were right," the woman said. "They're books."

Bug carefully opened the cover. Inside, beneath the date, Gail had written: "Sam: You're a very special person. There's nothing wrong with being different. Everything is going to be okay."

He felt his throat tighten. Unlike in the past when he forced himself to hold back the tears, this time he let them escape. The woman next to him pulled him into her arms before he knew what had happened. She didn't feel like his grandmother, but she felt safe nonetheless. She rocked him slowly back and forth, murmuring that it was going to be all right, that he shouldn't be sad, that he would see his "mom" again soon. It took Bug a moment to realize she was talking about Gail.

"She's not my mom," Bug said, his voice muffled by the woman's polyester blouse. "My mom is . . ." He stopped, unsure how to explain the situation. He sniffed and pulled away. "I'm going to stay with my Aunt Sarah until my mom can . . ." He shrugged. "Until she's better."

The woman nodded and gently squeezed his arm. "Does your aunt live in New York City?"

The gesture reminded him of how Gail had squeezed his arm earlier that morning. He leaned forward and placed the books in the backpack. He cleared his throat and wiped at his face with the heel of his hand before sitting back up.

"Boston," he said without meeting her gaze. He focused on folding the tissue paper into neat, increasingly smaller squares until it was too thick to fold.

"Well, how about that," the woman said.

Bug looked up to see that she was smiling.

"That's where I'm headed, too." She sat up straighter and extended her hand. "My name is Marilyn. What's yours?"

Jimmy

JIMMY STARED DOWN at his cell phone and wondered if he should send a message to Helen to ask how the trip was going. She hadn't sent her schedule, but he figured she should be getting close to Boston by now. If he remembered correctly from studying the map, it looked as if it was a straight shot along Highway 90 from Chicago to Boston. Granted, he didn't know what route the bus would take, but it stood to reason it would be the shortest.

They had said they would check in over the course of the trip. And because he didn't know what he was going to do when they met, he should at least keep up the facade until he was in Boston.

"Nut up," he murmured as he flipped open the phone and used the tip of his thumb to press the power button.

As he waited for it to boot up, he thought, not for the first time, that his phone was a commentary on his life. It was the same pay-as-you-go phone he had used for years—the cheapest one he could find. Whenever anyone commented on it, he would simply say he was old school and that all he needed was to call people or text. Anything else could wait until he got home and had a big screen and keyboard. But that was just a lie. He desperately wanted an iPhone or Android that he could casually pull out of his pocket and use in front of others. But that, he knew, was out of his price range. He could barely afford the burner phone he currently had.

Once the main screen loaded, he pressed the arrow key that took him to the text screen and entered Helen's name. Using his thumb, he spelled out his message.

> ER is crazy today. One kid came in with a pneumothorax.
> We saved him, though. How's your trip?

He hit the send button and watched as the little winged envelope flew away. Though they had agreed not to overuse their phones, he wondered if Helen's was on. He hadn't realized it when he made his reservations, but the buses today were much different than the ones he remembered. Today's coaches had outlets and

WiFi. Perhaps she had plugged hers in and had been waiting for his message. The thought of her responding both excited and sickened him. On one hand, he wanted to communicate with her. On the other, he knew the lies he was about to face up to and it made his stomach tighten with anxiety.

Jimmy looked down at the battery icon. He still had a full charge. He snorted softly. Battery life was one of the few perks of his no-frills phone. He ran his thumb back and forth over the power button. It made sense to turn it off. Despite having a full battery now, he might need it in Boston when he would need to have it to . . . what? Book a hotel room? His credit cards were maxed out. To call a friend? He didn't know anyone in Boston. To call a cab back to the bus station? He didn't have the money for that either. He snapped the phone shut. He would take his chances.

Jimmy leaned to the side so he could slip the phone into the front pocket of his pants. The position allowed him to catch the profile of the funeral director in front of him. He made her uncomfortable. He could tell when they boarded and he had hesitated in front of her, that she hadn't wanted him to sit next to her. Aside from the bag in the empty seat next to her that declared it subtly off limits, he could see it in her eyes. Granted, it had been a brief flash that she had quickly tried to hide, but it had been there nonetheless.

He'd chosen instead, the row behind her. His seat mate was a heavyset African American woman who was currently sitting with her eyes closed. An open Bible lay in her lap. She had given him a closed-lip smile in greeting as he slid into the seat before returning her attention to her Bible. When it had become clear that was going to be the extent of their interaction, Jimmy had turned his attention to the line of people shuffling down the aisle. It looked as if there would be few, if any, empty seats.

He had watched with interest as a young woman with a green leather bag stopped in front of the empty seat next to the mortician and said something. He had been only slightly mollified when she seemed to not want the young woman to sit next to her either. Their conversation, he noticed, had been brief.

That had been more than an hour ago and now, the dark-haired woman was working on her computer. He craned his neck to see her screen. She appeared to be using the bus's WiFi to surf the

Internet. He watched as she clicked through the main menu of the Boston University website until she reached the anthropology department. A picture of a woman's henna-painted hands filled the top of the screen. The woman clicked several links until she reached the faculty listing page. He couldn't see the name she chose from the list, but within seconds, a picture and bio appeared of a slender woman with shoulder-length red hair. Her eyes looked like Sinead O'Connor's in that video from the '80s. The name at the top of the page, in bold red letters, read "Sarah Talbott."

Jimmy wondered who the woman was. He leaned farther to the right and squinted to see the smaller type under the "Research Interests" heading. He couldn't see all of it, but it looked like she specialized in death and mortuary practices.

"Ha!" He grinned in satisfaction at figuring out the connection and sat back in his seat.

He felt the stare of the woman in the seat next to him and turned. She was looking at him with an expression that suggested distaste.

"What?"

The woman shrugged and then jerked her chin pointedly at the seat in front of her. Her light brown eyes were almost exactly the same shade as her skin. She scanned him up and down and then met his eyes, her expression defiant. Like Jimmy, she was fleshy. But unlike him, she wore her weight with power and self-possession. Her clothing—what he could see of it—was stylish and cut to make her look voluptuous rather than fat.

She pressed her lips together and raised one eyebrow slightly as she studied him. "You seem to be awfully interested in what's going on in front of you." Her voice was lowly pitched and she spoke each word distinctly with resonance, the vowels deeply rounded and weighty.

Jimmy blinked and lifted his chin. "I know her." Even to his own ears, the words sounded defensive.

"Do you now?" She held his gaze for another long second, the right corner of her mouth tightening so the shadow of a dimple appeared on her cheek.

"Yes. We were on the same bus from Harrisburg together. We talked about . . ." Jimmy stopped.

They really hadn't done more than exchange pleasantries. He

had talked more with Eddie than the woman in front of him. He didn't even know her name. He wondered if she had listened to his conversation with Eddie—if she had heard the introduction and knew his name. The thought made him feel strangely important. The fact that she might know his name and he didn't know hers somehow made him feel like she was more invested in him than he was in her. He smiled slightly at the thought and then realized the woman next to him was still watching him, waiting for him to finish his sentence.

He shrugged. "Stuff. Work."

"Umm hmmm." The woman nodded and gave a little snort before returning her attention to her Bible. "1 Thessalonians 4:11." The words were murmured, but Jimmy could still hear them. He had no idea what specific Biblical point she was referencing, but he guessed whatever it was, it was judgmental.

"Whatever," he said, his tone intentionally dismissive.

To punctuate the point, he faced forward and closed his eyes. He had gotten good at appearing as if he didn't care. He knew from his sessions with Diane that it was a defense mechanism. Pretending he didn't care . . . pretending like everything was okay . . . was the only way he could survive being raised by Sean Reilly, an alcoholic who was angry with his life and who blamed everyone and everything else for the fact that his wife had abandoned him and left him with a child to raise on his own.

Staying out of Sean's way and pretending not to feel his father's anger and resentment was how Jimmy survived. Still, it hadn't always worked. *Look at what happened with Boomer.* Even though he had talked about it with Diane, Jimmy still felt sick when he thought about that day.

He had stayed late at the school library. It was something he usually did because it was safe and quiet, but also because he never knew what he was going to find when he got home. Sometimes, everything was fine because his father would be gone or was on one of his attempts to drink less. He was tolerable then. His jokes were still cutting, but nothing like the nastiness that came out when he'd had too much or switched from Schaefer beer to Cutty Sark. Still, for the weeks prior to that day, things had been better. Sean had been limiting himself to a six pack an evening and had only lost his temper a couple of times.

Something about that day, though, felt wrong. Even as he stood at the foot of the concrete stairs leading up to the porch, he knew that something bad was going to happen. He stared up at the front door and observed, not for the first time, that the paint was peeling away from the wood.

"Gotta go in sometime," he muttered and shifted his book bag so it hung more evenly off his shoulders. He sighed and climbed the stairs to the stoop. He stopped in front of the door, shoved his right hand into the pocket of his jeans, and pulled out the key to the dead bolt. He was about to slide it into the lock when the door swung open.

His father stepped from the darkness of the foyer into the waning afternoon light. His bulk filled the doorway in a way that Jimmy knew was bad. He raised his eyes to look into Sean's face and knew immediately that his sixth sense had been correct.

"You're late." Sean's eyes were tired and red-rimmed.

Jimmy could tell he had already had a few beers if not something stronger. He lowered his eyes so he was looking at his father's chest. He was still wearing his gray uniform from the garage where he worked as a mechanic. His name was embroidered in blue script on the white name patch adhered to the front of his partially untucked work shirt.

"I went to the library," Jimmy said. "I had to do research for—"

"I don't give a shit why you were late," Sean interrupted. "Your god-damned dog has been inside all day and shit on the rug."

Jimmy leaned to the side and tried to look around his father into the house. From what little he could see, Boomer was nowhere in sight.

"I put him out, but you need to get your fat ass in here and clean up that shit." Sean's voice grew louder and more belligerent with each word.

Jimmy shrank—both from his father's anger and from embarrassment that this scene was taking place in front of the neighborhood. He forced down the urge to look to see who was witnessing it. Behind him, he could hear the slow *thump* . . . *thump* . . . *thump* of several of the neighborhood boys tossing a football back and forth. He hoped they couldn't hear his father's reprimand. The last thing he needed was for them to tell everyone at school. They already laughed at his too-tight clothes and the buzz cut his father made him wear.

Sean stepped back and jerked his thumb over his shoulder. "Get inside."

Jimmy stepped into the hallway and walked past his father. The pile of poop was in the middle of the rug. Even from where he stood, he could smell the pungent aroma of it.

"Pick it up," Sean said from behind him.

Jimmy shrugged off his backpack and set it against the wall. "Let me get a bag so—"

"No." Sean stopped him with a rough hand to his shoulder. "Now. With your hands. So you'll remember not to let this happen again."

"Dad, no. Just let me get a paper towel." Jimmy turned toward the kitchen, but was jerked backward. Sean spun him around so they were face to face.

His father's jaw was set and his eyes were hard. "Did you hear what I said?" His voice was low and menacing.

Jimmy knew that tone well. It meant there would be no argument or he would get the belt and then still have to do what his father said.

"You will pick it up now. With your hands. One piece at a time." His father stepped back and casually stuck his hands into the front pockets of his work pants.

Jimmy nodded slightly and then bent down and gingerly picked up the soft, brown pieces with one hand and placed them in the palm of the other. They were cold and sticky. Behind him he could hear Sean jingling the coins in his pocket. He straightened and, arms outstretched, carried them to the bathroom and flushed them down the toilet. He quickly washed his hands and then silently, returned to the hallway where his father waited.

Sean studied him for several seconds and then nodded in satisfaction. "It's time for dinner. I put a box of Hamburger Helper on the counter." He turned toward the living room and then stopped. "Make sure you wash your hands again before you start cooking. You still smell like shit."

Jimmy walked slowly into the kitchen and turned on the hot water. As he waited for the water to get warm, he leaned forward on his toes and peeked out the window. It had become dark enough that he couldn't see Boomer.

"I don't hear any pans in there," Sean called from the living room.

Jimmy ran his hands under the water and then picked up the grease-blackened bar of LAVA. He rubbed the soap between his hands and grimaced at the feel of the grit between his palms and fingers. He hated cooking, but ever since his mother walked out on them, he had been responsible for most of the household duties. Generally, their meals consisted of sloppy joes, Tuna Helper, or spaghetti. It wasn't much, but he did what he could.

He rinsed his hands under the water and then grabbed the stained dish towel that hung limply from a white plastic hook stuck onto the side of the cabinet. He considered getting out a new towel, but knew it would no doubt look like this one by tomorrow and it would only mean more laundry. Instead, he hung it back on the hook and then turned to the stove where he turned on the front coiled burner. As he waited for it to heat, he pulled open the metal drawer under the stove, took out a large skillet, and put it on the burner. From the refrigerator, he pulled out a package of ground round and poked his finger through the clear plastic wrap to open it.

The meat felt cold and slimy in his hands as he dropped it in the skillet. Before he thought better of it, he wiped his hands on his jeans. He sighed. He had hoped to get a couple more wears out them before having to put them in the wash. He could hear the sound of the evening news out in the living room. From the volume, which always grew louder the more Sean drank, Jimmy guessed he'd had several drinks beyond what had been his recent limit. If Jimmy was lucky, Sean would pass out right after dinner so he could sneak Boomer to his room and do his homework in relative quiet.

At the thought, Jimmy glanced again at the window and wondered how long Boomer would officially be banished to the backyard. Usually, by the time Sean had sobered up the next day, he had forgotten about whatever real or imagined infractions had occurred the night before. The same probably would be true in this case.

Jimmy poked at the sizzling hamburger and broke it into smaller pieces. The aroma of the browning meat made his stomach growl and he realized suddenly how hungry he was. He looked at the box of Hamburger Helper and calculated the time until dinner was ready. Probably another twenty minutes. If he was quick, he might be able to sneak outside and see Boomer.

He tore open the box, pulled out the pasta, and spice packet and went to the sink where he filled the measuring cup with water. When the hamburger was ready, he carefully poured the grease onto Boomer's bowl of dry food as a treat for being stuck outside, and then mixed the rest of the ingredients in the pan. He rummaged in the pan drawer again for a lid and then set the burner on low so dinner could simmer. He glanced up at the kitchen clock. If he was quick—and quiet—he could sneak outside and see Boomer.

Moving as quietly as possible, Jimmy tiptoed to the back door. As he went, he peeked into the living room. His father was in his battered recliner, his feet up as he stared at the television screen. He reached the door, slowly turned the dead bolt, twisted the knob, and gently eased the door open. Behind him, he could hear familiar jingle of a local car commercial.

Jimmy peered out the storm door into the back yard. The light from the kitchen made it impossible to see anything but his own reflection so he flipped on the porch light. Boomer wasn't on his usual spot on the frayed, muddy rectangle of carpet that functioned as a doormat.

He frowned, flipped up the metal locking mechanism on the door handle, and, as quietly as possible, eased open the storm door. He grimaced at the loud groan of metal on metal and quickly looked back over his shoulder into the living room. His father either didn't or couldn't hear anything over the noise of the television.

"Boomer?" Jimmy said softly as he stepped out onto the concrete porch. "Boomer? Where are you, buddy?" He peered into the darkness of the yard beyond the reach of the light. Nothing. "Booms? You okay?" He glanced back at the house and then hurried down the cracked cement steps into the yard. "Boomer?" he said louder, no longer caring if he was caught by his father and punished.

Something was wrong. He hurried to the corner of the small yard and looked into Boomer's dog house. It was empty. He walked the perimeter of the chain-link fence looking for spots where Boomer could have dug under. And that's when he saw the open gate, the padlock that usually was snapped shut, hanging unhinged from the latch.

Jimmy felt the familiar tightness in his chest. The gate was always locked—both to keep people out and to keep Boomer in. The only two keys were in the junk drawer in the kitchen. There was no way anyone could open the lock unless they picked it. But why would anyone do that?

He saw the movement out of the corner of his eye and turned quickly back to the house. His father stood, backlit by the kitchen light, his hands in his pockets, his face shadowed. Though he couldn't see his eyes, Jimmy knew Sean was watching him.

He had opened his mouth to tell him that the gate was open and that Boomer was missing, when Sean shifted his position. His face, which had been in the shadows, was now visible in the outside light from the porch. His expression was one that even now, as an adult, made Jimmy's jaw tighten in anger. Sean was smiling. And at that moment, Jimmy knew he would never see Boomer again. It was only one of his father's many offenses, but it was the one that cut the deepest and hurt more than any of the beatings or insults because, in that moment, Sean had broken Jimmy's heart.

"Fucker," Jimmy said softly.

He blinked away the memory. Past hurts were not an excuse for all the things he had done. And they were not a justification for what he was continuing to do. They might be explanations, but that was all. And, he reminded himself, it was like Diane said: you can only blame your parents and your past for so long. At some point, he had to step up and make amends. He had to be honest with Helen.

Jimmy sighed deeply and shook his head. There was no easy way out of this and no way he could emerge with any honor and self-esteem except to tell the truth. He wasn't his father. He wasn't the type of man to intentionally hurt someone. He wasn't mean. He was . . . broken.

He squeezed his hands tightly into fists and focused his attention on the sensation of each fingertip pressing into the flesh of the heel of his hand. Life wasn't fair, he reminded himself. And as hard as this was for him, the shame of admitting what he had done was nothing compared to what Helen was bound to feel when she learned the truth. She would feel deceived and victimized. And it would be his fault.

Jimmy looked again at the woman sitting beside him. Her head was tipped back against the headrest, her eyes closed. Her Bible was open on her lap, her index finger squarely in the middle of a block of text. The print was too small for Jimmy to read it, but he could see the boldfaced heading. She was reading the book of Revelation.

Despite himself, he snorted softly. Much was going to be revealed, all right. For better or worse, much was going to be revealed.

Helen

HELEN RUBBED THE tip of her index finger thoughtfully against the soft ridge of her upper lip. It was a habit that David had tried more than once to break her of because, as he often explained with authority, covering one's mouth was a subconscious indication that the person was lying. She had tried to explain she wasn't lying, but that something about the gesture, the feel of her fingers skimming across the bow of her upper lip, helped her to think. It was calming. She needed the calm right now, she thought as she looked down at her lap and James's text message. She'd received it an hour ago, had re-read it more times than she could count, and still had no idea how to respond.

> ER is crazy today. One kid came in with a pneumothorax.
> We saved him, though. How's your trip?

"Uh huh." Helen snorted softly, though out of anger, hurt, or disgust, she wasn't sure. She tapped the dimming screen and read the message again. She wanted to type a biting response that would let James know she knew about his lies and wanted nothing to do with him. But another part of her, the part that recognized that she had lied as well, understood somewhat that there were likely extenuating circumstances. She was invested enough to want to know why he had fabricated what appeared to be an entire life. What need or fear had driven him to create an entirely false identity? She sensed that James wasn't an inherently bad person; there was sincerity and a kindness that she believed was real. But what about the rest of it?

She studied the letters on the screen. She needed to do something—needed to say something in response. But what? That the trip was fine? That she was almost to New York City? That she somehow understood his loneliness and could forgive the lie if he would just tell her the truth? She needed to be calculated in her response.

The seat cushion beneath her vibrated as the bus decelerated.

She raised her gaze to look out the window. They were entering the corkscrew exit that, according to her research of the route, led to the Lincoln Tunnel and then fed directly into the Port Authority Bus Terminal. Next to her, the woman who boarded in Newark, began to organize her things.

Helen pulled out the folded itinerary and printouts of each of the terminal floor maps from her bag. She had been assured that the transfer to the #2534 to Boston could be easily accomplished as long as she didn't take too much time on the second floor where, she reaffirmed to herself, the gift shops, food stands, and restaurants were located.

Or, she thought suddenly, she could "miss" her connecting bus. She didn't have to go to Boston. She could spare herself all of this angst and simply throw her phone in the trash, get a new number, and start a new life. She could excise all of the things that weren't working by simply leaving the terminal, walking out onto 8th Avenue, and starting over. She had already quit her job and left her husband for someone—or more to the point something—that apparently didn't exist. David thought she was going to Boston. Why not cut her losses and take this opportunity to run away?

The bus pulled into the underground bays of the North Terminal and moved slowly between the lines of buses parked on either side in jagged, sawtoothed rows. Helen looked again at the schedule. If she were to make the connecting bus, she had forty-five minutes to transfer—which meant forty-five minutes to make a decision. She gave a tiny, ironic laugh. She had wanted change. Well, now she had it. She carefully refolded the papers and stuffed the itinerary back in her purse.

"Ladies and Gentlemen, we have arrived at the Port Authority Northern Bus Terminal." The driver's words were heavy, almost breathy, as if he were holding the microphone against his lips. "We will be arriving at Gate 71. Please let me remind you that if you are transferring to a connecting coach, your checked baggage is not automatically transferred. For those of you who are making this your final destination, welcome to New York City. For those of you who are making connections . . ."

Helen listened as the driver ran through the list of departure gates. The Boston Express was, of course, the last to be announced. Gate 84. Helen nodded to herself. Speech ended, the driver thanked them for their business and signed off just as the bus slid easily into one of the open, available spaces. Around her, people murmured and shifted in their seats. The moment the bus came to a stop, the passengers around her began collecting their things. The woman in the aisle seat next to Helen stood, stretched, and pulled an overstuffed tote from the overhead shelf. She dropped it heavily into the seat. Helen could see the corner of a wrapped present sticking out of the top, the ribbon and bow smashed from the trip. The paper on the corner of the box was slightly ripped.

"Dammit." The woman's voice was gravelly from what Helen guessed was too many years of smoking cigarettes.

Subconsciously, she ran through cancer- and smoking-related death statistics in her head. The woman looked up from the tear in the paper to meet Helen's eyes. Her face was haggard.

"He won't even notice. It'll be ripped off in three seconds flat, anyhow." She held Helen's gaze and shrugged. "Kids."

Helen hugged her purse to her chest and nodded in sympathy.

"You got kids?"

Helen shook her head.

"They make you old before your time." The woman gestured to the gift. "The best thing they can do is give you grandbabies. That's when it gets fun."

Helen smiled what she hoped was a polite smile. She didn't want to have a conversation about children or babies or family right now. The Xanax had calmed her, but she still felt the heat of anxiousness rising in her chest. She inhaled deeply through her nose and noticed that the people in the front of the bus were moving down the aisle. Still clutching her bag, she rose to her feet. The overhead shelf made it impossible to stand fully upright and so she stood, head and shoulders bowed uncomfortably forward, her bag dangling awkwardly from her right hand.

Her inability to have children was part of how she found herself in this situation. After the last miscarriage, both she and David had tried to pretend their relationship was strong. But the cracks that Helen had known were always there had widened. David had not actually said he blamed her for not being able to carry a baby to term, but he didn't have to. She could see it in how he looked at her and how he became critical of her in every way except her reproductive failures. Those, oddly enough, were off limits.

Helen thought about one of their most ridiculous and spiteful arguments. It had been over the water spots on the glassware. They had been sitting at the kitchen table. David insisted, even though it was just the two of them, that they sit down to dinner, complete with a set table, place mats, and cloth napkins. Dinner was always exactly forty-five minutes during which they would each have one-and-a-half glasses of wine. Helen had learned not to have more than that or suffer the passive-aggressive comments or disapproving looks.

The night of the argument that changed everything, Helen had just pulled the lasagna out of the oven. She carried it over to the table and set it on the acacia trivet. David was staring down at the place settings.

"What's wrong?"

"This glass," he said.

He grabbed one of the stemmed Bordeaux glasses and held it up to the light.

"Look, it's disgusting." He held it up in front of her in the direction of the overhead light. The glass was cloudy and dotted with white spots.

"It's the dishwasher. It's not doing a good job on the glassware. Or the plates." Helen shrugged. "I'll get some hard water tablets next time I'm at the store." She took off the oven mitts and tossed them onto the counter.

"This film is disgusting," David repeated. "We can't drink out of these. They need to be rewashed."

"That won't do any good without the additive." Helen turned back to the lasagna and removed the aluminum foil. Steam rose off the bubbling cheese. The aroma of garlic, oregano, and tomato sauce filled the air.

"You need to start hand-washing them," David said. "In vinegar and water. That's what my mother used and she never had a problem with it."

Helen faced David. "I said I'll get an additive, David. I don't have time to start hand washing our dishes on top of everything else. Especially since we have a fully-functional dishwasher."

"Which clearly, is not working," David said.

"I just told you the solution."

They glared at each other for several seconds.

"It may have escaped your notice, David, but I work a full time job in addition to doing the cooking, cleaning, and laundry," Helen said.

"I am aware." David's voice was tight.

"And I do it on my own."

"Not true," David said. "There have been several times I have helped out. What about when that family died of carbon monoxide poisoning? Or while you were investigating that plane crash in India. Who did everything while you worked?"

"You did," Helen conceded. "And you complained the entire time."

"Well, what do you expect when it took six months?"

"David, there were families relying on me—on my company—to make good on their loved one's policies. We had to investigate and then pay out their claims. That takes time. What was I supposed to do?"

"I know, I know." David waved his hand and walked to the sink. "It's just telling when a bunch of people you've never met take precedence over your husband."

Helen watched as he turned on the hot water, leaned down, and opened the cabinet. He pulled out the plastic bottle of dish soap and squirted some in the glass. He stuck his finger under the stream to test it and then picked up the blue sponge.

"You're seriously jealous of something that happened two years ago?"

David shoved the sponge inside the wine glass and scrubbed. "No, what I'm saying is that during that time I picked up the slack. So, for you to suggest you do everything is incorrect."

Helen threw her hands up. "Fine. You're right, David. You're always right."

Rather than answer, David continued to work on scrubbing the glass, his shoulders hunched forward over the sink.

Helen looked around the room that was a part of her life and felt a shudder of repulsion. She hated this room. She hated the border that David had insisted on when they painted. She hated the antique flowery Royal Doulton plate and the glasses. She hated her husband.

The realization took her by surprise. She. Hated. Her. Husband. Each word built on the one before it to create an inescapable whole. She hated David and the life they had created.

That moment had been, she realized in retrospect, the beginning of the end. She had gone on with her life, of course. She had made sure to work only the hours that were required. She continued to set the table with the ugly plates and listen to David's monologue of his day as they ate the healthy meals she prepared. And she hand washed the stemware.

But inside her, something had changed and she added other things to her routine—things that were solely for her. She took advantage of the corporate gym membership and worked out over her lunch hour. She changed her hair from dark brown to a lighter, almost honey-colored shade. And she began to flirt.

At first, it was nothing substantial or meaningful. Lingering eye contact with men she passed on the street—looks that she knew were subtly sexual. Flirtatious smiles with men at the gym as they mutually checked out each other's bodies. It was powerful, this push and pull of sexual energy. And that's all it was at first— an exercise in reclaiming her attractiveness and desirability. But then it got serious.

Andy was not what most women would consider handsome. He was not even what most women would give a second glance. He was tall with dark hair that was hinting at recession. He had soft, brown eyes and what her mother would have called a weak chin. He was fit, but not excessively so. And, as she learned later, he was kind. That was what she would come to find most attractive about him.

It had started at the gym. They had made eye contact and exchanged smiles, which led to greetings, which led to short, casual conversations. It had been harmless, until the day they ran into each other outside of the safe parameters of the gym.

Helen had been in line at the coffee shop two blocks from the gym. She was staring up at the chalkboard menu and debating between a smoothie and latte, when she felt a tap on her right shoulder. She turned. Andy stood behind her. She had never seen him in street clothes and almost didn't recognize him.

He smiled. "Fancy meeting you here. I know it technically goes against the rules of working out and healthy living, but after I'm done with my workout, all I want is sugar and caffeine."

Helen grinned. "Me, too. I try to stay away from it, but I have a huge sweet tooth. Especially when it comes to chocolate."

Andy leaned closer and pointed at the top row of the brightly lit cooler. Small white plates with Saran-wrapped desserts were displayed in tempting rows. "That's my downfall," he said, his mouth close to her ear. "I can resist almost anything but a lemon bar."

Helen could feel the heat of him against her shoulder. He smelled of soap and shampoo. She tried not to react and instead stepped forward to the counter where the barista waited.

"Cold press iced vanilla latte with skim milk and sugar-free syrup." She pulled out her scuffed brown wallet from her purse.

"Let me," Andy said and held out his credit card to the barista. "But do me a favor, give me the same and add to that a lemon bar and . . ." He looked at Helen and back at the cooler. "How about one of those double chocolate chip brownies. The biggest one you've got."

"Andy, that wasn't necessary," Helen said. "And besides, I'm trying to keep my sweet tooth under control."

Andy shrugged. "You were good with the sugar-free syrup and skim milk. And you inspired me to get the same thing. We have to be good so we can be bad."

Helen turned and studied his face to see if his statement had been innuendo or if he simply was referring to calories. He smiled benignly and accepted the credit card receipt which he folded carefully. He slid the receipt, along with his credit card, into a shiny brown leather billfold and then stuffed it into the back pocket of his jeans.

"I can help whoever's next," the barista said.

Andy stepped back and gestured for Helen to precede him to the pickup area. He rocked forward onto the balls of his toes as they waited for their orders.

"I feel like I've seen you and chatted with you a million times, but I realize I don't know anything about you." He grinned. "So, aside from training for the elliptical Olympics, what do you do?"

Helen laughed. "I'm an insurance investigator." She could tell Andy had no idea what she was talking about. "I investigate claims made on our company and ensure that there is no fraud or issues that preclude us from paying out."

Andy pursed his lips and nodded. "Gotcha. So, what's the most bizarre claim or investigation you've ever done?" He picked up the lattes that were set on the counter and gestured for Helen to get the desserts. "You realize since I bought your coffee that you're obliged to sit and talk with me."

Helen felt a tingle of excitement in her stomach and fingertips. She glanced down at her watch. If she stayed, she would be late returning to work. Still, she followed him to an empty table and watched as he used the side of his hand to brush crumbs off her chair. She decided she could stay for ten minutes.

"Do you need a fork?" Andy was already unwrapping his lemon bar. Helen shook her head. "Me neither. I prefer to eat with my fingers. It's more primal. More intimate. In fact, the Greeks and Romans ate with their fingers much of the time."

"Except for soup, I would guess," Helen said.

Andy laughed. "No, not soup. They actually had spoons. Same with the Greeks. Most people think the only utensils they had were knives. Not true."

Helen raised her eyebrows. "And why do you know all of this?"

"You wouldn't believe me if I told you," Andy said.

"Try me." Helen grinned. "You might be surprised."

"I'm a silversmith."

"As in jewelry or art?"

Andy wadded the Saran Wrap into a tight ball and raised his gaze to meet Helen's. "Some of both." He removed the plastic lid from his latte and stirred it with his straw. "I do commissions mostly. And lately, a lot for some creative anachronist friends."

"What are . . . creative anachronists?"

Andy raised the cup to his mouth, sipped, and then set it back on the table. "They're people who . . ." He paused and seemed to consider how to answer her question. "They're groups of people across the world that study and recreate pre-seventeenth century Europe."

Helen narrowed her eyes. "Are you joking?"

Andy shook his head slowly. "Nope."

"So, what do you mean they recreate pre-seventeenth century Europe? How? And what does that have to do with you?"

"There is an organization called the Society for Creative Anachronism and they have a sort of shadow world that is comprised of kingdoms that are drawn over the modern world."

Andy held up his hands. "Swear to god. And the people who belong
to the SCA create a persona for themselves that is as realistic and
authentic as possible based on the Middle Ages and Renaissance.
They study the time period and make clothing, weapons, tools,
whatever, that are as authentic as possible—no zippers or anything
that's not pre-1600s. They meet for weekend events and then live
as their characters. Many are tradespeople and they make goods
that they use for trade or barter. One aspect of it includes sword
fighting."

"Like a Renaissance Festival?" Helen leaned forward.

Andy bobbed his head from side to side. "Mmm . . . sort of.
But more serious and less for show. They take it very seriously
and are dedicated to being as historically accurate with their armor
and weapons as possible."

"And that's where you come into it?" Helen took a sip of her
latte and then unwrapped her brownie. Unlike Andy, she folded
the cling wrap neatly into fourths and set it on the table.

"Yes." Andy broke off a piece of lemon bar. "They come to me
with specific requests and descriptions of what their persona needs
or wants in terms of weapons or utensils and I make them."

The insurance investigator part of her couldn't resist asking,
"Don't people get hurt if they're going out and battling each other
with swords and knives?"

"They get bruised and beat up, but not seriously injured."
Andy swallowed the bite he was chewing. "They're wearing
padding and armor. Some even wear chain mail. And they stop
when everyone agrees the blow would have been fatal."

"And these are adults," Helen said. "Grown-ups."

Andy nodded. "I'll show you." He pulled his phone out of his
jacket pocket, tapped the screen several times, and then handed it
to Helen. "Scroll to the left."

Helen looked down at the picture. It was a tall, thin man with
curly hair and several days' growth of stubble. He was dressed in a
dark green tunic and was proudly holding a heavy looking sword.
She swiped her finger to bring up the next image. It was of the
same man, this time in armor. He was standing with his legs apart,
his arms out straight, the sword held vertically as if to fend off a
blow. She scrolled to the next picture, which was a close-up of the
sword. She noticed the elaborate handle.

"Usually I don't do such high end stuff, but the man who hired me for this one was a Baron in the Middlerealm." He broke off another piece of lemon bar and popped it into his mouth. "Look at the next one."

Helen slid her finger along the bottom of the screen. The image that appeared was of two shiny daggers with smooth wooden handles.

"Those are thwittles," Andy said. "They were also called peasant daggers because they were originally working knives. After a while, some were made with thicker blades and they were used as weapons."

"They're beautiful." Helen looked up to meet Andy's amused gaze. "And you do this a lot?"

Andy smiled. "Some. I also do jewelry and art with found industrial parts. I like to mix it up. But, we were actually talking about you and what you do."

"It's not nearly as interesting as your work." Helen waved her hand dismissively and picked up her brownie.

"So sayeth you." Andy leaned forward, his forearms on the table. "Tell me."

"I investigate insurance claims to determine payment." Helen bit into the brownie. "It's not that exciting."

"I'm sure there's more to it than that. Tell me about your most interesting investigation. And before you answer, just know I imagine you like a 1940s female sleuth, so don't burst my bubble."

He was flirting and Helen liked it. She tried to smile in a way she hoped was playful. "I don't know as it was interesting as much as impactful." She shook her head. "May 22, 2010. Air India Flight #812 from Dubai to Mangalore. It overshot the runway and 158 of the 166 on board died. Three of them had policies with us. I was responsible for investigating and navigating the lawsuits against the airline and the underwriters of their insurance." She snorted softly. "Meanwhile, the families of our policy holders were simply trying to get reconciliation."

"It sounds stressful," Andy said. "And sad."

"It was." Helen stared down at the table. "Two of the three were a married couple. They were from Indiana." She took a sip of her latte. "I dealt mainly with the daughter. Apparently, her father had just retired and they were on a second honeymoon. They were making up for lost time after so many years of working. They wanted to enjoy their golden years. And then, just like that . . ." She snapped her fingers. "Gone. They waited too long."

"At least they went together," Andy said.

Helen took another bite of her brownie and chewed slowly. "That kind of love," she said without looking up. "That kind of commitment . . . after so many years. I want that. I want that storybook romance with the knight in shining armor who rides in on his white steed. I want the happily ever after."

Andy gestured at the gold-and-diamond band on Helen's left hand. "And what about Mr. Helen? I take it his armor is less than shining?"

Helen looked quickly up. Andy's expression was sympathetic. She looked guiltily down at her ring finger and considered how to respond.

"I'm sorry," he said quickly. "It's none of my business. Just because I bought you coffee doesn't entitle me to all the details of your life." Andy looked down at his black, metal wristwatch and sighed dramatically. "I should be getting back to the studio, anyway. I have an afternoon meeting to prepare for."

Helen nodded. "I need to get back to work, too."

They stood awkwardly. Andy picked up the rest of his lemon bar, popped it in his mouth, and used his thumb and forefinger to brush the crumbs from the corners of his mouth. He swallowed dramatically and picked up his coffee. "After you."

They walked in silence to the door.

Once outside, Helen turned and looked up at him. "I'm sorry about—"

"No need to apologize. I get it. Believe me. I've been there. But if you need to talk, you know where to find me." Andy squeezed her shoulder.

Helen had nodded and watched as he turned and walked away.

That should have been the end of it. But prolonged looks at the gym led to coffee which led to heavy petting sessions wherever they could find someplace private. Helen had stopped it before they actually slept together—but just barely and only because her Catholic guilt began to weigh on her. She had stopped going to the gym and vowed that her brush with infidelity was enough to make her refocus on her relationship with David. And she had, until she stumbled on to James's profile.

"Finally," someone said from one of the rows behind her.

Helen's attention jerked back to the present. The line of disembarking passengers had begun to move and within seconds, she was able to step into the aisle and stand fully upright.

The man who stood between her and her seat mate cricked his head to either side and rolled his shoulders. The movement made her notice the tiny hairs that grew below the more severe line of his haircut. They looked soft to the touch and Helen had to stop herself from reaching out and running her fingertips across them.

The greasy smell of diesel exhaust assaulted her nose the moment she stepped off the bus. The echoing hiss of hydraulics and growl of bus engines filled the open concrete space. She winced at the noise and waited with the rest of the passengers for their bags to be unloaded. Hers was one of the first and she stepped quickly forward, collected it, and then hurried toward the door that led to the terminal. Once inside, the noise of people talking, the announcements, and the smooth sound of rolling luggage wheels replaced the cacophony of the loading bay.

Helen inhaled and exhaled deeply in an attempt to clear the taste of exhaust. Around her, people milled and talked loudly. She looked up at the directional signs for Gate 84 and then turned to walk down the corridor in that direction. As she walked, she looked around. There had been obvious attempts to make the terminal more appealing, though more than anything, it looked like a dirtier version of an airport terminal. She glanced down at her watch. It was eleven-thirty. There really wasn't enough time for her to go to the second floor for something to eat. She still had a Snickers Bar and a bag of Chex Mix in her purse from their last stop. If she got a bottle of soda or water, that would tide her over until she reached Boston. If, she thought again, she decided to go to Boston. Now was the time to decide.

Around her people continued to move hurriedly in all directions—parting on either side to accommodate her. It felt strange to be stationary in the midst of so much activity and she quickly moved until she was against the wall and out of the way. She pulled her phone from her bag and pressed the key that brought the screen to life. She went to James' text and read it again.

The blatant lie made her feel sick. She needed to make a decision and she needed to make it now. Staying in New York City

didn't really make sense. It would be expensive and she would be
alone. Better to go on to Boston where she at least knew Emma.
And as for James . . . she bit her lower lip. She was angry but she
had to know the truth. Only then could she move on.

"In for a penny, in for a pound," she murmured as she shrugged
her purse more securely on her shoulder. She would go with her
gut. She tapped open the text box and began to type.

Maggie

MAGGIE STOOD IN front of the glass doors for Gate 84 with the rest of the passengers and waited for the announcement they could begin to board the express bus to Boston. She looked down at her watch. In just a few hours she would be checking into her hotel. Her first order of business would be to check in at the conference registration table. And then she would go find Sarah.

She had considered simply calling Sarah and begging her to meet. But after the way she had treated her, the telephone simply wouldn't do. She knew that if she was going to do this, it had to be in person. She had to be able to look Sarah in the eyes as she told her the truth.

On the leg from Philadelphia to New York City, Maggie had searched the Boston University website and determined that Sarah had class that evening from five to eight p.m. in Room 312 of the College of Arts and Sciences building. Waiting for her outside of her class could come off as stalkerish, and probably it was unfair to ambush her at work, but it was her only option. She didn't know Sarah's home address and her faculty page didn't list her office hours. The class, something about Pre-Columbian burial practices, was the last one she taught for the week.

Maggie shifted the weight of her computer bag and looked around the waiting area at the other passengers. Near the glass doors leading out to the bay, next to a bored-looking gate agent who was tapping away on his phone, sat the boy who had traveled by himself from Philadelphia. Sam—she remembered from his name tag—sat quietly on the hard plastic seat. His enormous green backpack hung heavily off his narrow shoulders and seemed to anchor him backward to the seat. His sneakered feet dangled a couple inches off the tiled floor that he seemed to be intently studying.

Who, Maggie wondered, was he going to see? She thought back to the woman with the official-looking cluster of identification badges who had said good-bye to him at the bus station. She had been emotional. That much had been clear from the way she hugged him. But Sam had seemed neither happy nor sad about the situation. If anything, he seemed . . . resigned. She turned her attention to the gate agent who was frowning at the screen of his smartphone and then glanced around the terminal. Her gaze landed on the man who had sat behind her since Harrisburg—the man who had introduced himself to Eddie as Jimmy.

They had arrived at their underground gate five minutes earlier than expected and after collecting her bag, Maggie had opted to find a rest room so she could brush her teeth and freshen up. She stepped back into the chaos of the station and was displeased to see Jimmy limping stiffly in the direction of her gate. She had forgotten that he was going to Boston, too.

If she were nice, she would consider walking with him. She knew she had been borderline rude when she hadn't offered him the seat next to her on the bus, but given that he, too, was going to Boston, if they walked together to the gate, then she would have no choice but to sit with him on this final leg. She shook her head. Better to stick with the established boundaries.

She took a deep breath, lifted her chin, and focused intently on the space in front of her. She walked quickly, pretending not to see Jimmy as she strode past him, and then later, merely gave a quick nod of acknowledgement when he arrived, his face flushed, his forehead slick with perspiration.

Now, as she watched him look idly around the waiting area, she wondered again what had happened to him. Had he injured his back or his leg? Perhaps he had been in Iraq or Afghanistan. She tried to imagine him in a uniform and was mentally switching from blue to khaki to olive as she saw the color drain from Jimmy's face.

She blinked, wondering if he was having a heart attack before realizing he was staring at someone. She turned her head quickly to see who he was looking at and was surprised to see a very ordinary-looking woman standing by herself next to one of the support pillars. Her shoulder-length, blondish hair was thick and she pushed it back behind one ear as she frowned down into her phone.

Maggie returned her attention to Jimmy. His expression was a combination of what she could only guess was shock and perhaps horror. He took a stilted step backward, his eyes never leaving the woman. Maggie could see the fabric of his pullover stretch and relax across his stomach and chest as he breathed rapidly in and out. She looked back at the woman who now appeared to be typing out a message on her phone. After several seconds, she gave a final, exclamatory tap at the bottom of the screen, inhaled deeply, and then lowered her hand to her side.

Just as Maggie was about to look again at Jimmy, the woman raised her eyes and caught Maggie's gaze. She gave Maggie a half-hearted smile that was anything but happy. Maggie smiled in return and then quickly looked away. In her peripheral vision, she could still see Jimmy standing where he had stopped in his backward progression. She tried to appear casual as she looked first to the space between Jimmy and the woman, and then at him directly.

He was staring down at the screen of a flip phone, his head tipped downward, his chin almost to his chest. Maggie could see the flush at the tips of his ears and she wondered who the woman was. From his reaction, she must be someone that Jimmy knew— or more likely, resembled someone that Jimmy knew. Maggie glanced back at the woman who seemed lost in her own thoughts as she studied the other passengers, including Jimmy. She didn't seem to have a reaction. *Interesting*, Maggie thought. *He knows her but she doesn't recognize him.*

She glanced down at her watch. It was 11:50.

Four-and-a-half hours. The thought came unbidden and she realized in less than five hours she would be in the same city as Sarah for the first time in a year. The conference started at six p.m. with the typical meet and greet. She knew she should go and mingle, but more than anything, she wanted to see Sarah. She reconsidered her decision of just showing up. Maybe she *should* call. But what would she say?

"Hey, sorry I ignored you after our weekend of sex last year. It's just that I am terrified of relationships and I really like you so I decided not to have anything to do with you. Oh yeah, and I've been obsessed with you since then even though I pretended like you didn't exist. Sorry." Maggie shook her head. Yeah, nothing weird about that.

A part of her hoped by some stroke of luck, Sarah would attend the conference even though she wasn't scheduled to speak. That would be less awkward. And, to be thrown together would give her the excuse she needed to re-establish contact. Granted, it would also suggest that she wouldn't have made contact otherwise—which wasn't the case.

When had this all become so complicated?

Maggie didn't even know why she asked the question. It had become complicated the second night when she had met Sarah and Evan for drinks in the hotel bar. She had forced herself to be ten minutes late by finding things to do in her hotel room. First she organized her toiletries. Then she hung the clothing she hadn't made time to unpack the day before. By the time she changed into casual clothes, touched up her makeup, and sprayed on a little cologne, it was seven after nine. She put her driver's license, credit card, room key, and cash in the back pocket of her jeans, did a final scan of her room and headed for the elevator.

The bar was busy and as Maggie stepped inside, she was pleased to see that Evan and Sarah had secured three stools at a raised table near the back. Sarah's leather briefcase sat on the empty stool, protecting it from poachers. The place was packed with funeral directors who had not been ready to call it a night after the mixer.

"Hey," Evan said as Maggie approached.

Both he and Sarah were still in their work clothes and he looked enviously at her casual attire.

"I'm jealous," he said. "You look so comfortable."

Maggie smiled.

"Thanks," she said and gestured at the stool with Sarah's bag.

Sarah turned and met her gaze with an expression that was hard to read. As she reached for the bag, she scanned Maggie's outfit knowingly and gave what Maggie could only interpret as a smirk. She moved the bag so she could loop the shoulder strap over the back of her stool.

Maggie slid onto the seat and signaled a server who was walking in their direction with a tray loaded with drinks. The woman met Maggie's gaze and nodded as she stopped at a large table of funeral directors that Maggie noted included The Pontificator, to drop off all but two of the drinks. She smiled as she approached the table where Maggie, Evan, and Sarah sat. On the tray was a drink in a martini glass with three olives and a rocks glass with a lime wedge.

"A very dry dirty Ketel One martini, up, with three olives," she said as she placed it in front of Maggie. "And, a Beefeater and tonic."

"Thanks," Maggie said as the server walked away. She glanced at Sarah who raised her eyebrows but said nothing.

"We had a bet going as to what you would drink," Evan said. "You had a clear drink at the mixer so I said gin and tonic. Sarah thought you were a vodka girl." He leaned forward. "So, who was right?"

Maggie grinned. "Sorry, Evan." She grasped the stem of the martini glass. "Sarah nailed it."

"Damn," he said as he lifted his glass of beer. "You win." He drank deeply until the glass was empty and set it on the table. His upper lip glistened with beer and he used the bar napkin to dab at it as he stifled a belch. "So. You're from Indiana?"

Maggie nodded and forced herself not to look at Sarah. "Yep. Seymour, Indiana. Home of John Cougar Mellencamp and all his little pink houses."

"And you're a funeral director there?" Evan asked.

"I am. Anthony & Son. I inherited the business from my father." Maggie took a sip from her martini. "My brother had no interest in the home, so I bought him out. And here I am."

"And here you are," Sarah said softly.

Maggie looked at her and felt her cheeks warm as she remembered the lies she had told the night before.

"But I'm not really that interesting," she said quickly, hoping to change the subject. "Tell me about you two?"

"Well," Evan said as he held up his empty glass and signaled the waitress that he wanted another beer. "I'm currently in the Bay Area at a facility that is part of a chain. I love the climate and the people, but I really want to get back to Pennsylvania, which is where we're both from originally."

"Really?" Maggie turned to Sarah and smiled coyly. "I'm surprised. I would have guessed you're from around here. A local."

Sarah colored. Perhaps, Maggie thought, she, too, was recalling last night's half-truths. Though she hadn't actually said she was from Seattle, she definitely hadn't given the impression she was here on business.

"No," she said and looked quickly down at her drink.

"Harrisburg, Pennsylvania." She gestured at Evan. "We both went to Penn State and then I went to the University of Pennsylvania for grad school."

"And you studied anthropology," Maggie said.

"Yes," Sarah said. "Actually, I studied archaeology in undergrad and then got my graduate degrees in cultural anthropology."

"Studying . . . death?" Maggie asked.

"My dissertation was a cross-cultural study of death and mortuary practices in a number of non-industrialized nations," Sarah said in a way that indicated she had given that particular answer more than once.

"And is that what you're going to be talking about tomorrow?" Maggie asked as the server appeared and set Evan's beer on the table.

"Are you ladies ready for a second round?" she asked.

Sarah pulled the Beefeater and tonic toward her. "I'll just drink this one." She again looked knowingly at Maggie's outfit. "Will you stay for another or do you have someplace you need to be?"

Maggie tossed back the rest of the martini, plucked the toothpick skewer of olives out of the glass, and slid it toward the server. "I'd like another. Exactly the same."

Sarah raised her eyebrows, but said nothing.

"You were about to tell me about your presentation tomorrow," Maggie said, ignoring Sarah's look.

Sarah nodded. "I'll be talking about cultural sensitivity as it relates to non-traditional mortuary practices." She paused. "That sounds so academic. It's just that as more and more people come to the United States from non-Western societies, they bring with them cultural traditions that professionals in the mortuary industry need to be aware of and sensitive to."

"Sounds interesting," Maggie said.

"You should come," Evan said as he raised his glass and took a healthy swig.

Sarah raised her own glass and smiled slightly into it. "Yes, you should come."

Maggie looked sharply at Sarah. Was that a double entendre? Is she suggesting . . . ? *Don't even go there*, her brain said sharply. *You know the rules.*

"I might," Maggie said evenly. "When and where is it?"

Sarah took a drink and swallowed. "I speak at nine-thirty," she said around a piece of ice. "In Alcove A."

"I'll save you a seat," Evan said with a quick smile and then glanced down at his watch. "Shit."

"What?" Sarah asked, startled.

"I need to call Laura," he said and then looked at Maggie. "My girlfriend is in France right now. There's a nine-hour time difference and I want to catch her before she goes into her meetings."

He stood, pulled a thin leather wallet from inside his suit jacket, and removed a couple of bills.

Sarah waved him off. "Don't worry about it. I've got this one. You can pay tomorrow night."

He grinned and slid the bills toward her anyway. "See you in the morning?"

Sarah nodded.

"It was nice to meet you and get to know you a little better," he said to Maggie. "I'll meet you outside Alcove A at nine?"

"Nine," Maggie affirmed.

"Tell Laura I said 'hi,'" Sarah said.

Evan nodded and then turned toward the door.

Maggie and Sarah watched him go without speaking. They glanced at each other and then looked quickly down—Sarah at her drink and Maggie at the heavily-lacquered table.

"So," Sarah said finally as she picked up her glass and swirled the contents. "Have you ever even been to Omaha?" She took a sip and waited.

Maggie felt her face flush. "No."

"And the husband and kids?" Sarah asked.

"Not real either," Maggie admitted.

"So, you lied about everything."

"You know, you weren't entirely forthright either," Maggie said. "You acted like you knew the bartender—that you were just a local teacher avoiding grading papers."

"I do have papers to grade. And I do teach. Granted, I didn't tell you it was college, but . . ." Sarah shrugged. "At least I didn't fabricate an entire life."

They stared at each other for several seconds.

"I was surprised to see you at the mixer," Maggie said finally.

Sarah smiled and raised her gaze to meet Maggie's. "Probably not as surprised as I was to see you. I just wanted Evan to come save me from that loudmouth. And then when I looked over and saw him standing there with you . . ." She shook her head. "I was shocked."

"I was a little scared," Maggie admitted. "The way you charged over. I thought you were going to make a scene."

"Not my style," Sarah said and then grinned suggestively. "I prefer to make my scenes in private."

Maggie cleared her throat and nodded as she remembered Sarah's body beneath her, her hips arching upward against her thigh, her—

"So, is that your thing?" Sarah asked.

Maggie frowned, unsure what Sarah meant. She was about to ask but the server appeared at her shoulder.

"Dirty Ketel One martini, dry, with extra olives," she said as she placed the frosty glass in front of Maggie. "Would you ladies like anything else?"

"Just the check when you get a chance," Sarah said.

The woman nodded and disappeared into the throng of funeral directors. Maggie stared down at her drink for several seconds before lifting her gaze to see Sarah studying her. She blinked and then looked quickly down.

"What?" Maggie fished out the skewer of olives from her drink and ate them one by one.

"Is that your thing?" Sarah repeated.

Maggie swallowed the olives and then raised the martini to her lips and took a sip. She carefully set the stemmed glass back on the cocktail napkin and meet Sarah's gaze.

"You mean going to bars, lying about who I am, and having anonymous sex with strangers?" she asked calmly. "Yes, that's my thing."

Sarah nodded slowly. "And what about when it's no longer anonymous?" she asked the question so quietly Maggie almost didn't hear her.

Maggie swallowed. It would be so easy. It would also, she reminded herself, be against the rules.

"I don't do that," Maggie said finally.

"Ah," Sarah said. "Just love 'em and leave 'em, eh?"

"In my line of work, that's generally better," Maggie said.

"So, it's because of your work." Sarah's tone suggested that she thought otherwise.

"Yes," Maggie said, knowing she sounded defensive. "I'm a closeted lesbian funeral director in a small town in the middle of the Bible Belt. I have a reputation to maintain."

"Ah," Sarah said and took another sip of her drink.

"The people who come to Anthony & Son are small town, conservative churchgoers. They come because of my family's reputation. They don't want to think about a depraved lesbian doing ungodly things to the bodies of their loved ones." Even to her own ears the words sounded angry. "It's not like academia where everyone is liberal and open-minded."

Sarah smiled wryly. "Is that what you think? That we're all just a bunch of liberals running around celebrating diversity?"

"Isn't it?"

Sarah gave a short, sharp laugh. "There are still labels. People still judge. They're still petty. It's just manifested in a different form." She paused for several seconds. "But that's not what we're talking about. We're talking about you and why you don't do do-overs."

Maggie frowned. "I told you why."

"You told me why you don't do it in Indiana," Sarah said. "You didn't tell me why you don't do it in Seattle."

"The rules," Maggie murmured.

"Excuse me?" Sarah leaned forward.

Maggie looked up and was once again mesmerized by the thickness of Sarah's eyelashes and how they framed her dark green eyes. She looked quickly away.

"The rules," she said louder and cleared her throat. "I have rules that I follow. To keep it . . . manageable."

"To protect your reputation," Sarah said. Her tone held a hint of mockery.

"Yes," Maggie said.

Sarah leaned forward and gestured with her hand for Maggie to come closer. Maggie clenched her jaw and leaned in.

"So, if I invited you up to my room," Sarah said softly, her breath a light caress on Maggie's cheek, "the rules dictate that you would have to say 'no.'"

Sarah's words smelled pleasantly like gin. Maggie swallowed, blinked, and forced herself to give a short, tight nod.

"That's too bad," Sarah said as she sat back on her stool. "Because, I'd really like to spend the night with you. Again."

Maggie inhaled deeply and held the breath in her lungs. After several seconds, she slowly blew the air through her lips.

Sarah watched with an amused expression. She tipped the rest of the drink and the ice into her mouth and then turned toward Evan's vacated seat where her bag now sat. She pulled out a black leather wallet and extracted a couple of bills, which she added to the ones left behind by Evan.

The server appeared with the check and Sarah handed her the money without looking at the bill.

"Do you need change?" the young woman asked.

"No. The rest is yours." Sarah smiled and waited until the woman walked away before looking back at Maggie. "I should probably go. I have to present tomorrow and you're clearly dressed to go out so I won't keep you." She slipped the strap of her briefcase over her shoulder and slid off the bar stool.

Maggie nodded, feeling absurdly as if she had just been rejected. "Actually, I am." She finished her drink in one swallow, stood, and followed Sarah out of the bar.

"Going back to the WildRose?" Sarah asked as they stepped into the brightly lit hotel lobby.

"I'm not sure," Maggie said.

She looked past Sarah at the revolving door at the front entrance. The idea of going out was quickly losing its appeal. She turned back to Sarah. She felt suddenly like she was on a first date and neither of them knew how to end it.

Finally, Sarah hoisted her bag more firmly onto her shoulder and smiled. "Well, have fun."

Maggie pressed her lips together and tried to smile. "Thanks." She cleared her throat. "Sleep well."

Sarah opened her mouth to speak and then, as if thinking better of it, nodded and turned toward the bank of elevators. Maggie watched her walk away, slowly at first and then faster in an effort to catch the waiting elevator. Only after the doors slid shut did Maggie release the breath she hadn't realized she was holding. Around her, people continued to go about their business, unaware of the unspoken drama that had just played out. She turned back toward the revolving front entrance and the promise that awaited her outside the hotel. More than anything, she realized, she wanted simply to go upstairs and go to bed.

You're wasting a perfect opportunity, she reminded herself as she walked to the bank of elevators and pushed the button with the "up" arrow. It didn't matter. She was tired and, if she were completely honest, not sure she was ready to give up the memory of the night before. The same elevator she had seen Sarah enter dinged its arrival and Maggie moved to stand in front of it. The doors slid open.

Maggie stepped forward just as the woman in the elevator stepped out. They narrowly missed colliding and Maggie jumped backwards.

"Oh god, I'm sorry. I—" She looked up. It was Sarah.

"I was coming down for—"

"I decided I didn't want to—"

They spoke at once and then stopped. The silence that followed was, again, awkward. The elevator doors closed.

"The iron doesn't work," Sarah said and held up the iron and a handful of cord. "I was going to get a new one." She looked Maggie up and down. "I thought you were going out."

"I was." Maggie stepped backward a half step and smiled. "But the two martinis on top of not getting a lot of sleep made bed sound awfully good."

Sarah laughed. "Yeah. We were up late last night." She glanced at the iron in her hand. "If you wait a second, we can share an elevator. We're on the same floor." She grinned sheepishly. "Actually, I'm only two doors down."

Maggie smiled despite herself at the thought that rather than return to an apartment or a house as she had assumed, Sarah had only gone down the hall after she left.

"Be right back?" Sarah gestured toward the front desk. A few minutes later she returned and held up the new iron. "Let's hope this one works."

Maggie pushed the button and they waited. Three men in business suits, ties loosened, and faces flushed from drinking came to stand behind them. From their conversation, Maggie guessed they were conference attendees.

"It's just this push to go corporate," one man was saying. "And excuse me if I don't want to be a part of a conglomerate."

Maggie tried to ignore Sarah's proximity as they stared at the closed, metal doors. Behind them, the speaker's two friends were making noises of agreement.

"It's a death sentence to the family business," one of the other men said. "But, Jesus, do they make it tempting."

The elevator dinged and the doors opened. Maggie and Sarah entered first and stepped toward the back. The men stood in front of them. One leaned against the wall in front of the buttons.

"Five, please," Maggie and Sarah said at the same time.

The man punched the button for the fifth floor and then the buttons for the eighth and tenth floors.

"I don't even know if my son will want to take over the business," the shortest of the three said. "Sometimes I wonder why I'm even holding onto it."

Maggie looked at the speaker. He was short, a little overweight, but still boyish despite the gray that peppered his dark hair. She could see the cowlick in the back that he likely tried to tame with product. He rubbed his hand across his eyes and blinked wearily. A gold wedding ring shone dully on his finger. She glanced at Sarah who was looking pointedly at the floor.

The elevator dinged, signaling their arrival at the fifth floor. The doors slid smoothly open and Maggie stepped out. Sarah followed. They walked slowly without talking down the hallway to Maggie's room. She pulled her keycard from her jeans pocket and slid it into the reader. The lock disengaged with a soft click. She pressed down on the handle and pushed open the door. Sarah stood, looking down at the iron she clutched in both hands. She, too, looked tired.

"I . . ."

Sarah glanced up and for just a moment, Maggie saw her own loneliness reflected in her eyes. Before she could stop herself, she lightly touched the crest of her cheek. Sarah closed her eyes and turned her face slightly into the caress. They stood that way for several long seconds until Sarah sighed and turned her head just enough to press her lips against Maggie's palm. It was chaste in comparison to what they had done the night before, but the intimacy of it caused Maggie to tremble. She felt Sarah's smile against her hand.

"Look, I know you have your rules and all that." Sarah opened her eyes and looked at Maggie. "But I'm thinking maybe you should consider suspending them for the night." She smiled. "I don't want anything more than this. I'm not looking for a relationship."

Maggie blinked, momentarily stung at what felt like a rejection. *Hypocrite.* She wanted to laugh at the irony, but instead smiled. *Be careful what you ask for.*

"So, just to be clear," she said. "No strings. No emotional connection. No calls afterward. Just sex."

Sarah nodded slowly, her gaze unwavering. She stepped away from Maggie's touch. "Ask me into your room," she said softly.

Maggie swallowed. Her heart thudded in her chest and she felt each beat in her temples . . . in her neck . . . in her hands.

As if reading her mind, Sarah lowered her gaze to the hollow just below Maggie's jaw where her pulse fluttered. She shifted the iron to her left hand and gently brushed the fingertips of her free hand against the spot. Maggie inhaled sharply through her nose and Sarah smiled. "Ask me into your room," she said again.

"If I could have your attention, please."

The unexpected sound of the gate agent's voice over the loudspeaker jolted Maggie back into the present.

"In just a couple of minutes we will begin boarding Peter Pan Bus Line #2534 Express to Boston from Gate 84. Please have your tickets visible so we can see them. Thank you."

Around her, people began packing up their laptops and shoving books and papers into their bags. Maggie looked at Jimmy. He stood, his weight resting heavily on his uninjured leg, typing out a message on his phone. She could tell from his frown that whatever he was writing wasn't pleasant. She glanced back at the woman with the honey-colored hair. She had removed her coat and was standing with it draped over her forearm. She chewed idly on the thumb of her free hand as she stared off into space. The boy with the green backpack sat staring dully at the tiled floor.

Maggie inhaled deeply. This was it—the last leg of the trip. She hitched her bag higher on her shoulder and turned toward the gate. It was time.

Bug

"THAT'S YOU."

Bug looked up at the man sitting next to him. He had introduced himself as Matt when the driver of the bus from Philadelphia had led Bug through the bay and delivered him to the waiting attendant.

Matt. Bug had read the letters on Matt's scratched, plastic identification card when he reached out to shake his hand. They had barely talked during the trek to the gate and now Matt sat texting someone on his phone while they had waited. With the boarding announcement, Matt stretched out his right leg, turned slightly onto one butt cheek, and slid the phone into the front pocket of his too tight uniform pants.

"As soon as they give us the final go-ahead, I'll take you out and get you settled." Matt sat back into the seat. "You'll need to make sure that when you get to Boston, you wait for the driver or a bus employee to escort you off the bus, okay?" He leaned forward and raised his shaggy eyebrows.

Bug could tell Matt was waiting for an acknowledgement that he understood the instructions and would follow them. He nodded twice. Matt smiled without showing his teeth and then scratched the skin above his beard. Bug wondered what it would feel like to have a beard. Would it be like wearing one of those ski masks with the holes for the mouth and nose? Would it feel thick on his face?

"What's it feel like?" he asked suddenly.

Matt frowned slightly and tipped his head to the side. "What's what feel like?"

Bug lifted his hand and touched his own face with his fingertips. "Your beard. What does it feel like to have it on your face?"

Matt's frown deepened and Bug leaned slightly backward, preparing himself for the angry words he knew would come next.

Matt laughed, and Bug blinked in surprise at him.

"I don't know." Matt pursed his lips in thought. "I guess it feels like . . ." He shrugged. "It's like your head hair. Sort of. But not really. You don't notice it until you touch it. It's itchy warm." He smiled. His teeth were small and yellow.

Bug nodded. Itchy warm. He opened his mouth to ask another question but before he could get the words out, Matt stood. His phone was a rectangular bulge in his pocket.

"Time to get you in your seat," he said as he pulled Bug's ticket from the breast pocket of his shirt. He glanced down at the paper in his hand, nodded once, and then leaned down for the duffle bag that they had unloaded from the bus from Philadelphia.

Bug leaned forward against the weight of the backpack and slid awkwardly off of the seat. As he adjusted the straps on his shoulders, he looked up to see the pretty woman with the long, dark hair who had been on his bus from Philadelphia staring at him. He met her gaze, and she smiled. He felt his face flush.

". . . right to your aunt."

Bug jerked his attention back to Matt. Though he had missed the first part of the sentence, he guessed that Matt had said that when they got to Boston, someone from the bus company would lead him through the terminal to Aunt Sarah. He tried again to push down his fear that she probably didn't want him any more than Rhonda had.

He remembered the night when he realized his visit to Grandma Jean's wasn't temporary. He had been dozing when the peal of the telephone startled him awake. Grandma Jean's phone was different than Rhonda's. Rhonda's phone was gray plastic and could be carried around. But Grandma Jean's was about the size of a loaf of bread and it was attached to the wall. A long, twisted cord connected the receiver to the phone itself. And it had a very loud ring that reminded Bug of his alarm clock. It was that ring that woke him.

The phone rang several times before Bug heard the creak and muffled thump of the footrest of the old recliner clicking into place and then the soft *shhhing* of his grandmother's house slippers as she made her way into the kitchen.

"Hello."

Bug wondered who could be calling at this time of night. It was almost time for the local news to end, at which time, Grandma Jean turned off the television and all the lights except the one over the stove, and then slowly climbed the stairs to her room. It was the same routine every night and Bug took pleasure in its familiarity. No one called after nine o'clock—no one except Rhonda.

Bug's stomach tightened. If she was calling, it probably had to do with him. And the most likely reason was that she was settled into her job and was coming to get him. Although a part of him was excited at the idea that she actually wanted him back, a larger part was filled with dread at the thought of leaving the warm, loving predictability of Grandma Jean's house. Even as he had the thought, he felt bad. He should love his mother. And he did. But here was safe. Here, at Grandma Jean's, he was happy.

Downstairs, he heard the scrape of one of the wooden chairs on the linoleum floor. It wasn't a short conversation if Grandma Jean was sitting down. He wondered what they were talking about. He knew that it wasn't right to sneak out of bed and listen, but he had to know what was being said. As quietly as possible, he pushed back the covers, slipped from the bed, and tiptoed across the wooden floor of his bedroom, to the hallway, and down the stairs. He knew two of the steps squeaked, so he was careful to avoid them.

Midway down, where the outside railing met the wall, Bug stopped and sat in the shadows. If he leaned forward and to the side, he could see Grandma Jean's profile. Just to be safe, though, he drew his knees up and wrapped his arms around his legs.

"Yes, yes, I know."

Bug could tell that Grandma Jean was frustrated. He leaned forward and listened hard.

"And I understand that, Rhonda, but what you don't seem—"

Bug heard his mother's somewhat nasal voice cut Grandma Jean off. He couldn't hear all of what Rhonda was saying, though he was able to pick out enough words to understand what was being said. "Daryl . . . shifts . . . Bug."

Grandma Jean sighed. "I really wish you wouldn't call him that. It's a horrible name."

His mother said something else.

"And I'm happy to have him," Grandma Jean said. "My concern is that I'm not as young or as healthy as I used to be and I just worry that if something happens to me—"

Rhonda interrupted again and this time, spoke for several minutes before Grandma Jean stopped her with, "Well, you should have thought about that before you got pregnant."

Bug felt his heart beat faster and he strained to hear his mother's response.

"You don't deserve him," Grandma Jean said finally. "He's better off here where at least there is someone who loves him and takes care of him."

"I love him," Rhonda said in a loud voice that bordered on screechy.

"I'm hanging up now, Rhonda," Grandma Jean said. "I'm too old and too tired to listen to this. Don't worry about Sammy. I want him here with me. And if I have anything to say about it, he will stay here for good. Goodbye."

Bug heard the scrape of the chair as Grandma Jean pushed it back from the table and walked back to the phone. He could hear the sound of his mother continuing to speak loudly until Grandma Jean hung the receiver in the cradle and disconnected the call. She sighed heavily into the silence.

Bug waited for the sound of her footsteps heading back into the living room but was surprised when he heard the whirl of the rotary dial. There was silence for several seconds and then, "Hi, Hon. It's Mom."

Bug could tell from the way she spoke that she had called Aunt Sarah. Unlike his mother, Sarah spoke in a much softer tone. All he could hear was Grandma Jean's side of the conversation.

"Yes, I know. She called me, too." Bug heard the creak of the wooden chair as Grandma Jean sat back down. "I don't know, but she sounded completely out of it. Argumentative. I hung up on her."

There was silence and then, "It's no place for Sammy. She can barely take care of herself let alone . . . I know."

Bug wished he knew what his aunt was saying.

"No, we're all right. My retirement from the state and my social security covers everything we need." Silence. "No, Sarah, it's not your responsibility." Grandma Jean sighed. "Well, thank you."

Sarah seemed to talk for a very long time before Grandma Jean responded.

"It's not that. I just worry. I'm not as young as I used to be and I just worry that if I fall or get sick . . ." Silence. "No, of course not. I'm healthy as a horse." Grandma Jean laughed. "Or that, too, yes. So, how are classes?"

Bug listened for several more minutes before he understood that they were done talking about Rhonda and about his living situation. It appeared that he would be staying with Grandma Jean. He knew he should be sad that his mother didn't want him. And a part of him was. But more than anything else, he was relieved.

"What's she like?"

Bug blinked out of his thoughts and he realized he had been walking alongside Matt to the exit doors without thinking about where they were going.

He shook his head. "I only met her once."

"Right." Matt nodded. "Well, I'm sure she's great."

They reached the doors to the loading bay and Matt pulled it open with his free hand and stepped back so Bug could go through first. The acrid air outside the terminal was cold and Bug coughed as he walked into the loading area.

"It's worse in the summer." Matt pointed to a bus that looked almost exactly like the one Bug had ridden in from Philadelphia. "That's yours, there."

They walked up to the doors of the coach and Matt knocked on the glass window. Inside, the driver was bent forward over his phone. He looked sideways, held up a finger, and tapped the screen several times—the last time with a flourish. He slipped the phone into his jacket pocket and then leaned forward and pushed a button on the dash. The hydraulic doors opened with a hiss.

"Hey, Matt." The driver, a thin, older man with a creased face, jerked his chin in greeting. "Who's this?"

"This is Sam." Matt looked down at Bug and then back at the driver. "Sam. This is Tom. He's going to make sure you get to Boston safely." He gestured for Bug to climb into the bus.

"Hey, Sam." Tom grinned at Bug and then looked back at Matt. "You'll let them know to meet us?"

As the men talked, Bug shrugged off his backpack and settled into the seat directly behind Tom. He wondered if Marilyn, the woman from before, would sit with him again. He looked at the empty seat and considered putting his backpack in it, just to make sure no one else would sit there. He leaned down and was about to heave the bag up when he heard his name. He looked up to see Matt standing in the aisle.

"Have a good trip." Matt extended his hand and Bug reached out to shake it. "I've put your duffle bag in the luggage compartment under the bus. I'll make sure there is someone in Boston who will help you get it out and then will take you to your aunt. Until then, stay with Tom, okay?"

Bug nodded. "Thank you."

Matt winked, turned, and with a wave in Tom's direction, hurried off the bus. Outside, people were waiting in line to board.

Tom turned in his seat to face Bug. "So, here's the drill. I need to get everyone loaded. Don't get off the—" His phone pinged and he quickly slipped it out of his pocket. He looked down at the screen and then back up at Bug. "Sorry." He grinned. "My daughter is having a baby." He held up the phone. "They're on their way to the hospital." He quickly typed a response and then returned the phone to his pocket. "So, just stay here, okay?" He grinned again and then stood and bounded down the stairs.

Bug lifted the backpack into the seat and then sat back to watch people climb onto the bus. Most of them looked tired and cranky, like his mother did on the mornings after she had been out. A couple of the people looked familiar. The pretty woman with the dark hair smiled at him as she passed. There was also the man with the crew cut—the one who limped. He had been on the bus from Philadelphia, too, though, unlike the woman, didn't seem to notice him.

Bug sat straighter at the sight of Marilyn's gray bob and wondered if he should meet her eyes and smile or look down and let her choose if she wanted to sit with him. Before he could decide though, Marilyn caught his eye and smiled broadly. She waited until the man ahead of her passed before stopping next to the seat with Bug's backpack.

"Is this seat taken?" She smiled and Bug felt a rush of relief.

He quickly lifted his bag from the seat and placed it back on the floor in front of his feet.

"I was hoping you would save me a seat," Marilyn said as she stowed her tote bag in the compartment over their heads. "I saw you board early and I just thought to myself, 'I hope he knows I want to sit next to him again.'" She slid into the seat and held up her novel. "I thought we could each read our new books."

Bug nodded and leaned forward to unzip his bag. He carefully pulled out one of the books Gail had given him and then zipped the bag closed. As he sat back, he turned to meet Marilyn's gaze. She smiled and patted his arm.

"Thank you," he said softly as she gave his wrist a quick squeeze. "Thank you for being nice to me."

"No need to thank me," Marilyn said. "It's what friends do."

Bug nodded and turned to look out the window. Now that he was seated and didn't have to change buses again, his eyes and arms felt heavy. After laying awake most of the night and then the excitement and stress of the morning, his body was demanding sleep. But sleeping on the bus, surrounded by strangers, where anyone could take his bag, was out of the question. He needed to stay awake. It would only be a couple of hours anyway.

He turned to look at the woman next to him. Marilyn apparently had no such concerns. She sat, her hands crossed over the book in her lap, with her eyes closed. She couldn't have fallen asleep already, he knew, but he could tell, just as he could tell with Grandma Jean, that she was tired. He could see the tiny pulse in her neck and the slow rise and fall of her chest. He knew she was alive. But something about the way she sat, so still, made him wonder if that's how she would look when she was dead.

He remembered how Grandma Jean had looked during the family visitation. He hadn't been able to see her as he had walked beside his Aunt Sarah down the carpeted aisle that ran between the pews. He'd had to use the small step stool in front of the casket to see her face. Bug had stared. Seeing her like that, so still, her skin the color of the vanilla candles she used to burn in the kitchen, made his heart hurt.

"It's not her," his Aunt Sarah had murmured. Rhonda hadn't come home the night before and it was just Bug and Sarah at the viewing. "It's her body. But it's not her. She's . . ." She gestured vaguely toward the ceiling.

"Is she in Heaven?" Bug knew that Grandma Jean had believed in God even though they had never gone to church.

Sarah pulled her lips together in a sort of smile and made a soft noise the back of her throat. Her eyes narrowed at the corners. "Is that where you think she is?"

Bug looked back at the body in the coffin. He would like to think that she was in Heaven but it was hard to imagine that a place where everyone was happy, with no worries or fear, existed. He shook his head.

"No. Not really. But Grandma did."

Bug glanced up at his aunt. She was looking down at her mother, her eyes wet with tears. He grasped her hand. She sniffed and used the crumpled tissue in her free hand to dab at the corners of her eyes. Her lashes looked dark.

"Do you want to say anything?" Her voice sounded thick and she cleared her throat. "Do you want to say goodbye?"

Bug shook his head. "She's not there."

Sarah had squeezed his hand, helped him down from the step stool, and led him to the pew behind them. They had sat for about an hour, not speaking and looking everywhere but at each other. Rhonda hadn't shown up for the viewing. In fact she had barely made it to the funeral, coming in just before the family was supposed to walk to the front of the church. Her wrinkled, black dress hung crookedly on her gaunt frame. Her hair was pulled back into a pony tail and her eyes had brown, hollow smudges under them. The odor of stale cigarette smoke clung to her so strongly that Bug could taste it.

He had dreaded going back to Philadelphia with Rhonda. She was his mother and he loved her, but after the cleanliness of Grandma Jean's, the stuffy smell of body odor, discarded meals, and old carpet that permeated the narrow row house on Addison Street made him feel like he was going to vomit. Unlike the welcoming warmth of Grandma Jean's home, Rhonda's house was cold and unfriendly. Rhonda had said she was going to use some of the money from the sale of Grandma Jean's house to make some changes, but Bug knew not to get his hopes up. He had learned that only led to disappointment.

Bug jerked awake as his head made contact with the cool glass of the bus window. He looked anxiously down at his bag and then at Marilyn. She was again reading her book. Bug rubbed at his eyes with the heels of his hands. He needed to stay awake. He needed to alert for whatever was coming next.

Jimmy

JIMMY SAT RIGIDLY in his seat and watched as Helen moved down the aisle in his direction. As had been the case before, he had chosen to sit behind the dark-haired mortician, though this time he had forced himself not to make eye contact as he walked past her and the unoccupied seat to her right. Helen, however, seemed to have zeroed in on the open seat.

What are the chances? His heart thumped wildly in his chest. Not only had Helen found out he had lied but now she was on the same bus to Boston. *What the fuck?*

Shock didn't even begin to describe how he felt when he had seen her standing in the terminal. It was as if the floor had dropped out from under him. And then he got the text. He had watched her type and send it, had heard the alert as it dropped into his mailbox. He had tried to be casual as he slipped his hand inside the pocket of his pants and pulled out the phone. The tiny screen was illuminated. His hand trembled as he flipped open the phone and used the thumb of his other hand to push the button that opened the message.

> I called the hospital. I know you lied. What I don't know is why.

He stared at the screen. How could he answer? What response could he possibly give to explain something he wasn't sure he even understood himself? "It's not you, it's me." "I didn't mean for it to go so far." "I'm sorry." They were all true, but none of them were the answer Helen deserved. He swallowed and then, without raising his head, looked back up at Helen. Her posture was rigid, her expression unreadable as she looked around the room at the other passengers. His stomach dropped when her eyes met his. She gave him a polite, tight-lipped smile. It was the acknowledgement of a stranger.

Jimmy had snapped closed his phone and put it back in his pocket. To reply to her message while she could see him, even though she would have no idea he was replying to her, had seemed too revealing. He would do it later, he thought, after he was seated and had had time to think about how to respond. But now, sitting in his seat, watching Helen move awkwardly down the aisle, her brows pulled together in a slight frown, he wasn't sure there was anything to say.

He lifted his finger to his mouth and gnawed at the cuticle. As she approached, she shifted her gaze and looked directly at Jimmy. Their eyes locked and he felt something in his stomach shift and tighten. He tried not to look away even as her lips tightened into deeper frown—not unlike the look the funeral director had given him hours earlier.

He jerked his finger away from his lips and dropped his hand into his lap. He felt his face flush as he lowered his gaze and began to pick at the wet flap of skin.

"Is this seat available?"

Helen's voice was richer in person than it was over the phone. He glanced up to see that she was talking to the funeral director.

"No. I mean, yes, it's available. No, it's not taken." Maggie laughed and Helen smiled.

Jimmy watched as she shrugged her purse off her shoulder and set it in the empty seat. She had been carrying her coat over her forearm and now she folded it into a neat bundle and slid it into the overhead compartment. The movement pulled the fabric of her blouse tightly across her chest and despite his best attempts to not be obvious, Jimmy couldn't help but notice the swell of her breasts. Snatches of their more racy exchanges popped into his mind and he felt his body respond. He shifted uncomfortably.

"I'm Maggie," he heard the funeral director say as Helen slid into her seat.

"Helen."

"Going to Boston or farther north?"

Jimmy leaned forward to better hear the conversation.

"Boston," Helen said. "You?"

"The same," Maggie said and then, after a pause, "I'm going to a conference. For work. How about you?"

Jimmy felt his pulse accelerate.

Helen snorted. "Long story. Let's just say I don't know why I'm going anymore. I was supposed to meet someone. But now, I'm not sure."

Jimmy could hear the anger in her voice. He didn't blame her. Hell, she had every right to be angry. If the situation was reversed and she had lied to him about something so significant, he would be furious.

"—do for a living?" Maggie was asking Helen a question.

"I'm an investigator for an insurance company out of Chicago," Helen said. "I look at the circumstances of claims to determine if they are legitimate and meet the criteria for the policy payout. And you?"

"Funeral director," Maggie said. "From a small town in Indiana."

Helen said something else, but she must have turned her head because Jimmy couldn't hear the words. He leaned forward in a way that he hoped was casual.

"—valuable service," Helen said. "I don't know what my husband and I would have done without Wojciechowski's. When our daughter was stillborn, they were so kind."

Jimmy jerked his head up in surprise. Husband? He frowned. Surely she meant ex-husband, although that was news. They had talked about everything and Helen had never mentioned being married. Nor had she ever mentioned anything about a child that had died.

"—so sorry for your loss," Maggie was saying. "Death is never easy, but a baby is probably the hardest."

Helen said something in a tone too low for Jimmy to hear and then both women were silent.

Why, he wondered, had Helen never shared any of this? Was it because she was Catholic and ashamed of being divorced? He knew she had been raised in a very conservative household, but things she had written or said indicated that she was long past all of that. As far as he knew, she hadn't gone to Mass in years. And besides, wasn't that sort of thing less of a big deal in the Catholic Church now? He didn't care if she had been married; what bothered him was she hadn't told him.

Like you have any room to talk?

Jimmy blinked at the hypocrisy and sat back in his seat with a sigh. Unlike Helen, he didn't have Catholic guilt to use as justification for his lies. And his hadn't simply been an omission of parts of his past. He had out and out lied—had fabricated a life for himself that was so far from the truth that it was embarrassing.

Granted, he hadn't meant to fall in love with Helen. There was just something about her that filled the void of everything that was missing in his life. The warmth of her eyes and smile in her pictures. The depth of her words. They had connected on a deeper level almost from the start. She had felt it, too. Later, after they had become intimate, Helen had admitted that she had known she was attracted to him before they had even communicated.

I have to confess something.

Her typed words had terrified him and Jimmy remembered hesitating before responding.

You know you can tell me anything.

The wait had been almost too much to bear. He could tell from the Google chat message that she was typing her answer and given the time it was taking to compose, he braced himself for the worst. He blinked in surprise when what came through was a single line.

I knew who you were before I contacted you.

Jimmy felt his heartbeat accelerate. Did she mean that she knew he wasn't the man in the picture? Or did she mean that she knew his heart or . . . He needed clarification.

Could you elaborate on that?

He waited for what seemed like forever while the cursor blinked. Finally, he saw that she was typing. Within a minute, her message appeared.

It's true that I contacted you after reading your posts on the parasailing forum, but I also went to your Facebook page beforehand and looked at your public posts and pictures. I couldn't help myself. There was something about you that drew me.

Does that freak you out?

Jimmy grinned. Helen had cyberstalked him before contacting him. He wasn't sure why he was so happy about that fact, but he was. She had been drawn to him. *Drawn to someone else's picture, don't you mean?* The voice in his head was that of his father. *Do you think she would have given you the time of day if she knew what you really looked like?* Jimmy felt his grin fade. The voice was right. His father had been right. He wasn't worth Helen's time—or at least the real him wasn't. But Helen didn't know that. She could never know that.

> Not freaked out at all. Actually, flattered. Everything happens for a reason. I often think about the symmetry of life while I'm doing yoga.

Jimmy hit *send.*

> I love that you do yoga. Have I ever told you that?

Jimmy sent a smiley-face in response. He considered sending a more provocative message—something about how flexible he was. Or how his flexibility allowed him to get those hard-to-reach places. But he hadn't. This was more about intimacy than it was about sex. Still, he had to admit, the flirting was addictive. It had become the lone bright spot in his otherwise gloomy existence.

Even when he had been in rehab, his tenuous connection to her had been the only thing that gave him hope. He had ignored the fact that it was based on a lie. It was a connection—a tether to the man he intended to become once he got clean. Once he got in shape. Once he . . . what? Became someone else? Again, the voice was his father's.

"You need to toughen up, boy." It had been a common refrain when Jimmy was growing up. "Life's a bitch and you can't be soft. You gotta always be ready to fight."

It wasn't his father's fault that he was so gruff, Jimmy reminded himself. He was the product of a time where men were supposed to be hard—especially when they grew up in the gritty, working-class neighborhood of Shipoke.

"It was one shit sandwich after another," Sean Reilly was fond of saying after a few beers. "But it made us tough—made us men."

Often it was a segue into stories of the Army and Vietnam. Jimmy knew that many of them were embellished if not out-and-out lies. But he also knew that past valor was the only thing Sean had. It was the only thing that made him feel special. Getting his girlfriend pregnant hadn't. Working for the railroad and later, the transit authority hadn't. Raising Jimmy certainly hadn't.

His life really had been one shit sandwich after another, Jimmy thought as he stared at the back of Helen's seat. It was not unlike his own. The only difference was that Jimmy's misfortune was of his own making. He couldn't blame poverty because, despite not having much, his father had always made sure he never went without the basics. He couldn't blame the atrocities of war for his addiction. No, he had no one to blame but himself. He was the one who had made bad decisions.

So, what are you going to do about it? This time the voice wasn't his father's. It was Diane's.

Jimmy frowned in concentration as he tried to reconcile the realization that was forming in his head. Was the solution really as simple as that? He shook his head. He had heard the words before but until this moment, they hadn't really made sense. He was the one who could make all of this stop. He was the one who could make the decision to change. Sure, he had gone through rehab because he had to. He had worked the program because he had to. But he hadn't owned any of it. Not really. Not until now.

"I can stop this," he murmured softly.

The realization took his breath away and for the first time since graduating from the paramedic program, he felt as if he was in control. He felt the bubble of hope deep in his chest as he leaned to the side and pulled the phone out of his pocket. He stared down at it and for the first time didn't resent that it wasn't fancy. It was what it was. And so was he. Recognizing what he had to do and for the first time not dreading it, Jimmy flipped open the phone and began to type.

Helen

"I AM SO sorry for your loss," the woman next to Helen said in a low voice. Her eyes were compassionate and Helen had to force herself not to look away. "Death is never easy, but a baby is probably the hardest."

Helen nodded. "Thank you. It was . . ." She shrugged and shook her head. "It was difficult."

Maggie gave her wrist a gentle squeeze and then dropped her hand back into her lap. More to end the conversation than anything else, Helen pulled her compact out of her purse. She fumbled with the release mechanism and finally had to use both hands and her fingernail to pry it open.

Maggie took the hint and returned her attention to whatever she had been doing on her phone.

Helen held the mirror up and examined her reflection. There were circles under her eyes. She pinched the round, foam applicator between her thumb and forefinger, rubbed it on the creamy circle of foundation, and then smoothed it along the underside of her eyes and across the bridge of her nose. She tipped her head back, studied the rest of her face critically, and then dabbed a bit on the blemish on her chin that seemed determined to erupt.

The familiar actions calmed her. She couldn't believe she had told Maggie about the miscarriage. She never talked about it. Most of the time, she tried to forget that it had even happened. Dwelling on it, she knew, wouldn't bring Alex back. Even the name brought with it a stab of pain. No one, not even David, had known that Alexandra, Alex for short, was the name she had given to the baby she had carried inside of her for four-and-a-half months. She had been certain it was a girl though they hadn't known for sure until she miscarried. She shuddered at the memory of having to "give birth" to the baby that had died inside her two weeks earlier.

Part of her thought she knew the moment that Alex had died. She had been making dinner. She was supposed to be resting, but David liked coming home to a warm meal and she had become bored with lying around all day with her feet up. She had just put the homemade kopytka into boiling water when she felt the first wave of nausea. She flipped off the heat, stumbled backward to one of the wooden kitchen chairs they had gotten at an estate sale, and eased herself down. She dabbed at the sweat on her forehead and neck with the tail of her apron and chastised herself for standing over a boiling pot of water. She closed her eyes and breathed slowly in and out until the nausea passed.

She ran her hand along the soft swell of her belly. She had begun to show a couple of weeks earlier and never ceased to take pleasure in touching the bump that was going to be her daughter. In the past, she had miscarried before even reaching this milestone. Her daughter. They had made the decision not to find out the sex of the baby, but Helen knew without a doubt that she was carrying a little girl. She was about to stand when the second wave of nausea hit—this time accompanied by a strange pain. It was almost as if she were being pinched from inside her womb. And then, just as quickly as the pain had come, it disappeared. Helen felt her nipples harden and her skin seemed to prickle. She shivered.

It had been exactly four months.

Of course, she hadn't known at the time that Alex was gone—not for sure anyway. Instead, she convinced herself that it was just part of the experience, a subtle change inside her that, because they had never made it this far, was normal. Everything they were experiencing in the second trimester was new. And it was then that they had made their first mistake. They had allowed themselves to hope. And with each new milestone, that hope grew. The fact that they had made it to the second trimester, that they had been able to see the baby on the ultrasound and hear her heartbeat—that had made the loss more devastating than any of the others.

Two weeks later, the pain and contractions began. She had been asleep when the cramps came with such intensity that she had cried out. She had rolled onto her side, her hands clutched against her belly.

"No," she cried softly. "Not again. Please . . . not again."

She tried to slow her breathing. She watched the luminescent blue numbers of the clock radio change from 3:15 to 3:16 to 3:17. The pain passed, but only for a moment before a rush of blood saturated the sanitary pad she'd worn to bed. She could feel it trickle wetly from between her thighs and down the skin just below her buttocks. She could feel the warm stickiness as it soaked into her nightgown and the mattress.

"David." She reached back and blindly slapped at his sleeping form. "David. Wake up. We need to go to the hospital."

"S'rong?" he mumbled.

"We need to go to the hospital," she repeated. "Something is wrong with the baby."

The mattress beneath her shook as David sat up and turned to lean over her. "Do you need 911?" She could hear the fear in his voice.

"I . . ." Helen shook her head. "No. Maybe."

She calculated how long it would take David to get her down the stairs, to the car, and then to the hospital. If they called the ambulance, they would be able to start working on her immediately. They might be able to save the baby.

She felt another sharp pain and gasped. "Yes. Ambulance."

The wait had been short—as had the trip to the emergency room. It was a rush for nothing, though. The news had not been good. Alex had been dead for two weeks. The cramping and bleeding was simply Helen's body beginning the process of expelling the fetus. As would have been the case with a live baby, the contractions intensified until, after four hours of hard labor, Helen had delivered their daughter.

"I want to see her," she had murmured to David.

He had been with her the entire time, holding her hand, coaching her through the breathing and the pain, encouraging her to continue pushing despite knowing the outcome.

"I want to see her." Helen remembered repeating the request and David had squeezed her hand before standing and going over to the nurse who was standing with her back to the delivery table. David spoke to her in low tones and then, after what seemed like forever, turned. In his hands he held something that looked as if it were wrapped in a washcloth.

"You were right," he said as he placed the tiny bundle in her hands. "It was a girl."

Helen stared down at the tiny, perfect face. She was surprised at how light Alex was in her hands. She was barely as long as a chocolate bar and weighed about the same.

"She seemed so much bigger inside me," she said softly. She

reached out a fingertip and gently touched the tiny, bald head. She felt David's hand on her shoulder.

"I'm so sorry." His voice cracked and Helen tore her gaze away from Alex to look at her husband. He was staring down at the baby, his eyes wet with tears. "We were so close this time. We can try again."

Helen had nodded even as she knew that this was the last time they would do this—the last time she could do this. Each missed period, each positive result on the E.P.T stick only to have a violent period weeks later, left her feeling just that much more empty and bereft. The loss, she knew, had become too much to bear. And so she did the unthinkable.

She let David think they were trying even as she took birth control pills to prevent it from happening. She would never be a mother. She had given up that right when she had the abortion all those years ago.

They had debated whether or not to have a service—whether to bury or cremate the body. Ultimately, they had decided to have a cremation. Wojciechowski's Funeral Home had performed the service for free. And now, Alex's cremains rested in the mausoleum at All Saints Polish Cemetery. The niche, with its brass plate, was a reminder of what she could never have because of what she recklessly threw away in her youth. Her barrenness was, she knew, her punishment. It was God's way of letting her know that for every action there are consequences and wrongs must be righted.

The hand holding the compact trembled and Helen realized she had been staring unseeingly at her reflection for quite some time. She replaced the foam applicator, snapped the compact shut, and glanced sideways at the woman next to her.

Maggie was still tapping away on her phone.

Helen dropped the compact back into her purse and then pulled out her own phone. There were several new texts from David. She swiped her finger across the bottom of the screen and tapped on the most recent.

Just come home, for Christ's sake. We can work this out.

She deleted the message and was about to begin deleting the rest of them when a new message popped onto the screen. It was from James. She stared at the alert, aware that usually when she saw his name, it filled her with excitement. Now, all she felt was anger. And shame. She had sent a message telling him that she knew the truth and asking why he had lied, but now she wasn't sure she wanted to know the answer. She hesitated, her finger hovering over the message. *Fuck it.* She took a deep breath and tapped the screen.

> You're right. I lied. I am so sorry and never meant to hurt you. I just didn't know how to tell you the truth. Nothing about me is what you thought. I am not a doctor. I don't parasail and I don't live in Boston. I also am not going to come meet you. The best thing I can do for you is leave you alone. For what it's worth, I really am in love with you. I'm sorry.

Helen stared at the message, unsure if the tightness in her stomach was shock, disappointment, or relief. Part of her wanted to scream at James, to insist that he meet her so she could take out her frustration on him. Part of her wanted never to hear from him again. And, if she were honest, part of her wanted to see him in person, to see what he looked like and to try to understand why he lied. She hit reply and typed her reply.

> You still didn't answer my question. Why did you do it? Why did you lie to me? I think I deserve an answer.

His reply came within a minute.

> You do deserve an answer but I don't know why. I'm being totally honest.

Helen shook her head.

> I don't believe you. Tell me why you lied to me.

She waited for his reply. When it didn't come, she reached into her purse and pulled out the Snickers Bar. She peeled the wrapper down as if it were a banana and took a big bite. If she was going to be unhappy, she might as well get fat, too.

Thursday Afternoon
November 13, 2014

Maggie

MAGGIE TRIED NOT to be obvious as she looked sideways at the woman sitting next to her. They had spoken briefly when she had first asked to sit in the empty seat next to her, but hadn't really spoken since. In fact, she had gotten the impression from the way Helen had ended the conversation after sharing the death of her daughter that she was wishing she hadn't opened up.

It wasn't uncommon when people learned what Maggie did for a living that they shared their own funeral experiences. It was, even if it had been years before, cathartic. What most people didn't understand was that funerals weren't for the deceased. Maggie was always adamant about that when she spoke to the staff. Funerals were for the living—the people who were left behind. It was their chance to see that it was real, to say goodbye, and often, to make amends.

Maggie had always known death; she had grown up with it. But she hadn't truly understood it until the summer she began her internship at Anthony and Son. It was a requirement of her program at Ivy Tech that after the two-year program, they complete a year-long internship. For most of the students, it was a chance to get hands-on experience and apply what they had learned in their classes. For Maggie, though, it had been the next step in the natural progression of assuming her position in the business. She had done more than her fair share of answering phones and running errands while in high school, but this was the first time she would be a part of the business as a mortuary professional.

"It's different working on people you know," her father had warned her on the first day.

They were standing in front of Stanley Frission, her grade school principal and the first body she would work on that wasn't a stranger.

"Part of it has to do with the fact that you have a connection to them, but a bigger part of it is because you have a connection and obligation to their families." He had looked at her, then, his expression serious. "Never forget, Maggie. It's not about the dead.

What we do is for the living." He gestured to Mr. Frission's body. "He's gone. But his family and friends, the people who loved and cared about him, they're still here. And it's our job to make what is one of the worst moments of their lives, manageable."

It was a philosophy Maggie had upheld throughout her career. She wasn't prepared, however, for the day she would be the person experiencing the loss. She had been in the embalming room, taking inventory of the supplies. She had her back to the door and was counting bottles of liquid sealer when her father stepped into the room. He cleared his throat.

"Maggie, I need to talk to you about something."

Maggie remembered that she had nodded, made note of the number of bottles they had on hand, and then turned to face her father. His expression left no doubt that whatever he had to tell her was bad. She stuck the pencil under the clasp of the clipboard, set it on the counter next to her, and leaned back, her elbows bent, bracing herself with her palms.

"I just got a call from Andrew Gleason." Franklin stepped around the stainless steel embalming table and walked toward her. "Your friend from high school . . . Rachel . . . She died last night."

Maggie gripped the edge of the counter tightly and forced herself to maintain her composure.

"How?" Her voice sounded hoarse and strained. She cleared her throat.

"She hanged herself."

Maggie exhaled sharply, the emotional blow was shocking as if she had been physically punched in the stomach.

Franklin placed his hands on her shoulders and squeezed gently. Maggie blinked several times and stared numbly at the buttons of his starched, white dress shirt. He continued to speak and she frowned, trying to make sense of the words.

"—know you two were close and I think, given the circumstances, it would be best if I handle the embalming and prep. You'll have to do it someday, but I'm not sure this is the time."

Maggie forced herself to meet her father's gaze. Was he doing this because he knew she and Rachel had been lovers or was it because he simply thought she had just lost one of her best friends? His expression was compassionate—the same one he used with all their clients. He was, she realized, consoling her the only way he knew how. She nodded.

"I'm going to go get her in about ten minutes." He squeezed her shoulders again. "Why don't you take the rest of today off? Tomorrow you can focus on office work or wash the cars. Maybe you could help with the obituary if you think it would make you feel better."

Maggie tried to swallow the lump in her throat. "I . . . um . . . I think I might go for a drive or something." She knew she was about to cry and she didn't want to do it here.

Franklin dropped his hands to his sides and stepped backward. "Just be careful. If you get too upset, pull over. Okay?" He glanced down at his watch. "Call if you're not going to be back for dinner."

Maggie nodded again and then turned and walked dumbly out the door into the hallway. She stopped in the office, grabbed her purse, and then walked out to her car. She clenched her teeth, forcing herself not to cry until she was alone.

Once in the car, Maggie drove west out of town on Highway 258 until she reached County Road 200. Though she hadn't been to the abandoned house and the small freshwater lake behind it in years, she could have driven the route with her eyes closed. She came to the familiar gravel road, turned left, and followed it until she reached the overgrown driveway that led to the ramshackle structure she and Rachel had found years before when they prowled the countryside with their newly minted driver's licenses.

Maggie parked the car in the grass in front of the weed-choked gate that led to what once must have been the front walk. If possible, the house, which had always been faded and gray, seemed to have sunken even more inward onto itself. She stared at the building. She and Rachel had spent hours exploring the house with its warped and damaged wooden floors, graffitied walls, and exposed pipes and wires. It was here that they found the ancient Playboy magazines with their provocative images that led to their first awkward kiss and later, their love making. And, it was here that they'd had their last, tearful argument.

Maggie pushed open the rusted gate and wove through the weeds and tall tufts of grass to the front porch and its low set of steps. The warped wood moaned under her weight and she was careful to avoid the exposed heads of the rusty nails. The second step from the top was missing a plank and she stepped carefully over it and onto the porch. The smell of cool, dank decay tickled her nose and she resisted the urge to sneeze. She hadn't been out here since the day Rachel insisted she publicly acknowledge their relationship.

They had been lying on a blanket in the bed of Rachel's battered Ford Ranger pickup truck—a hand-me-down from her older brother who was in the Army. They had just made love and Maggie lay on her stomach, her arms above her head, her face turned away from Rachel. She had been deliciously languorous.

"I wish it was always like this." Rachel traced her finger along the sharp edge of Maggie's shoulder blade and down her naked back.

Maggie turned her face to see Rachel lying on her side, her head propped up against her elbow. Her dark green eyes, framed by thick lashes, were serious. The golden light of the Indian summer sun revealed the complexity of reds and browns in her hair. She loved Rachel's hair. Even when they were in grade school, it had been a thing of fascination that she longed to touch. It had never been that painful carrot orange so many redheads had as children, but instead, a rich reddish auburn that had only deepened as she got older.

"What do you mean?" Maggie smiled up at her and tucked an errant strand back behind her ear. "Lying around naked in the back of your brother's truck?"

Rachel laughed softly. "No. This. Us." Her soft smile slowly dissolved into a tight frown.

Maggie sighed inwardly and tried to keep her expression and words light. "Who's to say it won't be?"

Rachel was quiet for several seconds and then finally, shook her head. "It won't." Her tone was dull and almost petulant. "Now that we're back in school, we're going to have to go back to pretending to be just friends."

This was becoming a familiar discussion and one that Maggie knew had no acceptable resolution. She tried to smile. "I know. But it won't be that bad. We're in all the same clubs and we can meet up after I finish cross country practice."

Rachel pushed herself into an upright position. Maggie could see the beginning of a bruise just below her collarbone where she had sucked too hard. "What about the Homecoming dance?"

Maggie frowned, unsure of what Rachel meant. "I don't know. What about it?"

"Who are you going with?"

"I don't know." Maggie sat up and grabbed her t-shirt and track shorts. "It's months away. Why are you asking?"

"You're going to be up for Homecoming Queen," Rachel said. "Everyone is going to expect you to go with Josh."

"So?" Maggie quickly pulled on her shorts and then shook out her Seymour High Owls t-shirt.

"So, you're my girlfriend. I want you to go with me."

Maggie pulled the shirt over her head and tried to decide how to answer. "Rachel, you know we can't do that. This isn't New York City or San Francisco. What would people think?"

"Who cares?" Rachel's eyes flashed.

"I do," Maggie said. "My parents do. Your parents do. Rachel, we can't tell people what we do."

"Do you love me?" Rachel's chin was set in a way that Maggie knew meant she was angry, defiant, or both.

"Yes!" Maggie reached clumsily for Rachel's hands. "You know I do." She laced together their fingers and stroked the side of Rachel's thumb with her own. "But don't you see that this is a bad idea? We can't tell people about us."

"Is it because you're ashamed of being a dyke? Because that's what you are, you know. That's what we both are."

Maggie gasped at the harsh angularity of the term. Neither of them had ever said it out loud and the way Rachel said it now sounded like an indictment.

"I know." The words were sharp and she knew she sounded defensive. "But that doesn't mean that everybody else has to."

Rachel gave a short, harsh snort. They had talked several times about the pressure of hiding their relationship—about what would happen should anyone find out. But this was the first time Rachel had taken the conversation out of the abstract. "I want you to come to the dance with me. I want people to know we're together."

"I don't want to do that," Maggie said.

"Why not? It's the year 2000 for chrissake. Hell, Ellen DeGeneres came out three years ago on national TV."

"We're not Ellen DeGeneres and I don't want people to know." Maggie braced herself for what she knew would be an angry reaction. She was surprised then, when rather than yelling, Rachel simply took a deep breath and looked down at their joined hands.

"I can't do this anymore."

Though she spoke the words softly, Maggie felt as if she had screamed them. Her skin tingled as a rush of adrenaline coursed coldly through her body.

"What do you mean?"

Rachel disentangled their hands, sat back, and reached to the side for her own shirt. As she stretched, Maggie could see the even ladder of ribs, prominent under the smooth, pale flesh. She watched as Rachel tugged her bra free, slipped her arms through the straps, and reached back to hook it closed. Still without speaking, she pulled on the blue-and-white striped oxford and buttoned it from the bottom up.

"What do you mean?" Maggie asked again, this time louder.

Rachel finished buttoning her shirt and reached for her jeans. She shoved her feet into the legs and then flipped onto her back to pull them over her hips. She buttoned and then zipped them closed before rolling onto her knees and patting lumps in the blanket in search of her shoes.

"Rachel, stop!" Maggie grabbed her arm. "Talk to me."

"What I mean," Rachel said as she jerked her arm from Maggie's grasp, "is that I can't do this anymore. I can't pretend to be someone I'm not. I can't pretend not to love you. I can't spend all my time worrying that someone is going to find out. I can't love you in secret. I can't watch you date boys to cover us up. I can't pretend like it's okay that you are dancing with Josh when you should be dancing with me."

"You're making too much out of this," Maggie said quickly.

"Or maybe you're not making enough," Rachel said. She faced Maggie. "Be with me."

"I am with you," Maggie insisted.

She searched Rachel's eyes for something that signified that this was just another one of their arguments—that they would agree to disagree for now. What she saw instead was resignation.

"I'm going to tell people, Maggie. About me. I'm going to tell them that I'm . . ." Rachel shrugged. "I'm going to come out." She held up her hands. "Don't worry. I won't tell them about you. But if you're worried what people will think, then you probably shouldn't be my friend anymore."

"Wait," Maggie said. "No. You can't do this. If you do, we can't . . . I can't. You can't do this."

Rachel smiled softly. "You just don't get it, do you? I have to be true to myself—even if that means losing you."

"But I love you," Maggie insisted. "I'm in love with you."

"And I'm in love with you. But I can't live a lie and you can't live the truth."

And she hadn't. Neither of them had.

The raw truth of the realization struck Maggie as she stared at the ramshackle house where, in the blink of an eye, she had lost her first and, if she was honest, only love.

They had, of course, continued to talk politely to each other at school. But never again had they kissed, touched, or been alone. Rachel had refused anything less than a public acknowledgement of their relationship and when Maggie couldn't give that to her, she found someone who could—a girl from another school who she brought to the Homecoming dance. From that point on, Rachel was the subject of gossip, ridicule, and discrimination. Though Maggie never took part, she also didn't go out of her way to defend or protect her.

She had also never stopped loving her. More than once, while she was living in Indianapolis, she had considered calling Rachel to see how she was, to talk about what happened, to see if they could fix things. Several times she had even picked up the phone to invite her to the city where there was anonymity and they could go out without everyone knowing who they were or judging if they touched too often or for too long. But in the end, she hadn't. Nor had she sought her out when she returned home for the internship.

It had only been by accident that they happened to run into each just last week at the Circle K. Maggie had been filling the tank of the hearse when the familiar pick-up pulled up at the pump next to her. Maggie had blinked in surprise when Rachel stepped out of the cab. Gone was the long wavy hair she had loved to touch, replaced instead by a boyish pixie that made her look a little like Peter Pan.

Though she couldn't see Rachel's eyes through the dark lenses of her sunglasses, Maggie could tell from her exaggerated nonchalance that she had seen her as well. Her heart beat faster—though from desire, anxiety, or surprise, she wasn't sure.

She cleared her throat. "Hey, Rachel. How are you?"

Rachel, who had circled the back of the truck and was unscrewing the gas cap, didn't acknowledge the greeting. She set the gas cap upside down on the edge of the truck bed and turned to the gasoline pump.

"This is ridiculous," Maggie muttered as she pushed the hold-open clip on the nozzle so the hearse's tank would continue to fill. She stepped awkwardly over the hose and walked to where Rachel now stood, one hand braced on the side of the truck bed, her head bowed forward as she stared down at the hand squeezing the nozzle.

"Hi, Rachel." There was no way this time that Rachel could pretend not to hear her. Maggie could see the quick rise and fall of her chest and knew she was just as flustered at the unexpected interaction. "How have you been?"

Rachel swallowed, sighed in what seemed like resignation, and, after a moment, straightened. She flipped down the hold-open lever and turned to Maggie. Her expression, at first devoid of emotion, seemed to soften as they looked at each other.

"I heard you were back in town. Working for your dad?"

Maggie nodded. "Yeah. Interning. It's a requirement of the program. And since I'll end up here anyway . . ." She shrugged. "How about you? What are you up to?"

"I'm working for Biggs Construction."

Maggie raised her eyebrows in surprise. "You're a construction worker? Wow. That must be—"

"In the office," Rachel interrupted. "Just because I'm a dyke doesn't automatically mean I'm on the crew, Maggie."

"I'm sorry. I shouldn't have . . . I didn't mean . . ." She sighed. "I'm sorry." They stood in silence for several seconds. Maggie tried to figure out how to say what she really wanted to. "Could we talk?"

Rachel tipped her head slightly to the side and studied Maggie. "I'm not sure what there is to say."

"We never really talked about what happened." Maggie reached out to touch her but stopped as Rachel took a step backward. She let her hand fall to her side. "You made your decision and that was it. You never gave me a chance."

"Because if I had waited, you would have . . . what? Come

out, too?" Rachel pushed her sunglasses up onto her head. Dark circles smudged the delicate skin beneath her eyes. She scanned Maggie's body. "Look at you. You're still not out."

"I don't hide who I am," Maggie said in a low voice. "I just don't advertise it. It's different in Indy. There are places where it's okay to be gay. Bars. Coffee houses. Bookstores."

"Places where it's okay to be gay," Rachel repeated and snorted softly. "So, what do you want, Maggie?"

Maggie took a deep breath. "I'm moving back after graduation. I thought maybe we could be friends. Maybe we could go out. There are some great places in Indy where we wouldn't have to hide." The words tumbled out of her mouth before she realized what she was saying. "Rachel, I'm still . . . I still love you. I've never stopped loving you. And I want to be with you." A gust of wind blew her hair into her eyes and she brushed it back in irritation. "We'd have to be careful because of the business and Dad, but we could try again."

Rachel stared at her for several seconds, her expression stricken. "No," she said finally, her voice tight. "You don't get to do this. After everything I've been through, you don't get to just blow back into town and say this to me at a fucking gas station." She flinched at the unexpected *thunk* of the pressurized pump snapping off the flow of gasoline. "Unbelievable."

She jerked the nozzle from the tank, returned it to its cradle on the pump, and angrily twisted the gas cap into place. Maggie reached out to touch her shoulder just as Rachel spun to face her, her expression a combination of sadness, heartbreak, and fury. Maggie took a step backward.

"When I came out, you abandoned me. I never expected you to tell people about us. I gave you that out. But you didn't even try to be my friend."

"I—" Maggie began.

"No. I have endured more shit than you can possibly imagine. I have been made fun of, gossiped about, beat up, and almost raped. Half of my family refuses to talk to me and the other half, though they won't admit it, are ashamed of me. Most of the women in town don't want to be seen talking to me because of what people might think. I have endured all of this because I refuse to live a lie. So don't you *dare* think that you can tell me that you still love me and that you want to be with me, but only if we sneak away where no one knows us."

She pushed the sunglasses back down onto her face, spun around, and circled the front of the battered truck. "Oh, and for the record," she yanked open the driver's side door, "you broke my heart once. I refuse to let you do it again."

That had been their last conversation. It had been ugly and bitter. And now, Rachel was gone.

Maggie walked to the edge of the porch where rusted bolts in the ceiling suggested a porch swing had once hung. She brushed away the few remaining flakes of what had once been white paint and sat carefully on the railing. They had made so many promises on this porch.

"This was all my fault." She closed her eyes and tried not to hear Rachel's angry words. *"You abandoned me." "You didn't even try to be my friend." "You broke my heart."*

Maggie tasted the bile in the back of her throat and knew that she was about to vomit. She stood quickly, leaned over the rail, and, while grasping the support post, emptied the contents of her stomach into the weeds. Her breaths came in short pants as she waited for the second wave to come. When it didn't, she spit twice and then wiped the thick saliva from her lips with the hem of her shirt. She turned back to the front of the house, bent forward with her hands on her thighs, and forced herself to breathe more slowly.

Rachel was dead.

Maggie shook her head and tried to push away the tears. She straightened and paced the length of the porch, hoping the movement would help her get her emotions under control. A part of her had always thought that somewhere down the road, she and Rachel would get a second chance—that they would find their way back to each other.

She wondered what Ben would say if he were here. *He'd probably say that this is just another example of how love kills.* It occurred to her that perhaps his solution of avoiding love was a good one.

Maggie looked down at the black sports watch she used when running. Her father had likely picked up the body from the Gleasons. Rachel might already be in the cooler at the funeral home. Or maybe, she was on the embalming table. It would be like her father to do it as soon as he could so Maggie would be spared being a part of what was going to happen to Rachel's body. In the end, though, it hadn't really mattered. Rachel was dead and nothing could change that. Nothing could assuage her guilt or the nagging feeling that she somehow had let Rachel down.

Even though her father had asked her not to see Rachel's body before it was ready for viewing, Maggie had crept downstairs later that night, after her parents had gone to bed. She had tried to stay away, but after hours of tossing and turning, she gave in to the need to see her.

She moved as quietly as possible down the stairs, making sure to avoid the squeaky spots she had identified years before when she and Rachel would sneak out to meet. Once downstairs, she eased open the heavy, metal door to the preparation room and stepped inside. The hum of the refrigeration unit was the only sound. She stood in the dark for several seconds before flicking on the overhead lights. Rachel's was the only body in the room and it lay on a gurney, embalmed and dressed, but without the final preparation of hair and makeup.

Maggie studied Rachel's still form from just inside the doorway. She looked pale and unnaturally still in the harsh fluorescent lighting. She walked forward until she stood over the body.

She pulled away the cloth of Rachel's blouse. The incision in her neck near the collarbone where they hooked up the machine that pushed out the blood and pushed in the formaldehyde and embalming fluid was sewn neatly up and covered with sealant. Her father had done a good job on the embalming. The furrow from the noose was almost unnoticeable, though the same couldn't be said for the faint, half-inch bruise that circled the front of Rachel's neck.

"Why did you do this?" Maggie asked as she brushed her fingertips over the half-moon ligature mark. Rachel's skin was firm from the embalming fluid and she knew that the stylist would use makeup to cover the injury. The knowledge that she would be one of the last people to see the evidence of Rachel's suicide, to see her at her most vulnerable, seemed somehow appropriate and unfair.

Beneath her touch, she could feel the slight indention in the skin and tried to imagine how the noose had looked. What she had used? How the knot had been tied? Had there been a note explaining why? She shook her head as she realized that the cause really didn't matter. It didn't change the reality of the situation. Her first love—her only love—was dead. And deep down, she suspected it was partially her fault.

Against her father's advice, Maggie had attended Rachel's funeral, though not as a mourner. She had insisted on working it. She had arranged the flowers, handed out the memorial cards, and driven the hearse to the cemetery. She watched Rachel's family struggle with the fact that they would never have the chance to make amends for the way they had treated her. She watched their grief just as she, herself, struggled to say goodbye to someone she loved and whose body she knew as well as her own.

And it was during those days that Maggie came to understand the hardest truth of all: love couldn't last. Whether it was what her parents experienced as they drifted apart or what happened to the people who came into their funeral home to say goodbye to their dead, love didn't stand a chance against life.

Maggie looked again at the woman who sat in the bus seat next to her. Intuition told her that if she shared her philosophy with Helen, she would understand. And it wasn't just the loss of her daughter, though clearly that had marked her. It was more than that. It was something deeper and more intrinsic that had been taken from her. Was it possible though, to get through life without losing the better parts of one's self? Weren't they all in some way broken? And didn't they all spend their lives trying to fix themselves? Nurse the hurts? Find the people who could fill the holes left by others? Wasn't that what she was doing with Sarah?

Maggie knew that part of her attraction to Sarah was her physical resemblance to Rachel. But it was more than just that. It was the way she held her head, upright with her chin thrust slightly outward in defiance. It was the way she had moved her hands and how they had looked on Maggie's skin. It was the way she made her feel. She was, Maggie had come to realize, her second chance. It was her—

The swerve of the bus jerked her to the side and caused her shoulder to bump into that of the woman beside her. Around her, several people gasped. Beneath her, the bus seemed to undulate as the driver tried to gain control. Like Maggie, the other passengers swayed back and forth as the bus fishtailed out of control.

So this is how it ends, Maggie thought as she gripped the armrests on either side of her seat. The woman in the seat next to her also gripped her armrests and their forearms touched as the bus began what felt like an almost painfully slow series of barrel rolls down the steep embankment.

"We're all going to die."

The murmured words were so low Maggie was surprised that she even heard them. She turned her head to stare at the woman next to her. Everything seemed to be happening in slow motion now and the elongation of time gave her an opportunity to take in the tiny details of the person with whom she had made pleasant conversation off and on for the past two hours.

The woman was small and efficient looking, with blondish hair that was glossy and probably very silky. She had green eyes . . . thick lashes . . . a blemish she had tried to cover with makeup. When the woman had slid apologetically into the seat next to her in New York City, Maggie had noticed that she had seemed anxious. *Helen*, Maggie thought suddenly. She had said her name was Helen.

The bus rotated and Maggie, who had the window seat, was thrown against Helen who let out a *whoosh* as Maggie's right elbow and shoulder slammed into her chest.

We're like those numbered balls in that round Bingo cage thing, Maggie thought as the force of the rotation flipped her upwards— or downwards given that the roof of the bus was suddenly below her. Helen was on top of her, but only for a second before they were separated and jerked sideways.

Everything happened faster now and suddenly, the noise was deafening—the groan of bending metal, the crunch of breaking glass, the screams and the rush of air as she was flung forward. Around her, the passengers bounced against each other and the seats of the bus. Purses and bags bounced, too, their contents spilling out and spraying like shrapnel.

"Grandma!"

It was, Maggie thought dimly, the little boy—the one she had seen with the sticker on his chest, his name written in Sharpie, sitting in the seat directly behind the driver. *Unaccompanied minor* she had thought when she first saw him. Why that phrase occurred to her now, she didn't know.

"Fuck!"

This came from the heavyset man who had sat behind her. He had been on her connector bus to New York City. He'd boarded in Harrisburg, she remembered. She had gotten off the bus to stretch her legs and to use the bathroom at the station. When they got back on the bus, he had chosen to sit directly behind her. He had small brown eyes that were lost in the pale flesh of his face. Something about him made her uncomfortable and she considered switching seats before deciding it would be too much work to move all of her things. When they changed buses in New York City, he had again chosen the seat behind her.

Why these thoughts . . . not my life flashing before my eyes . . . tell Sarah.

The questions came to her in snatches—half-developed thoughts that she understood without completion.

The bus was flipping again, on the second, perhaps third rotation. Maggie wasn't sure. And there was Helen again, her eyes wide, her lipsticked mouth in a perfectly round O.

Maggie thrust her arms out to soften the impact of their bodies crashing together again. One or both of them groaned as they came together and Maggie thought, oddly, that at least Helen was softer than the hard angles of the seats. They held onto each other and once again, Maggie was on her back on the roof of the bus.

Around them, coins and pens and a hundred other bits and pieces from pockets and bags rained down. The bus had stopped rolling and was now just gently rocking from side to side. Then silence for what felt like a ten seconds as everything and everyone came to rest. And then the moans and cries began. Helen was sprawled halfway on top of her, loose-limbed and unmoving.

I'm alive.

The thought occurred to Maggie just as a sharp pain shot through her head and down her spine. Her body tingled, every nerve suddenly aware and too sensitive. Adrenaline. Helen's weight was too much. She tried to move but didn't have the strength. *Move, dammit.* She tried again to force her body to do something . . . anything. She felt another stab of pain. This time it was excruciating and she moaned. She knew she had broken bones and likely internal injuries. She wondered what her face looked like.

I hope they do a good job on the restoration.

She imagined her naked body on the cold, shiny funeral home gurney—imagined the work that would go into making her broken body and damaged face look presentable. She should have gone with cremation. Besides, who would go to the funeral anyway? Ben? Sarah? Would Sarah even know that she had died? After the way Maggie had treated her, would she even care?

Now is not the time to feel sorry for yourself.

Maggie tried to raise her head again and gasped when the pain and nausea hit her simultaneously, followed by the white noise and tunnel vision. The chaos of the other passengers was obscured as she felt herself lose consciousness. The escape was welcome, she realized as she gave into it and felt herself let go.

Suddenly, she was looking down on the scene—at her bloody and broken body with Helen curled on top of her as if they were lovers. To her right was the man who had sat behind them. His face was bloody and his head was cocked at a strange angle. His eyes were open but he wasn't moving. Maggie knew that expression. Toward the front of the bus was the little boy, curled into a ball, crying. The old woman who had taken so long to board lay sprawled limply on her stomach, her limbs at unnatural angles. Maggie saw all of it and felt nothing. It was a nice change to see death and not to feel sadness.

Maybe dying is not so bad after all. Maybe . . . She had trouble forming the rest of the thought. The scene below her faded and then, before she could be troubled to summon up the words to describe what happened next, there was nothing.

Sarah

SARAH WOVE THROUGH the chaos outside of Newton-Wellesley Hospital and hurried toward the automatic doors of the emergency room. She had been on her way to the Greyhound station to pick up Sam when she heard the radio news story of the crash. Her phone rang several minutes later. It was Tara, the social worker with whom she had been working to coordinate Sam's relocation.

"Hi, Sarah." Tara's tone was calm although Sarah could tell she was upset. "I don't know if you've heard the—"

"Was it Sam's bus? Is he okay?"

"It was," Tara said. "There's no word what caused the crash, but as far as I can tell, Sam is alright. He's banged up and has a broken arm. They're sending the injured to various hospitals depending on their injuries. Sam is being sent to Newton-Wellesley Hospital in Newton."

"Right." Sarah looked for a place to pull over so she could put the coordinates into her GPS. "Do you have any other details?"

"Just that they were outside of New Pond on I-95 when they crashed." Tara cleared her throat. "Last I heard, there were five dead and several injured."

Sarah sighed. "Well, thank god Sam is all right. Are you at the hospital?"

"I'm trying to find some place to park. I'll keep an eye on who they're bringing in and when Sam gets here, I'll start the paperwork." Tara made a *grrr* sound. "Listen, I've got to go but I'll see you when you get here."

The trip had taken about thirty minutes, though, to Sarah, it felt much longer. She was, frankly, surprised at the increasing anxiety she felt as she got closer and closer to the hospital. She'd had mixed feelings about taking on the role of guardian for Sam. She had never really wanted children and part of her feared he would sense that. But now, at the thought of him alone and injured, she was more concerned about his well-being than any shortcomings she might have as a guardian. The realization he could have been killed was terrifying.

Ambulances were lined up at various angles around the entrance. A thin, red-haired woman in her early thirties, wearing a black belted trench coat stood just outside the doors. Her laminated badges hung from a bright blue lanyard around her neck. Though Sarah had never seen Tara in person, she sensed this was the social worker.

"Tara?"

"Sarah." Tara nodded and extended her hand. Her grip was firm, her palm dry. "Hi. You look just like your picture. It's nice to meet you. I haven't seen Sam yet." She held up a file folder. "I have all the paperwork here so we can get him admitted."

Sarah nodded. "Any word what happened yet?"

"No," Tara said. "I've heard several people say something about the driver texting, but I don't have that on authority so don't repeat it."

"That's—"

The sound of sirens became deafening as another ambulance pulled under the emergency entrance. She and Tara both turned and watched as it rolled to a stop.

The back doors flew open and a woman in a blue paramedic's uniform jumped out, pulled out the end of the gurney, and extended the retractable legs of the frame. Sarah heard a male voice inside the ambulance say something just as the driver, a burly man with blond hair, hurried from around the side of the ambulance. Together, the three extracted the gurney from the ambulance. The patient, a woman from the looks of her hair, was conscious and in a slightly upright position. They turned the gurney and wheeled her toward the hospital entryway.

Sarah stared. Despite the blood from the head wound and injuries to her cheek and mouth, the woman on the gurney looked like . . . Maggie Anthony. Sarah blinked. No. It was impossible. There was no way Maggie would be on the same bus as Sam. It had to be a mistake.

She resisted the urge to try to move closer even though she continued to stare. She jerked in surprise when the woman who looked like Maggie, the woman whose memory had haunted her for the past year, met her gaze.

The look on her face was a mixture of shock, pain, and disbelief. "Sarah?" The woman, who apparently *was* Maggie reached out her hand. It was streaked with blood. "Sarah? How did you know?"

Sarah opened her mouth to ask what Maggie was doing on Sam's bus, but the paramedics wheeled her into the hospital before she could form the words. The doors slid shut behind them. Without thinking, Sarah turned, as if to follow her but then stopped. She was here for Sam. That was her responsibility. Next to her, Tara's phone rang. She turned to see Tara pull it from her pocket and raise it to her ear.

"Hello?" Tara listened for several seconds. "Okay. Yeah. Thanks." She turned to Sarah. "That was a friend of mine. Sam should be here in a few minutes."

"Okay." Sarah turned to look back at the closed doors and resisted the urge to go to Maggie and find out the extent of her injuries and why she was on her way to Boston.

"Did you know her?" Tara asked.

"I . . ." Sarah shook her head in confusion and turned back to Tara. "Yeah. Sort of. She—"

In front of them, another ambulance rolled to a stop.

"Is that him?"

Both of them leaned forward as the paramedics worked together to pull the gurney from the back of the ambulance. This time, the patient, a woman, was fully supine, her head held immobile by the cervical collar. Even though she knew it was inappropriate to gawk, Sarah snuck a look at the woman as she was wheeled past. From what she could see, she was fairly attractive with shoulder-length blondish hair. Her eyes were open, her gaze skipping frantically from face to face as the paramedics talked over her to the doctor who appeared from inside the hospital.

". . . thirty-nine-year-old female . . . positive loss of consciousness . . . obvious fracture to left leg . . ."

The rest of their words were drowned out by the short *whoop whoop* of the incoming ambulance.

"I'm guessing that's him," Tara said as the now familiar routine of the back doors opening and the paramedics removing the gurney commenced.

The figure they brought out was, indeed, Sam. His eyes were

large and red. He had been crying. His face and clothes were smeared with blood. His right arm was in a splint of some sort. Sarah rushed forward, Maggie forgotten.

"Sammy! Hi." She put her hand on his leg. "I'm right here, okay? I'm not going anywhere and we're going to get you all fixed up. Okay?"

Sam nodded and looked like he was going to burst into tears. His vulnerability and fear made tears well up in Sarah's eyes as well. He looked so frail. Sarah felt as if her heart were going to burst. Everything in her wanted to protect him. And she would, she told herself as she and Tara entered the hospital alongside the gurney. She absolutely would.

FIVE HOURS LATER, Sarah sat in the vinyl-covered chair in the corner of the room where Sam would be spending the night and watched the muted television coverage of the crash. It was still unclear what had caused it, though Tara had confirmed the driver was texting. Apparently, he had looked up in time to see the car in front of him brake suddenly and had swerved to avoid hitting it.

In addition to the broken arm, Sam had suffered several cuts and bruises, and a concussion. He was lucky, the doctors said. He had been protected by the partition that had separated him from the driver. The woman sitting next to him though, Marilyn Shaw, apparently hadn't been as fortunate. According to the paramedics, he was crouched over her body when they found him, his eyes blank as he grasped her lifeless hand. It had taken two of them to pry his fingers loose so they could treat him.

On the bed, Sam slept, his narrow chest gently rising and falling in a smooth rhythm. Sarah took advantage of the quiet to think about everything that had happened over the past few hours. Not only had she almost lost her nephew before she even had a chance to take him home, but also, she had seen Maggie in the most unexpected of places.

Of course, everything about Maggie had been unexpected. Meeting her at the bar that first night. Committing the ultimate sin of cheating on Emma. The one-night stand that became a second, and then a third.

Everything about her behavior when it came to Maggie was

completely out of character. She couldn't articulate it but there was just something undeniable in their attraction that made her powerless. She had known it the moment she had seen her at the bar, drinking her martini and flirting with the bartender.

And then they had danced.

The way Maggie felt pressed against her was intoxicating. She had never felt that with Emma. Not even close. It wasn't an excuse for her infidelity; what she had done was unforgivable. But it was the truth. And she knew, without a doubt that if she didn't take the opportunity to be with Maggie, she would regret it for the rest of her life.

They'd had a remarkable weekend—had made a connection that Sarah was convinced was reciprocated. She believed it so much so that she had gone back to Boston, admitted the affair, and ended her relationship with Emma. She waited until she was free before contacting Maggie. And then . . . nothing. No response to the phone calls or e-mails except a couple of short messages and one long, clearly drunken voice message in which Maggie said she couldn't see her because of her reputation in the community and the fact that someone named Rachel was proof that love couldn't last so it was better not to care in the first place. Maggie had also asked that Sarah stop contacting her.

Sarah knew it was unhealthy to still care about someone who clearly didn't feel the same way. But even now, just knowing that Maggie was injured and somewhere in this hospital made her heart beat faster.

"How did you know?" Sarah still didn't understand Maggie's question. *How had she known . . . what?*

Sarah glanced at Sam and then stood. She crept silently out of the room and pulled the door softly closed behind her. She debated the effectiveness of walking the halls of the floor to see if she could find Maggie's room, but knew the chances of her being on this floor, let alone finding her, were slim. Instead, she walked to the nurse's station where one of the nurses, an athletic woman with short blond hair, sat, tapping industriously away on a computer keyboard. She had smiled knowingly at her earlier and Sarah wondered if she could use it to her advantage.

"Hi," she said with a smile as she leaned against the counter. "I wanted to thank you for everything you're doing for Sam." She gestured over her shoulder at his room. "He's a great kid." She shook her head. "This is just so horrible."

The nurse—Jessica, according to her name badge—nodded. "He's a lucky little guy."

"He is." Sarah broadened her smile in a way she hoped was charming and trustworthy. "I was actually hoping I could beg a favor. Sammy was traveling with a family friend. I saw her brought in just before Sam got here, but I didn't get a chance to talk to her. Her name is Maggie Anthony. Do you know or do you think you could tell me what room she's in?"

Jessica studied Sarah for several seconds and then grinned. "Sure. Technically we're not supposed to, but I think it's all right." She spun back to the computer terminal and typed in Maggie's name. "I'm glad she was only injured. Several people were killed."

Sarah nodded. "I know. Do you know how many were killed and injured?"

"Five died at the scene and two died en route." Jessica picked up an orange notepad. "Another twenty-eight were injured." She squinted at the screen and then scribbled down the room number. She ripped the note off the pad and handed it to Sarah. "She's in room 504. Take the elevator up and when you get off, take a left at the waiting room and then a right."

"Thanks." Sarah smiled and then looked back at Sam's room. "He'll be okay, right? I don't want him to wake up and be scared or think he's alone."

"I'll keep an eye on him," Jessica said and then grinned. "If you give me your phone number, I can call you if he wakes up. Or maybe for dinner sometime after he's released?"

Sarah smiled even though she had no real desire to go out with Jessica. "That would be great except I'm going to have my hands full over the next few months getting Sam settled in and figuring out how to be a parent. I'm taking him because my sister . . . can't."

Jessica studied her for a moment as if trying to determine if she was telling the truth. Finally, she nodded. "I understand. It's a lot to take on. I know I'm exhausted after just an afternoon with my sister's boys."

"Exactly." Sarah exhaled. "This is all so new. I just need to focus on him for now. "

"You'll be fine," Jessica said and winked. "I have confidence in you. Now, go check on your friend and I'll keep an eye on Sam."

"Thanks," Sarah said. "I'll be quick."

"Take your time." Jessica rolled her chair back to face the computer screen. "In fact, go get some coffee and something to eat."

Sarah nodded and then turned and walked down the hall toward the elevators. The thought that she was going to actually see Maggie and talk to her after so much time both excited and overwhelmed her.

She punched the "up" button. The doors slid immediately open and she stepped inside. She pushed the button for the fifth floor—the same floor number, she thought, as both of their rooms in Seattle. She remembered how they had negotiated that second night together.

"I know you have your rules and all that," she had whispered as they stood in front of Maggie's hotel room door. "But I'm thinking maybe you should consider suspending them for the night." She had smiled, and before Maggie could protest, added, "I don't want anything more than this. I'm not looking for a relationship."

What she hadn't said was that she was already in one and that anything more than this weekend couldn't happen until she was honest with Emma. But Maggie hadn't known that. Instead, she had raised her eyebrows as if surprised and slightly offended. And then she had smiled.

"So, just to be clear," she said. "No strings. No emotional connection. No calls afterward. Just sex."

Maggie had been touching her cheek. Sarah nodded slowly and then had taken a step back.

"Ask me into your room."

Hours later, after Maggie had fallen asleep, she had slipped from the bed and crept to her own room. It had been just like they had agreed. Tidy. A clean break. She had been sure that any further interaction with Maggie would be nothing more than a polite hello as they passed in the hall—which was why she was more than a little surprised to see Maggie standing with Evan outside the large double doors of the conference room where she was scheduled to speak.

"You look very scholarly this morning," Maggie had said with a playful smile. "The glasses are a nice touch."

Sarah remembered she had flushed at the compliment. She had chosen a camel-colored pants suit that matched the leather bag slung over her shoulder. She had pulled her hair back into what she hoped was a slightly academic-looking bun. She shrugged. "I slept in my contacts and couldn't get them back in this morning after I cleaned them."

Maggie held out a cup of coffee. "I thought you might need this."

Sarah glanced at Evan who was watching the interaction with more than a little interest. Like Maggie and the rest of the participants, he was wearing a dark suit, though his was, she could see as she leaned in to give him a hug, pinstriped. His starched pale blue shirt was open at the collar and he smelled like soap and spicy aftershave.

"Hi," she said quickly. "How did you sleep?"

"About as well as you would expect in a strange bed with a bunch of drunken funeral directors partying in the next room. And you?"

"I slept well," Sarah said as she ignored his knowing grin. She looked around him at the nearby table with fruit, coffee, and pastries. "I didn't get a chance to eat, though."

"Allow me." Evan turned and walked to the food table.

"Ready for your presentation?" Maggie raised the cup to her lips and took a sip.

"I think so. I would have liked to have gone over it one more time but I was busy doing other things." Sarah smiled. "I have to admit, I'm a little surprised to see you. I figured that after last night I'd only see you in passing."

Maggie studied her with a serious expression. She seemed to be debating whether or not to share what she was thinking. After several seconds, she sighed. "I like being around you. You remind me of someone."

Sarah blinked, unsure how to respond. "I hope that's not a bad thing."

Maggie gave a quick shake of the head. "Not at all. In fact—"

"So I brought back fruit if you're feeling healthy and a cheese Danish if you aren't," Evan said as he held out both hands. A Granny Smith apple lay in one and in the other was a Styrofoam plate with an oversized pastry.

Sarah chose the apple and took a bite. "Thanks."

"I was hoping that's what you'd choose." Evan pinched the pastry between his thumb and forefinger, lifted it to his lips, and took an enormous bite. "Man." He chewed quickly and swallowed. "Looks like you're going to have a full house."

Sarah nodded. "I should probably go get set up." She handed the apple to Maggie and grinned. "For you, Eve."

It had taken every ounce of willpower she had not to look at Maggie during the presentation. She could feel her attention, though. Her energy. It had been hungry. And, even though Maggie had her rules, they had ended up in bed an hour later. Unlike the previous time, however, something about their lovemaking had changed. There had been an unexpected familiarity, a knowledge of where to touch and how that had made the experience somehow more intimate. They hadn't really left the room for the rest of the conference.

Ding.

Sarah was shaken from her reverie by the sound of the elevator reaching the fifth floor. The doors slid softly open and she stepped out. Immediately in front of her was a large, glassed-in waiting room with clusters of people staring blankly at the television, tapping away on their phones, or speaking to each other in soft voices. She wondered if they were relatives of people who had been on the bus.

She turned to the left and walked to the hallway where she took a right. As much as she wanted to see Maggie, she walked slowly, forcing her heartbeat to slow. She stopped outside of Room 504 and looked inside. In the bed closest to the door lay the woman who had come in after Maggie. One of her legs, encased in a full-length cast, was propped up on pillows. She appeared to be asleep, her face slack, her mouth slightly open.

The occupant of the other bed—the person she could only assume was Maggie—was hidden from view by the privacy curtain that had been drawn closed. Sarah took a deep breath and walked as silently as she could past Maggie's sleeping roommate to where the edges of the curtain met.

Her heart throbbed loudly in her chest and in her ears as she lifted a trembling hand to the edge of the curtain. *You can do this.* She took a deep breath and parted the curtain.

Maggie lay sleeping in a partially inclined position on the hospital bed. Her face was bruised and misshapen, her right cheek and jaw puffy and swollen. A gash above her eyebrow had been neatly sewn closed, as had a half-inch cut that ran lengthwise alongside her ear. Around the head of the bed, machines hummed and clicked. The monitor to her left showed what appeared to be a rhythmic and steady pulse. Her blood pressure, too, seemed normal. Clear tubing ran from a suspended bag of saline and snaked to the needle in the back of Maggie's hand. Sarah remembered those hands.

She closed her eyes. Coming up here had been a mistake. Seeing Maggie now, after she had made her position clear, would serve no good purpose. Everything had already been said.

She opened her eyes and jerked in surprise to see Maggie watching her, her eyes glassy from the painkillers the doctors had undoubtedly given her. She blinked slowly.

"Are you real?"

The words were spoken softly and Sarah stepped closer to the bed so she could hear. The curtains that she had been holding open fell closed behind her with a soft whoosh.

"I think so." Sarah smiled.

She stepped fully to the side of the bed and looked down into Maggie's pale face. Despite the injuries and everything else that had happened, she still felt an unexplainable attraction to her.

"How did you know?" Maggie's words were thick and slurred.

"How did I know what?" Sarah gently touched Maggie's forearm.

"That I was here? That we crashed?"

Sarah tipped her head slightly to the side and frowned. "I didn't."

Maggie's brow furrowed. She seemed to be trying to concentrate. "But you're here. You came." She blinked in confusion.

"I'm here because my nephew, Sam, was on the bus," Sarah said. "He was coming to live with me. In Boston."

Maggie blinked slowly and then mumbled, "Unaccompanied minor."

"What?" Unable to understand what Maggie meant, Sarah leaned down.

"I saw him. He sat in the front." Maggie paused and licked her lips. "Is he okay?"

Sarah nodded. "He is. Broken arm, cuts, and bruises, a concussion, but he'll live." She glanced up at the machines. "What about you?"

Maggie grimaced. "Broken ribs, punctured lung, dislocated shoulder, and my back is messed up. But I'll live, too." She hesitated as if trying to decide what to say or, given the painkillers, how to say it. She cleared her throat. "I almost died."

Sarah nodded and gently squeezed Maggie's arm. "I know. But—"

"I made a mistake," Maggie interrupted. "Before. When you called. I was coming here to tell you why I ran." She moved as if she were trying to sit up and Sarah pushed her shoulder gently, but firmly, back against the bed.

"You need to try to stay still," she said.

Above Maggie's head, one of the machines made a noise that sounded like a whirl or a hum. It must have administered a painkiller because her body seemed to relax. "I was wrong, Sarah." Her voice became thicker. "I felt it, too. When we were together, I felt the connection." She tried to lift her hand but managed only to move it a little to the side. "Promise me you'll give me a chance." She blinked slowly.

Sarah leaned forward and gently touched Maggie's uninjured cheek. "I promise." Even as she spoke the words, she knew that they were as much for her as they were for Maggie. She watched as Maggie closed her eyes and surrendered to the oblivion of unconsciousness.

Realistically, she knew that making that promise could turn out to be a huge mistake. But, just as she hoped she could heal the pain and sadness of the little boy downstairs, she had hope, too, that things could be fixed with Maggie. She didn't know what had happened that made Maggie so broken, but she was willing to try to understand. For herself as much as Maggie.

And Sam . . . Sam needed love. He needed stability and safety and a sense of home. Sarah sighed. They were strangers to each other. But they were all connected. And they all, each of them, needed something to hold onto—someone to hold onto.

Silently, Sarah slipped from the room. She would take Sam

home and they would fumble their way through creating a life
together. And Maggie . . . they would talk and see what happened.
It wasn't any kind of resolution, but it was a start. She had no idea
what the future would bring, but she was hopeful. And in the end,
wasn't hope all that anyone had?

About the Author

Sandra Moran is an author and assistant adjunct professor of anthropology at Johnson County Community College in Overland Park, Kansas. A native Kansan, she has worked professionally as a newspaper journalist, a political speech writer, and an archaeological tour manager. In her novels, she strives to create flawed characters struggling to find themselves within the cultural constructs of gender, religion and sexuality. She is the author of *Letters Never Sent*, *Nudge*, and *The Addendum*, and can be contacted at: Moran.Sandra.D@gmail.com or via snail mail at PO Box 19622, Lenexa, Kansas 66285.

· Compelling start.
Could 'feel' the bus accident.
Nice development of characters

CPSIA information can be obtained
at www.ICGtesting.com
Printed in the USA
FSOW01n1455021215
13743FS